# Blind Influence

*By*
Linda Riesenberg Fisler

*I hope you enjoy the adventure.
All the best,
Linda Riesenberg Fisler*

Published by Linda Riesenberg Fisler
DBA Kit-Cat Press
Middletown, OH

Copyright © 2015 by Linda Riesenberg Fisler

All Rights Reserved.

Without limiting the rights under copyright reserved above, no part of this publication may be reproduced, stored in or introduced into a retrieval system, or transmitted in any form, or by any means (electronic, mechanical, photocopying, recording, or otherwise) without the prior written permission of both the copyright owner and the publisher of this book.

Dog Ear Publishing
4011 Vincennes Rd
Indianapolis, IN 46268
www.dogearpublishing.net

ISBN: 978-1-4575-3572-7

This book is printed on acid-free paper.

Publisher's and Author's Note:
This is a work of fiction. Names, characters, places, and incidents either are the product of the author's imagination or are used fictitiously, and any resemblance to actual persons, living or dead, events, or locales is entirely coincidental.

Printed in the United States of America

## Acknowledgments

My thanks and endless love
To my husband, Thomas,
And to many friends and family;
You are the wind beneath my wings.

# Foreword

*I* first met Linda Fisler at a wonderful art conference called Weekend with the Masters. She was hosting an art chat show interviewing some of the most prominent artists in the country. At the time, I had just written and directed a movie entitled *Local Color* which was screened at the event. When I did my interview with Linda, we found that we had a lot in common. Over the years, I've gotten to know her very well.

If there's a word to describe Linda, that word would be passion. She lives to create, both with her brushes and paints as an artist and with her words as a writer. Doing both of these vocations myself, I understand how wonderful and difficult this can be. To see the world through the eyes of someone who not only wants to capture its best moments but celebrate them is exhilarating and exhausting all at once. Also, to find that you spend much of your quiet time hearing the voices of characters you've created in your head carrying on conversations can be both pleasurable and maddening. I think every creative person at some point wonders why they are torturing themselves. Why are we trying to find the right words for a sentence, the right note for a song, the right color for a painting? After a lot of self-examination, I think we come back to the same place, which is, "Who knows? Who cares? Just get on with it." Linda and I have had endless dialogues about art and life, and her thoughts are always sharp and insightful. It's a trait I've found carries through all of her writing.

So sit back, relax, and enjoy her debut novel.

—George Gallo

*"In a closed society where everybody's guilty, the only crime is getting caught. In a world of thieves, the only final sin is stupidity."*

—Hunter S. Thompson

# Day One

## Paris, France

*T*he alley was dark and littered with trash from the overflowing waste cans and with drunken, unconscious patrons of the saloon located at its end. The amber light, which seeped from the cracks in the door and boarded-up windows of the dilapidated building, provided enough light for passersby to avoid stepping on any undesirable objects. Noise from the saloon was muffled, but still audible, as it drifted down the alley to one of the many streets of Paris.

A man, whose face was still handsome though hiding the youth that had been beaten from him by the life he had chosen, prepared to tiptoe his way through the maze to the saloon door. His short dark hair blended with the misty night. The collar of his raincoat flipped up, its belt tightly securing the taut raincoat around his sinuous body to protect the clothes beneath it. He stood at the corner of the street and alley, surveying them both. Had he been followed? Who was waiting for him in that dark alley or in that raucous saloon? Did he have his gun loaded? He withdrew the firearm, a Beretta, checking it and his surroundings. It was now ready in case he needed it. He glanced up and down the main thoroughfare before sliding around the corner into the misty darkness of the alley, toward the amber light that betrayed the presence of some of the lowest life of Paris.

As he tiptoed to the door, he heard a screech. He didn't bother to look. He had heard those types of screeches before. It was a rat, something he despised intensely and saw far too often. It was beyond this well-educated, well-dressed man why Jacques preferred to squander his life in such vile places. In this man's estimation, Jacques was paid rather handsomely for his information.

Another screech caught the man's attention and pulled him from his thoughts. He paused as he waited to hear additional steps on the wet pavement. There were none, only the snorts and swat of a man awakened by the vile, dirty creature trying to steal a breadcrumb from the drunk's shirt. The man again started for the door of the saloon.

He reached the door and breathed a quick sigh of relief. Just before placing his hand on the doorknob to enter the raunchy establishment, he took in a very deep breath. He winced from the stench, which made him wish he hadn't done that. He opened the door slowly, trying not to attract any attention with swift movements. He entered the room cautiously but calmly. He stood momentarily in a darkened corner at the entry of the room, surveying it and all the chaos. No one was the least bit interested in him. The room was lit with sconces and lamps, all draped with red and orange chiffon-like material. The man wasn't sure what kind of effect the owner was going for, but he was quite sure he had walked into a badly reproduced opera. The amber light danced with the smoke created by just about any type of smoking device he could think of, all being used by various patrons of the bar. In one corner of the room was a very badly abused grand piano, which was annoyingly out of tune. Most of the patrons were around this piano, while a sloppily dressed overweight woman sang as if she were an opera diva, complete with fan and headdress, screeching a very bad rendition of the *Casta Diva* aria, which sprang from her heavily red lipstick-laden mouth. Like fingernails scratching down a chalkboard, the woman's attempt at singing grated on the man's nerves. As the shrill sound of a high note accosted the man's ears, he turned his head to see a darker area, far from the offending racket of the opera impersonators who, he surmised, were pretending to be performing at Covent Garden.

As the man reached the darkened corner booth, he untied his coat and slid onto the stained and tattered velvet bench, his back to the wall, facing the door to the saloon. His form seemed to disappear in the darkness, his hands seen only as he called the bartender over to the booth. He thought of ordering gin when the bartender arrived but somehow felt whiskey was more appropriate. He found that thought strangely odd, but it didn't matter anyway. He had no intention of drinking it.

Shortly after the bartender returned with his shot, a short Frenchman, complete with at least a three-day growth on his face and the body odor to match, slid into the bench across from the smartly dressed man. The Frenchman's smile wrinkled the skin around his eyes and revealed missing teeth.

"Monsieur Adkins," the Frenchman greeted the man, eyeing the shot of whiskey.

"Jacques." Adkins adjusted the collar of his coat as he watched Jacques begin to salivate. Jacques's eyes never strayed from the whiskey. "Consider it an advance," Sean Adkins added in his proper English accent, a stark conflict to Jacques's very common and broken English.

"Some advance!" Jacques retorted, grabbing the shot. "You no like whiskey anyway." He threw his head back as he downed the shot.

Sean smiled. "What do you have for me?"

"I have some information on your blue-eyed friend, monsieur." Jacques paused as the bartender arrived to take a drink order from Jacques "Bring two more whiskeys," Jacques instructed the bartender.

"Bring the bottle," Sean corrected.

The bartender left to retrieve the bottle. "You are very good to me. That is why I work so hard for you, no?" Jacques said.

"You have been very helpful in the past. I've yet to hear what you have for me today."

The bartender returned with the bottle. He set it on the marred table, placing a second shot glass in front of Sean. Jacques was still fondling the first glass. The bartender waited to be paid as Sean eyed Jacques and his nervousness. Jacques was almost too anxious for the drink, and this piqued Sean's curiosity.

"Monsieur, it is the policy—," the bartender began.

"Yes, I'm sorry." Sean pulled out some cash and peeled off a handsome amount of money to pay for the bottle and secure their privacy. "There is extra for you. I trust you won't bother us or remember …"

"I don't remember anything or anybody. It is how I stay alive," the bartender answered as he walked away.

Jacques grabbed the bottle and began to pour himself a shot, licking his lips. "You will be pleased with what I have for you," Jacques said and then downed the shot, wincing as the cheap alcohol burned his throat. He wiped his mouth on his dirty sleeve.

Sean watched as he poured his third drink. This behavior was very strange indeed. Although Jacques enjoyed the benefits of drinking, Sean had never considered him to be an alcoholic, and this behavior was that of an alcoholic or someone drinking to seek comfort from something terrible, something haunting. Had Sean's blue-eyed friend double-crossed his stoolie, his informant? Or was Jacques about to double-cross him? Sean confidently and covertly looked around the saloon. The very bad opera was continuing. No one seemed out of place. And yet Jacques threw his head back, wincing after his third shot of what Sean figured was close to grain alcohol. "Well?"

Jacques had begun to pour his fourth shot when Sean tipped the bottleneck up in Jacques's hand. The meaning was clear. "Your friend left for America this morning," Jacques spat out quickly and then forced his hand to pour another drink. Very quickly and quite effectively, Sean wrestled the bottle out of Jacques's hand, applying just the right amount of pressure around the wrist. Jacques grimaced and released the bottle. He looked up at Sean as the Englishman placed the bottle just out of his reach, continuing to hold it. Jacques's eyes moved from the bottle along Sean's raincoat sleeve to his face, which showed a flash of anger.

Sean was trying very hard to control that anger, which was welling up inside him. "This morning?" Sean asked through his clenched teeth.

"Yes," Jacques answered, again licking his lips and fidgeting in his seat.

"And you wait until now to tell me this. I question your loyalty to me, Jacques."

"Monsieur, I am offended! I called you at your hotel this morning. You did not return my call until 5:30 this evening. I have been here waiting for you ever since. You are the one who is late. This is not my fault."

Sean knew Jacques was telling the truth, but it didn't make it any easier and it certainly wasn't calming his anger down. He had been tracking down a bad lead. The frustration of knowing that he had again been misled by informants he thought were more reliable than Jacques was just one more way the Serpent kept one step ahead of him. Sean had given the blue-eyed Serpent a full day's head start to America. Had he not been in the French countryside staking out a chateau where he had been told the Serpent was vacationing, he would instead be on a plane, hot on the Serpent's trail.

He ran the fingers of his free hand through his hair as his other hand continued to hold Jacques's precious nectar. Sean inhaled deeply, trying to calm his mind. "Where?"

Jacques eyed the bottle. He knew that the next answer was not to be given to Sean immediately and without some difficulty. The Serpent had been quite clear on that. Jacques needed to think how to throw him off that thought. "My memory is not too good. Maybe another drink … "

Sean felt his blood pressure climb rapidly as if his head were about to burst from the anger. He was going to lose control quickly if Jacques continued this stupid cat-and-mouse game. Through clenched teeth and desperate attempts to keep his voice civil, Sean spoke slowly. "You better think harder, my friend. You are not getting another drink until you tell me where in America your employer has gone."

Jacques sat back. He had never see Sean so angry. Jacques hadn't realized that Sean knew he was working for the Serpent. He wondered what his employer had done to make Sean react so, to harbor this much hate for him. Jacques was merely following the orders that had been given to him, just as he had done many times in previous years. He saw no reason why this reaction was warranted. His employer had never given him any reason to suspect that Sean would be this angry. The Serpent's instructions had been to tell Sean only that the Serpent had gone to America and to make Sean work for the information on the general area the Serpent was traveling to. Then Jacques would be paid handsomely and his family would be spared. "He did not tell me where, monsieur."

Sean eyed Jacques with contempt. He knew now that the Serpent had led him on a wild goose chase again to cover his escape to America. Was it an escape? It didn't matter. Sean knew that Jacques knew more. Jacques had to know what city the Serpent was landing in right this minute. Jacques may not know where the assassin would go after the Serpent's plane had landed. The Serpent enjoyed allowing Sean this close. It was their game, and the Serpent wasn't about to end it. Sean's green eyes flashed only a hint of the anger he was now harboring as he realized that Jacques had been a part of this ploy all along. He began to pour the two shot glasses full of whiskey. He let a little maniacal laugh leave his lips. As he poured the second shot glass full, the glass closest to Jacques, he let the precious nectar flow over the glass and onto the marred table while letting another maniacal chuckle leave his lips. The whiskey began to slip through the cracks and rush to the end of the table. It began dripping onto the disgustingly dirty floor, to the horror of Jacques's disbelieving eyes.

Scared by the scene unfolding before him, Jacques tried to stop the wastefulness of his precious liquid. Sean had never hurt him before, and Jacques felt Sean would not do so now. He wanted that whiskey to forget about his miserable life and his failures to care for and support his family. Earlier in the day, he had pleaded with the Serpent in Jacques's home. The Serpent had fondled his children, threatening his wife's life to ensure that the Serpent's message to Sean was completely understood. Jacques had pleaded with the Serpent that this would be his last errand in this fool's game. The Serpent had agreed. Jacques had wanted to celebrate that the Serpent's hold on him would be ending in the bottle Sean was now wasting. As he reached for the bottle, Sean smashed it on the side of the table, sending glass and whiskey in all directions. Jacques shielded his eyes, or tried, but Sean had grabbed the collar of his shirt, in front by his neck, with his free hand.

In the rush of adrenaline from his anger, Sean lifted Jacques off the seat of the bench and suspended him over the table. Jacques began to whimper, but none of this was heard over the opera being screeched from across the room.

Sean brought the jagged edge of the bottle up to Jacques's neck. "Is it getting any clearer," Sean started, spitting out the last two words, "my friend?"

"Monsieur, please. I have a wife and children … "

Sean wondered if Jacques had pleaded with the Serpent as he was pleading now. A fleeting thought that didn't persuade Sean for one minute. "I know that, Jacques. Do you think I give a fuck about them? Does the Serpent? What I don't know is where in America he is."

"Monsieur, please … I do not know … "

"Do you think your life is any more important to me than it is to the Serpent? Do you really think I care if you live or die?" Sean began to press the jagged edge of the bottle into Jacques's neck.

"Why do you treat me so? Yes, I believe you are a better person than the Serpent, but that is not the issue. I do not know where he is going. Please, I do not know!" Jacques began to whimper more loudly as tears began to fill his eyes.

Sean forced the jagged edge deeper, and blood began to run from the wound. "Can you feel how close I am to ending your life, Jacques?" Jacques let a little scream escape from his lips, but the position of Sean's hand on his throat kept it from being audible by anyone except Sean. Sean's voice was cold, calm and betrayed how ruthless he could be. "Where is he, Jacques?"

The stakes were too high for Jacques. He wanted this nightmare to be over. He wanted to never be bothered by either of these two evil men again. "Washington!" Jacques answered, defeated.

"State or city?" Sean asked, keeping Jacques suspended in the moment.

"Washington, DC," Jacques said, almost in a state of panic, wondering if Sean was going to take his life anyway. "Please, monsieur, I beg you. I know no more!" Jacques said as tears streamed down his face. "No more … "

Sean held him a moment longer, staring into his eyes. Then he sent Jacques's quivering body to the back of the booth. Jacques reached for and felt the blood that was trickling out of the small cut on his throat.

"You have never treated me this way before." Jacques looked at Sean, stunned. In the years that he had been playing his double-crossing informant game, he had never thought that Sean could be so mean, so deadly, and so cold-blooded. It was what made Sean different from the Serpent. But now, something was different in Sean. Something must have snapped. "Why?" It was the only question Jacques could form as his eyes welled up with tears again.

Sean stood. He threw some money on the table. He looked at Jacques. "Maybe you better decide whose side you are on, Jacques. I'm tired of being fucked with." Sean began to take a step, then stopped. "If the Serpent was with your family today, if they saw him, then I pity them for what he did to them after you left with this information that you were paid handsomely to give me." He looked at the broken bottle in his hand. "Your life is worthless." With that, Sean walked to the door and quit the saloon.

Outside, he smashed the remaining part of the bottle by throwing it against the wall. He flipped up his collar and wrapped his coat around him to protect himself from the elements of the Parisian night. He wiped the remains of the whiskey from his face as he began to walk out of the alley. With each step, his mind raced. He began to make a list of things he needed. By the time he reached the street, he was almost in a dead run. Just as he reached the head of the alley, he heard screams behind him. It was Jacques, screaming the names of his wife and children. Sean was right. The Serpent spared no one, not even Jacques. The Frenchman's days were numbered.

Sean ran to his hotel through the Paris night air. He had to get to America, and only one person could keep him from doing so. This person couldn't stop Sean if he went directly to Washington. Yes, Sean would go directly to Washington. It was the only way.

# Washington, DC

"Tony," the voluptuous, brown-eyed, cinnamon-haired beauty started. "I don't understand why you insist on taking me to dinner party after dinner party when you know I'll only insult every Republican within earshot." Nicole Charbonneau was as intelligent as she was beautiful. After leaving a promising career in Washington, DC's District Attorney's office, Nicole had become the star attorney at Rosen, Shafer, and Pruett. At this firm, she handled high-profile cases, and her name was recognized throughout the beltway. A promising future in politics was hers for the asking, if she desired it.

There are a number of ins in Washington. The "in crowd", "insiders", and "inside the beltway" are just some of the *ins* that indicate part of the envied elite. There are those who are *out* and relish the thought of being *in*. They desire to be part of this chosen closed circle. But the word "in" appears in the word "blind." While Nicole Charbonneau's boss, Tony Shafer, who was lustfully in love with Nicole, thought he was part of the insiders, he really was blind to what was taking shape in his small but powerful circle of friends. As a result of his partnership in the most powerful law firm within the beltway, his many connections made his law firm *the firm* to seek out for making those, shall we say, embarrassing indiscretions disappear without publicity. His firm had rescued many politicians, lobbyists, and corporation chairmen from the kind of publicity that had ruined many an individual's career. If Tony really wanted to be a power broker in DC, he had enough dirt on those creating the laws of the nation to fashion whatever position he desired. It was a good thing that all Tony wanted was his yacht, his large salary to spend the way he wanted, and Nicole.

Nicole had an interesting life and never gave a thought to being part of the in crowd, and in a rather odd way, she shunned the concept of the two factions in Washington. She didn't care if she was in or out as long as it meant that she had a job and could provide for herself as she had done for most of her life. She had always felt that one has to be blind to be a part of any particular group. This was one reason why she had never fancied being part of the crowd or a follower. Her life had been a series of consequences that left her with a series of black-and-white, yes-and-no decisions, made through weighing the outcome of each path. She never could understand how being in, or out, could even enter into one's thinking process. Unlike Tony, however, Nicole was only partially blind to what was developing around her.

Nicole's brown eyes scanned the athletic sixty-year-old man sitting next to her. She waited patiently while he formulated his response. Tony Shafer was one of the founding partners of Rosen, Shafer, and Pruett. His sun-bleached hair against his tan skin gave him a distinguished look. There were times when Nicole could see the damage forming deep creases around his eyes from the extended sailing excursions aboard his yacht. Many women found him very attractive. Maybe it was his money they found attractive. Nicole had to admit that Tony had a wonderful sense of humor and was generally a fun-loving guy. They shared a quality that both envied in others: perseverance—a trait that Nicole witnessed firsthand as Tony relentlessly tried to persuade her to become a Republican. Their relationship was purely platonic; Nicole was not interested in someone old enough to be her father, much to Tony's displeasure. He thought he truly loved Nicole, although what he really loved was the power she unknowingly commanded.

"Nikki," Tony started, fidgeting with the cummerbund of his tuxedo, "I've told you time and time again that with your reputation and the right connections, you could enter politics. I'm merely providing you with an opportunity to meet the right people who could provide you with those connections."

Nicole studied him further. She did not deny her interest in politics. She couldn't picture herself as a politician, though. As a matter of fact, that image made her laugh out loud. "Me? A politician?" She shook her head, still chuckling. "My God, Tony, I'd be shot in no time!"

"That's why you have people, who ... " Tony faltered, trying to find the proper word, knowing how Nicole would react to the words that had almost escaped his lips.

"Handle me?"

"For lack of a better word, yes," Tony answered.

"I suppose that is where you come in?"

"Only if you switch parties and become a Republican," Tony answered with a wink and a wry smile.

Nicole laughed again. "Ah, Tony, there is that sense of humor of yours! Me as a Republican is almost as funny as me being a senator."

*Blind Influence* | 11

"Think about it." Tony handed the invitation to the driver as the limousine came to a stop at the White House gate. The driver showed the invitation to the guard, who inspected it, then handed it back to the driver. The guard motioned for the gates to be opened, and then the limousine moved to the front entrance of the White House.

It was a crisp, clear fall evening, with the full moon adding its splendor to a beautifully lit, pristine building. The White House staff had outdone themselves once again. A red carpet had been extended to the driveway to greet the guests. A canopy had been erected to protect the visitors from falling leaves and the rain, which had been incorrectly forecasted by the weatherman earlier in the day. As the limousine came to a stop, Nicole's door was opened by a Marine in his dress uniform. He offered his white-gloved hand to Nicole, who accepted it, gracefully exiting the car. Her long bronze evening gown, which shimmered in the light, accentuated her figure with a slit up the side that stopped teasingly at mid-thigh. A teardrop neckline accentuated her bust. Her hair swept away from her face to a cascade of cinnamon curls, which stopped just below the shoulder blades of her naked back. She was stunning, and Tony knew it. He enjoyed the envious looks he received whenever Nicole was on his arm, and he wasn't about to stop enjoying them any time soon. He arrived next to Nicole, offered his arm, and led her inside.

The foyer of the White House was brilliantly lit, again setting Nicole's evening gown dancing. Tony and Nicole moved to the reception line. The president and first lady, along with the vice president and his wife, were greeting their guests with the typical rhetoric that was bandied about between the two political parties. Nicole glanced around the room and noticed that the guest list was composed predominantly of senators and representatives. She breathed a small sigh of relief, deducing that the conversations for the evening would be limited to current affairs and legislation pending in both houses. While Nicole found these conversations interesting, she rarely took part in them.

The dinner guests were milling around, some with drinks, talking about various subjects; their voices echoed in the open foyer, making it impossible to eavesdrop on any of the conversations. As Nicole entered, a number of the men's eyes were turned by her beauty. Two men in particular gazed unabashedly at her. Nicole was unaware of this, but Tony wasn't as he quickly moved to the receiving line.

President Andrews and his wife made a perfect couple, in Nicole's estimation. They looked to her like a Midwestern couple, very plain and very conservative. The president was in the middle of cleaning his wire-rimmed glasses when Tony approached. The Marine guard waited until the president had finished before announcing them, accepting the engraved invitation from Tony. Nicole took the opportunity to find something she could compliment the first lady on, noticing first the powder blue chiffon evening gown she was wearing. Nicole didn't care for the outdated dress, so she moved on to the hairdo, which had so much hairspray that a hurricane couldn't blow a bit of wind through it. Nicole sighed. It didn't appear to be an easy night after all.

The Marine started the introduction, but it was not needed. The president and first lady knew Tony from previous engagements and from his close friendship with the vice president. "Hello, Tony!" The president extended his hand. "How are you?"

"Fine, Mr. President. You remember Nicole Charbonneau?"

"Why, yes, of course." The president shook Nicole's hand.

"Hello, Mr. President." Nicole smiled graciously, not really sure if the president remembered her, and moved on to the first lady. She greeted Mrs. Andrews and complimented her on the evening gown she was wearing. Determining it was the lesser of two evils, she almost couldn't keep from laughing when she heard the "this old thing" reply. She smiled graciously instead. The vice president and his wife were next for her to greet. While Nicole really had no feelings toward the president, she had a strong dislike for the vice president.

"Tony!" Vice President Mark Stevens greeted the lawyer with a smile and an extended hand. "Good to see you! How are you?"

Tony shook his hand, answering, "I'm fine, Mark. You remember—"

The vice president's eyes followed Tony's hand as Tony gently grasped Nicole's elbow, moving her closer to himself and the vice president. The vice president's eyes were now scanning the rest of Nicole, starting at her hips and lustfully enjoying every voluptuous curve. When his eyes reached her face, they were met with her disapproving scowl.

*Blind Influence* | 13

"Ms. Charbonneau." Mark Stevens finished Tony's sentence. He took Nicole's hand in his, holding it with both of his hands. "You're hard to forget."

Nicole withdrew her hand forcefully. "I take it your ears are still ringing, Mr. Vice President?"

"They are indeed still ringing, Ms. Charbonneau."

"Then maybe I'm making progress."

"Progress?" the vice president questioned, taken by surprise by what he selfishly thought had been a flirtatious remark.

"Yes, Mr. Vice President. I now know that what I am saying is getting into your head. The next step is to make sure you process the information." Nicole smiled, satisfied that she had again caught him off guard. "Have a good evening," she said to Mrs. Stevens as she turned away from them, walking toward the dining room.

"I'm sorry, Mark," Tony started. "I don't know what gets into her when she's around you."

The vice president raised his eyebrows as he lustfully watched Nicole walk away. "Don't apologize, Tony." He glanced at his wife to ensure that her attention was elsewhere. "The chase is the best part, the most fun."

Tony was somewhat shocked, although he showed nothing. He merely smiled and excused himself to catch Nicole. He briskly walked through the crowd, briefly greeting those he knew.

Upon reaching Nicole, Tony was greeted rather rambunctiously by another friend, Norman Sipes. Sipes had a booming voice, a protruding belly, a burr haircut, and a drink in his hand that he certainly didn't need. Sipes was president and CEO of one of the fastest growing oil companies in America. Tony had urged Nicole about two years ago to invest in Sipes's company, as well as in other interests, but Nicole's instincts told her not to do so. She had suspicions that Sipes's success had been gained through illegal scams. By the looks of things, she felt she was right.

"Tony! You old dog! How do you do it?" Sipes called, winking an eye and pointing toward Nicole. Sipes's voice and actions managed to grab the

14 | *Linda Riesenberg Fisler*

attention of almost everyone in the foyer. He didn't care. He had waited patiently, by his estimation, to talk to the young beauty, staring at her non-stop since she had entered.

"Norm, how are you?" Tony asked, trying to ignore his friend's atrocious behavior.

"You never mind that. What did you promise her this time?" When Sipes could see he was not going to get an answer from Tony, he decided to use the direct approach. "You can tell me, sweetheart," he said to Nicole. "I know I can triple what was promised." He clumsily tried to wink alluringly at her.

Nicole was about to answer when Tony, knowing her answer would be less than pleasant, interrupted. "Norm," he started, turning his friend around with both his hands to face the bar, "I think you better ask that gentleman for a pot of coffee, or you might not make it into this dinner party either." A few couples within the immediate vicinity laughed at Tony's remarks. In any case, everyone's attention was returning to their own conversations. Tony turned back to Nicole, taking her arm and leading her into the din-ing room.

The room seemed to be an endless sea of white tablecloths, which shrouded the round tables and hung midway to the floor. The high-backed dining room chairs, eight at each table, were pulled back slightly, inviting the guests to be seated. The centerpiece of each table was a pristine single white candle encircled in a glass canopy with a ring of pastel roses. The guests could see their reflections in both the china and silverware, which had been meticulously polished and placed. Tony and Nicole scanned the eloquently printed name tags that were suspended in front of the china by silver holders.

Finding Nicole's seat, Tony left to get their drinks. Nicole took the oppor-tunity to scan the other names of the people she would be sharing dinner conversations with this night. She was horrified to discover that Norman Sipes was seated next to her. She quickly glanced around the table for a suitable replacement. Senator Robert Jenkins, a Democrat from North Carolina, was seated a few seats away from her. She had always wanted to meet him, and now seemed the perfect opportunity. Cautiously, Nicole switched the name tags, unaware that the other gentleman who couldn't keep his eyes off her was watching her even now. She placed the senator's

*Blind Influence* | 15

name tag next to her seat. Pleased with herself, she smiled at her deviousness and then suddenly she heard a voice behind her.

"I hope this means you wanted to meet me," Senator Jenkins stated in the refined southern draw that made him so irresistibly charming, a hint of hope in his voice. Nicole jumped at the sound.

She turned to face him, feeling her cheeks warm from embarrassment. "Senator Jenkins … " She blushed even more, having been caught in the act.

"I'm sorry. I didn't mean to startle you."

"That's quite all right." Nicole decided to quickly change the subject. "I saw your speech yesterday regarding ANWR, I mean the Alaska National Interest Lands Conservation Act." The Alaska National Interest Lands Conservation Act, ANILCA, was a comprehensive act designed to preserve the untamed Alaskan wilderness, native peoples, and animals for the enjoyment of all. Albeit in the early stages of development in the fall of 1979, this large, encompassing act was being boiled down to one very polarizing issue. One stipulation, falsely portrayed by media and politicians alike, was now the rallying call for numerous protests and hotly contested discussions around the world. While ANILCA created more than one hundred fifty seven million acres of national parks, wildlife refuges and wilderness areas from federal holdings, the act also allowed for the drilling of black gold, the blood that kept the United States producing and warring. This act allowed for the drilling of oil in the Arctic National Wildlife Refuge, the ANWR, unconditionally. Those who opposed this greedy land grab knew ANWR was nineteen million acres of extraordinary wildlife and wilderness void of scars of human intervention and destructiveness.

"Please, let's not discuss politics." The senator was impressed that Nicole could recall the name of the act rather than reducing it to the simplistic idea of drilling for oil in ANWR as the media had done. He used his hand to replace a lock of brown hair back in its wanted place. The senator had brown eyes that Nicole determined that any woman could easily get lost in, and a personality that made anyone who spoke with him feel at ease. She could see why he had earned the reputation of being the most eligible bachelor on Capitol Hill.

He moved down the table to see with whom he had been switched. "I'm afraid that speech is what got me invited to this dinner." The senator men-

16 | *Linda Riesenberg Fisler*

tally noted the name. Not wanting to cause any further embarrassment to Nicole, he simply smiled at her. "Besides," he said as he moved back toward her now, "if we talk politics, it will be a very boring evening."

"I think that depends on which side of the issue you are on, and by the looks of it, I'd say we're out numbered."

"Exactly the reason I was invited. If they persuade me to vote for this act, they feel I'll lead the rush of Democrats in their direction."

"I see Senator Barker is here as well."

"Ah, yes. If you get Barker, you definitely get all the Democrats. With me, you will get enough for a majority."

Tony returned with Nicole's drink, unhappy to find her speaking with the young, handsome senator. He arrived just as Nicole started to ask her next question.

"Thank you, Tony. Senator, you're not considering the possibility to allow drilling in ANWR, are you?"

"He must have some doubts; otherwise, he wouldn't be here, Nicole," Tony interrupted, smiling.

"On the contrary, Mr. Shafer, I have no intention of changing my vote. I believe your attention would be better served preparing for Mr. Sipes's appearance before my committee."

"Wait a minute, Senator, Norm Sipes has not been subpoenaed as of yet."

"'Yet' is the key word, Mr. Shafer. We are working on that." He winked at Tony. It was no secret that Jenkins's committee was investigating illegal price fixing within the oil industry. Everyone in the industry was being called before the committee.

The senator's attention was caught by Senator Barker. "Excuse me," he said.

When the senator was safely engaged in conversation with Senator Barker, Nicole chuckled, saying to Tony, "Way to go!"

*Blind Influence* | 17

"That wasn't any worse than what you said to Mark."

"Yes, but Senator Jenkins has a brain."

"Damn it, Nikki!"

"I'm sorry, Tony. I forgot. You call him a friend."

"And he is a damn good friend." Tony tried to settle himself down before continuing. "Will you do me a favor?"

"What?"

"Keep your mouth shut tonight. You have some influential people at your table. If you handle yourself appropriately this evening, well, you know."

Nicole couldn't believe Tony couldn't finish the sentence. "I'm not interested, Tony." She set her drink down on the table. "And I'll always be a Democrat."

"Hear, hear!" Senator Jenkins answered as he returned to their table. "That's the kind of talk I like to hear."

Nicole smiled. Tony, however, was not amused. "Just try and not insult everyone."

Nicole did her best imitation of a child's pout, answering, "I'll try."

Tony angrily moved to his table. Nicole rolled her eyes and took her seat next to the senator, who, with perfect manners, helped Nicole into her seat, then seated himself.

A few minutes later, more of the guests entered the room, finding their seats. As the president and vice president entered the room, all stood. They moved to their seats along what Nicole determined was front of the room. A long rectangular table, with a podium centered on it, was where the president and his honored guests were to sit. The president moved to the podium and urged everyone to be seated.

As the room became silent, nearly everyone in their assigned seats, Nicole took the opportunity to scan her table. Tony was right. Besides the senator, who underestimated his influence in the Senate, and Norman Sipes, there were Donald Tipperman, a multimillionaire who had acquired his wealth through the stock market and some business ventures that Nicole hadn't really kept up with; Karen Johnson, a Republican representative from Kansas, who was also on a joint committee with the senator and had her eye on Senator Davidson's seat in the Senate; and Joseph Engle, the founder of First US Bank and a financier, who reportedly helped Norman with financing his company in the beginning, seated next to Congresswoman Johnson. To Nicole's surprise, Senator Barker's wife was also at this table, and last but certainly not least, there was someone Nicole knew nothing about. He was a man in his mid-fifties, she guessed, nicely dressed in a blue herringbone suit, with some very nervous and annoying traits. His sniffling alone and the nervous readjustment of his thick glasses were just two of the irritating habits he performed almost constantly. She felt like she should know him, but she just could not place him.

The president cleared his throat and began his speech. Nicole, feeling her first hunger pangs, hoped for a short speech. She truly hoped she would be interested in what the president had to say. He started out mentioning various world political shake-ups, the downturn in the economy, the inevitable fall of Communism in the not too distant future, and the need of the world for the United States to provide strong, consistent leadership. He stated that because of these reasons, it was imperative for the United States to get its "house in order."

Then the president made a statement that shocked not only Nicole but Senators Barker and Jenkins as well. The president stated that his support of allowing companies to drill for oil in the Alaskan National Wildlife Refuge was waning, citing that the end didn't justify the means. He felt that the short-term goals were not worth the cost. He continued, saying America's only true answer to the crisis was to lose its dependence on oil—not just foreign oil.

The president, aware of the disapproving looks from not only the vice president but also every other Republican in the room, continued, stating that it would be impossible for the United States to lead from strength with its own people disillusioned in its leaders. "How can you ask a young man or woman to potentially sacrifice his or her life for the US when that person has no respect for the people leading him?"

Many in the room felt that the statement was far from reality. Nicole even overheard the whispered, cold response from Representative Johnson to

*Blind Influence* | 19

her colleague at another table; "They go because we send them and it is their job" seemed to hang in the air. The callous comment also caught the attention of Senator Jenkins, who stared in Johnson's direction until her eyes met his. A former Navy Seal who had paid dearly for the freedoms enjoyed by all Americans by losing the lower portion of his right leg on a secret mission during the Vietnam War, Jenkins was angered by this frivolously cold remark and wanted the Representative to feel just how much he resented it. His contemptuous stare continued until Representative Johnson felt uneasy, maybe threatened, and squirmed in her chair. Satisfied that his unspoken point had been made, the senator turned his attention back to the president.

Nicole felt as if she were in a dream. This position was so radical for the president, it was as if he had switched parties. Nicole glanced at Senator Barker, who was smiling, already counting a victory. She then looked at Mark Stevens, who, oddly enough, was exchanging a disparaging look with Tony. Nicole watched Mark's eyes move to Sipes and the man Nicole didn't know.

Nicole casually turned her head to catch Sipes's reaction. Oddly, he smiled and gave a flippant wave of his hand. He then reached for his water glass. He glanced at the unknown man, who nervously smiled, adjusted his glasses again, and turned his gaze to the president. The whole scene gave Nicole the chills but still somewhat intrigued her. After all, Norman Sipes had the most to lose by this legislation. She finally shrugged it off, realizing she never would figure the three of them out and had no real desire to try. She hadn't realized she was staring at Sipes until suddenly her stomach rumbled, catching Senator Jenkins's attention.

"Excuse me," Nicole said, once again embarrassed.

"That is quite all right." The senator reached into his coat pocket. "Here, this should help." Smiling, he produced and handed her a peppermint. "I always come prepared. You just never know how long he's going to talk."

Nicole smiled. "Thank you," she told the senator, popping the mint into her mouth. She leaned closer to the senator and whispered, "Isn't this a surprise?"

"It certainly is. Dinner will be very interesting," he replied. Jenkins caught the scent of Nicole's perfume, finding the aroma very pleasing.

They both turned their attention back to the president, who continued to belabor the point. Nicole kept a continued watch on certain influential Republicans, monitoring their responses. The overwhelming reaction was anger and irritation. The senator was right. Dinner was going to be very interesting.

After another fifteen minutes, the president, satisfied that he had emphasized all his points, ended with, "And for all these reasons, but most important of these reasons, that the US should lead the world in alternative fuel development, I shall veto the Alaska National Interest Lands Conservation Act when it reaches my desk if the provision to drill with reckless abandon in ANWR is still attached." With that, he called for everyone to enjoy their dinner and sat down next to his wife, who smiled approvingly at her husband.

The room was quiet until Nicole started to clap. Others joined her in an unenthusiastic and polite round of applause. Nicole watched as Congresswoman Johnson stared disapprovingly at Senator Jenkins. The senator, not willing to start yet another one of their countless arguments, remained calm and tried to start a pleasant conversation with Nicole.

"How long have you been practicing law, Ms. Charbonneau?"

"Please, call me Nikki," she interjected. "For about eleven years now." The senator smiled at her.

"All with Rosen, Shafer, and Pruett?"

"No. I was with the United States Attorney's Office for about three and a half years. The rest has been with Rosen, Shafer, and Pruett."

The representative from Kansas couldn't stand it any longer. "Tell me, Senator, how did you do it?" She placed a very unpleasant emphasis on the word *did*.

"What did I do, Congresswoman?" the senator asked calmly.

"Convince the president that this act will absolutely destroy the country, when you know that it will decrease US dependency on foreign oil. It is inconceivable to me that you and Senator Barker can't see that. Once again, you and the rest of the Democrats intend on hurting the many by protecting the few."

Nicole wanted desperately to answer the congresswoman but decided against it. The last thing she wanted was to be part of a political debate with Senator Jenkins at the table. Besides, she had seen him in action enough to know he could handle this himself.

The senator simply smiled and decided to try to defuse the situation. "Ms. Johnson, I fear you give me far too much credit. The president arrived at this decision himself. I'm sorry to say, we Democrats had nothing to do with it. Besides, this isn't the proper place to discuss it."

The senator tried to return to his conversation with Nicole but was interrupted in mid-sentence. "On the contrary, Senator," Sipes chimed in. "I'd like to hear your answer. After all, I counted at least six references to me in that speech."

Joseph Engle shot a nervous look at Sipes, of which Nicole caught only a glimpse. "I think we all felt we were referenced, Norm," he added, trying to gain support. A few heads nodded in agreement.

Nicole couldn't resist a good fight and wanted it clear that her support, even though it could be for a losing effort, was for Senator Jenkins. "I'm sorry, Mr. Engle, I have to disagree. I don't feel I was referenced at all in the president's speech."

"Well," Engle chuckled, "you're just a lawyer."

*And good at defending assholes like you from being thrown in jail!* She thought.

"Let's not get away from the initial question, Senator," Sipes said to Jenkins.

"I hate to disappoint all of you, but I really had nothing to do with it," the senator answered.

"Come on, Senator," Tipperman started, "are you trying to tell us that stirring speech you gave yesterday was written without any collaboration with the Oval Office?"

"You flatter me, Mr. Tipperman. Yes, it was. As a matter of fact, I wrote that speech myself. My aides were busy researching another issue." Jenkins shot an accusing look at Norman Sipes.

22 | *Linda Riesenberg Fisler*

"Senator, a majority of the points you made in your speech were also in the president's speech," Congresswoman Johnson charged.

"Maybe he was watching C-SPAN," Nicole chimed in, trying to ease the growing tension. The attempt failed, even though Mrs. Barker and Senator Jenkins laughed.

Mrs. Barker gave a pleasant chuckle before clearing her throat. She was beginning to take a liking to Nicole.

The senator added a quick comment after Mrs. Barker cleared her throat. He was still smiling at the remark when he said, "Quite possibly."

"Oh please!" Johnson replied, annoyed. "What do you take us for, Ms. Charbonneau, a bunch of idiots?"

Nicole had all she could do to keep from answering in the affirmative to *that* question. It struck Nicole as odd that the congresswoman reacted the way she had to Nicole's statement. In any case, Nicole wasn't about to pass up a golden opportunity to insult a politician. "Well, Congresswoman, when someone discounts the effects of certain legislation on the majority of indigenous people who live there, I can only assume that they are either ignorant or incompetent."

The congresswoman at first wasn't sure if Nicole had insulted her or the senator. Nicole, aware of this, decided to make it very clear. "The Alaska National Interest Lands Conservation Act serves only those interested in oil and does very little to provide refuge to a way of life. While setting aside a rather large amount of land for parks and refuge, the gains of allowing companies to drill for oil unconditionally does nothing for the people who live off that land except destroy their very existence. It allows for drilling before surveys can be conducted to determine if the amount of oil is of sufficient quantity to warrant the cost of excavation, that cost being not only the cost to the companies who want to drill, but its effect on the D2 lands, which were lands withdrawn from a previous act by the Department of Interior and designated for development. These D2 lands have a greater degree of ecological diversity than any other similar-sized area of Alaska's North Slope. I'm not even mentioning the effect this would have on the native people that have lived there for generations. In the meantime, the world's economy is lulled into believing that the US dependence on foreign oil is relieved, only to quite possibly discover in a few years that dependence never disappeared as promised. The economic repercussions could be devastating for a mere tap dance of so-called relief. Focusing our efforts on long-term answers is the only true way to lessen America's dependence." Nicole felt a need to add while looking at Norman Sipes, "And the more this is done by companies not already involved in the current production of oil, the better."

"That is precisely why I am in the process of writing an amendment in that regard," the senator finished. He was impressed by Nicole's knowledge of the act. "Not bad for an attorney," the senator added, looking at Engle, who cringed. Representative Johnson and Sipes were not pleased with this turn of events. Johnson was so mad, she couldn't think of a response to Nicole quickly enough.

"Nikki, is Tony aware of your politics?" Sipes asked.

"Yes, painfully aware, Mr. Sipes." She smiled as she answered.

The senator smiled at Nicole's remark. "Mr. Sipes, I'm curious, why do you feel you were singled out by the president's remarks?" Nicole's comments had shifted the momentum and allowed him to focus on Sipes's comments.

"Not just me, Senator. As Mr. Engle pointed out, we all did."

"And as Ms. Charbonneau pointed out, not all of us felt that way," the senator countered.

Little beads of sweat began to appear on Norm's forehead as the two men were locked in a stare-down.

By pursuing this, the senator put Nicole in a precarious situation. Sipes was a client of the firm for which she worked. Although she had no intention of ever representing him, she felt she had to intercede. But she needed to determine how to do this without compromising her previous position.

"You can either answer that question here or in front of the committee, Mr. Sipes," the Senator prodded.

"I was probably overreacting. It was a big surprise," Sipes answered, taking a drink of his whiskey.

"To what were you overreacting? The president was making general statements. If you overreacted to general statements, then I would have to assume you have a guilty conscience. Am I to assume that perhaps your company is already doing what might now be prohibited by this act?" Jenkins continued his stare into Sipes's eyes.

Nicole was relieved to see their dinner arriving.

Mrs. Barker, who noticed the tension at the table, tried her best to end it. "Dinner is served. Senator, couldn't this wait?"

The waiters swarmed around the table and were gone in a matter of minutes. Almost everyone started picking up their silverware to cut into the grilled marinated chicken breast.

"No, Mrs. Barker. I'm afraid it can't wait. Mr. Sipes, I would like an answer."

Nicole was about to place a long-awaited forkful of food into her mouth when Sipes slammed his fist on the table. Nicole, startled, accidently dropped her fork as she inadvertently jumped at the loud noise. Water lapped at the sides of the glasses holding it, and the silverware jiggled, landing slightly askew.

"Damn it!" Sipes's booming voice caught everyone's attention at the surrounding tables, including Tony's. "I am not on trial, Jenkins! I know what you are trying to do, and I'll be damned if I will answer your stupid questions, here or in front of your pathetic little committee!"

The room was quiet.

"Mr. Sipes, I am merely asking what you found offensive or accusatory in the president's remarks." Jenkins continued to stare at Sipes.

Sipes looked at Nicole for help. Nicole returned to her food, vowing to herself to keep out of this argument. Tony was aware that Sipes was treading on thin ice. Nicole, however, didn't want to give the impression that she was willing to defend him.

"I believe," Sipes started, trying to keep his temper in check, "that the president's remarks were offensive to anyone whose business is oil."

*Blind Influence* | 25

"Did you find the president's remarks offensive, Mr. Van Der Merck?" the senator asked the owner of one of the biggest oil producers in the world, who was seated at a table nearby. Jenkins placed a forkful of food in his mouth while he waited for the answer.

"Surprising would be a better word," Mr. Van Der Merck replied, very uncomfortable at being drawn into the public conversation. Trying to deflect the conversation away from his table and back to Jenkins, he added, "Wouldn't you agree, Mr. Jefferies?"

*Michael Jefferies!* Nicole had heard his name before but had never seen him. Jefferies was the director of the FBI. "It is very surprising," Jefferies answered in an annoying voice. Nicole almost wanted to shudder at the sound.

"So, that leaves you as the only one being offended, Mr. Sipes," Senator Jenkins stated.

"Offended?" Tony questioned, now standing beside Nicole's chair. He tried to give an unconcerned chuckle. "He is the only one in this entire room that is offended?"

"Yes, Mr. Shafer." The senator turned to face Tony. "It seems Mr. Sipes feels the president referred to him at least six times in his speech tonight. I was merely asking why he felt that way."

Tony studied the senator carefully. Although his blood pressure nearly doubled, he outwardly remained calm. He couldn't believe that Sipes, in a matter of seconds, had destroyed the many months of work he had performed to keep the subpoena at bay. Tony had called in a number of favors to keep Sipes from appearing before the senator's committee. "I'm sure you misunderstood him, Senator."

"No, I don't believe so."

"Nikki?" Tony questioned, hoping she would be a team player and back up her superior.

Nicole couldn't believe Tony. It was not only a slap in the senator's face but an insult to her as well. Now she had a choice to make. She decided to face Tony's anger rather than to have the senator think she was a patsy. "The senator didn't misunderstand him, Tony." Nicole could see Tony's anger grow another degree. "I'm sorry."

"Don't apologize for speaking the truth, Nikki," the senator tried to console her. "I'm afraid I've ruined everyone's dinner. If you all will excuse me, I will take my leave." Senator Jenkins pushed himself away from the table and got up, dropping his napkin in his vacant chair, turning to Tony. "Good evening, Mr. Shafer." He turned and looked at Norman Sipes. "Mr. Sipes, you'll have a subpoena in the morning."

Nicole sat back, dreading the ride home. She glanced around the table. All eyes were shifting between Tony and Sipes—everyone's eyes except Mrs. Barker's. She was looking at Nicole. She smiled when their eyes met, as if to say *well done*. Nicole smiled back, briefly.

"I think we better call it a night, Nikki."

Nicole didn't answer Tony. She stood, bidding her dinner companions farewell, and exited the room with Tony.

Sipes followed them into the foyer. "I want her fired!" Sipes yelled in the foyer.

"That won't solve anything," Tony answered dismissively.

"What are you going to do?"

"Me?" Tony questioned. "Sipes, I am getting sick and tired of defending your fucking ass, especially when you are so liquored up, you have no fucking idea what you are saying! I'm half tempted to let you appear in front of Jenkins's committee!"

"Tony, you know I can't do that."

"I think I'll wait for you outside, Tony," Nicole interrupted. "I really don't want to know anything about this."

"Oh sure, scoot right on out of here, you little slut! You had a chance to keep this from happening," Sipes said to her.

Nicole smiled at Sipes, withholding her response only to let him guess at what she wanted to say. She simply turned to walk out the door. Tony quickly came to her defense.

"That's enough, Sipes! I've told you every time you have asked she doesn't want to represent you, and she certainly isn't going to fuck you, so knock it off. As for what I'm going to do, I don't know yet." Tony readjusted his tux jacket and brushed off some lint in an attempt to settle himself. Then he said in a calmer, lower voice, "I've just about run out of favors." He turned and walked outside to wait for their limousine with Nicole.

The ride home wasn't as bad as Nicole had anticipated. She got the usual speech of how she should be a team player, after which she reminded Tony that she had told him years ago that she would never lie to protect one of his slimy clients. As far as she was concerned, Norman Sipes fell into that category. After that, nothing more was said between them. As they arrived at Nicole's condo, she bade him a rather cold good night in the car and retired to her condo, alone, with her mind at peace and her reputation intact. That was much more important to her than representing scum, and even the six-figure salary she was earning at Rosen, Shafer, and Pruett.

# *London, England*

$C$harlie Dawson, a middle-aged plump and proper Englishman with lots of gray hair and a goatee, had just settled into his huge leather chair behind his old wooden desk to catch up on world events. He picked up his freshly brewed cup of tea and the sealed envelope that contained intelligence reports, placed on his desk by his secretary. The sun, for once, was shining through his window behind his desk. For once, reading the reports could be accomplished without the use of his desk lamp. He picked up the envelope, swinging his chair carefully around to look out the window and catch a few of the sun's rays. He propped his legs up with one foot on the windowsill and the other crossed over the top. He sipped his tea, opened the envelope, and placed the stack of reports on his lap. He picked up the top one.

He felt almost cheerful as the sun warmed his face. *Amazing what the ole sun can do! London looks absolutely marvelous on sunny days!* he thought. He read the first page of the report. There didn't seem like much happening in the United States. "It's a waste of paper, really," he said out loud as he kept reading. He chuckled when he read yet another headline regarding the huge deficit and how so-and-so wanted to remedy the situation. Something about a new banking act. The mention of the president's announcement to veto an act that was to allow drilling for oil in Alaska. Charlie turned the page, stifling a yawn. Nothing there, either.

He picked up another report and flipped through it while sipping his tea. He picked up a third report, thicker than the previous two. He could see by just skimming through the first page that his counterparts on the domestic side were going to be busy in Northern Ireland again. It seemed the IRA was up to its old tricks. There were claims by the IRA for at least six bombings, and threats of dozens more if their demands were not met.

"Morning, Charlie," Kent Chapman, a tall man in his thirties with blue eyes and blonde hair, said cheerfully as he entered Charlie's office. Kent's biceps rippled as he picked up a cup to pour himself some of Charlie's tea.

"Morning, Kent." Charlie dropped his legs off their perch and swung his chair around. He placed the intelligence reports in a drawer, then closed the drawer. "Looks like you boys will be busy."

*Blind Influence* | 29

"I'm not on that detail anymore. I'm on the international side, so you don't have to hide those reports, Charlie," Kent said as he sat down. "Heard anything from Sean?" Kent and Sean had gone through training at Fort Monkton. He had even worked with Sean when they were undercover agents infiltrating the IRA on their first assignment.

"No, I'm afraid not," Charlie answered. Even if he had heard anything from Sean, his answer would still be the same. Sean's work was so confidential, only those who needed to know already knew. Kent wasn't on the need-to-know list.

Kent thought for a moment. "That is strange. Sean always checks in with his superiors. He always felt it was one way to keep the old man off his back." Kent paused to see if he got any kind of reaction from Charlie. "Is he all right?" Kent's mind threw him back to the time when he and Sean had worked together.

Kent felt as if he were the older brother to Sean, even though they were the same age. It was a feeling not shared by Sean; although Sean had felt close to Kent at one time, he didn't feel that Kent had the skills to become an impactful resource for the Secret Intelligence Service, the SIS. In Sean's estimations, Kent was a bit reckless and sought recognition far too frequently. What Kent lacked in that area, Sean felt that Kent made up for in loyalty; however, Sean also realized that sometimes Kent was too quick to give his loyalty to those he would have been better off not knowing. Kent sought recognition, monetary reward, and, to some extent, fame a little too often in Sean's eyes. While working with him undercover, Sean trusted Kent with his life, and Kent had always delivered—except for one fateful night that Sean understandably would never forget.

Kent shook his head to rid himself of his thoughts.

"He's fine," Charlie reassured Kent, wondering what the agent now sitting across from him was thinking. "His judgment is flawless. However, I am concerned that he may be working too hard. His brother and father feel he is too obsessed—" He was interrupted by a knock on the door. "Come in," he called.

"Hello, Charlie," a well-dressed man said as he entered Charlie's office.

Charlie immediately stood up and shot a look to Kent for him to do the same. "Lord Adkins." Charlie moved around his desk and extended his hand. "It is always a pleasure to see you, sir."

"Kent, don't you have some work to do?" a voice from behind Lord Adkins asked. It was the voice of the director of SIS, Jack Kensington.

"Yes, sir," Kent stuttered and made his way out of Charlie's office. Lord Adkins smiled congenially as Kent moved past the two powerful and imposing men.

Lord Adkins shook Charlie's hand, which had never retracted during all the commotion. "Thank you, Charlie. I believe I have seen that chap before." Lord Adkins looked puzzled as he tried to determine if he had indeed met Kent previously. "Have a seat, please."

Charlie stood his ground in his office and acknowledged his superior's presence as well. "Director," he said, his hand extended to welcome Kensington. It seemed that very little ever upset Charlie. "What brings the pleasure of your company to my humble office?" Charlie ignored the opportunity to refresh the memory of Lord Adkins with the information that Kent had worked with his son prior to his current assignment. Charlie was use to the special attention that Sean Adkins received from these two men. He understood that Director Kensington was a friend of the family. Peter Adkins was in the House of Lords and head of the Joint Intelligence Committee.

"I'm afraid it isn't a social call," Lord Adkins started. "Have you heard from my son?"

"As I told you before, sir, Sean is in France. The nature of his work prohibits him from checking in regularly." Charlie opened his desk drawer and pulled out a file. "The last we heard from him was about a week ago. He stated he was getting closer to apprehending the Serpent. He had made contact with a new informant that evidently knew where he was going to be in a week or so. Sean wasn't sure if it was a new job that the Serpent would be on or if it was just his location in France."

"Yes, yes. We've heard all this before," Lord Adkins answered with a wave of his hand, clearly annoyed. "I have to say I'm concerned about my son's mental health. This is an obsession, and I don't believe he should be on the Serpent's trail."

*Blind Influence* | 31

"I'm not sure how I could keep him off it, Peter," Kensington remarked.

"Well, if that is the case, Jack, I'm not sure you are the right man to lead this organization," Peter snapped. "He is off the case because you say he is off the case. If he doesn't like that, then he can be dismissed from his duties here."

"And you think that will stop Sean from hunting this assassin down?" Jack Kensington smiled at Lord Adkins. He sat forward. "Look, Peter, Sean has done everything by the book. He is not showing any signs of becoming a vigilante or—"

Peter stood up and adamantly stomped his foot on the floor once, interrupting Jack. "My son's wife and child were murdered in cold blood, and you don't think his hunting that cold-blooded bastard hasn't turned him into a vigilante?"

Jack sat back. He looked to Charlie for reassurance. Charlie gave a quick no with one shake of his head. "No, we don't think that has turned him into a vigilante. Yes, he has a personal stake in bringing this assassin to justice, but Peter, until he does something that would warrant his being removed from this case, I won't do it. He is the only one who knows what this bastard looks like. He knows his moves. We take him off the case now, and who knows how many other assassinations will take place before we pick up a trail as close as Sean has to him. Besides, if I take him off the case, he'll resign and hunt that bastard down outside the law. He will then become a vigilante, not to mention a criminal." Jack paused, wondering if his friend was really listening. "He *is* working within the parameters of SIS."

Peter turned and looked at Jack, surprised by his comment. "My son would—"

"Would do anything to make that assassin pay for what was done to your son's wife and child," Jack finished. "Peter, let your son do his job." He looked at Charlie. "Let us do our job."

Peter sat back down in his chair. Both Charlie and Jack could tell that Peter was contemplating all that had been said. "Gentlemen, I lost my wife six years ago when an IRA bomb went off at a train station where she was waiting. There were countless other bombings, and when Sean was in the IRA undercover, I never felt this ill at ease. This all seems so personal. I have seen my son change from a carefree, loving father to a cold-hearted robot of a man whose only purpose is to find this assassin. I've lost my son. I want him back." Peter looked at Jack.

"The only way you are going to see him back is if you let him get the revenge he is seeking. He will seek it either within the law, as he is doing now, or outside it. Peter, I know Sean. We've talked about this for the many weeks he spent at my home recovering from that tragic night."

Peter sat back. "Yes, well, I consider that a time when you were possibly brainwashing him."

Jack sat silently as he eyed his colleague and longtime friend. He was trying to not explode at Peter's accusation. He quickly gathered his thoughts and anger to give a striking, calculated response. "You know, there are times when I forget just how much of a son of a bitch you can be."

Charlie was surprised by his superior's remark. He knew Kensington and Adkins had been friends for a long time, but to make a comment like that in front of him was out of line. Charlie stood as he said, "Perhaps I should leave you two alone to discuss this—"

"Sit down, Charlie," Jack commanded. Charlie obeyed. "I did not brainwash your son into tracking down the Serpent. I brought him back from the hell he enshrouded himself in and gave him a reason to live. I didn't tell him he had to track down the Serpent. In fact, I pleaded with him to just give us a description. Your son knew that wouldn't work because the Serpent is a master of disguise. What you don't know, Peter, is that the Serpent started his career in the IRA. You don't know that Sean and the Serpent worked together in the IRA. For Sean's whole career, he has been tracking the Serpent, getting closer and closer to him so that this cat-and-mouse game they are playing would be possible. You don't know all that happened between the two of them and the reason why the Serpent killed and mutilated Sean's family. And why don't you know? Sean didn't want you to know. Sean knew you and his brother wouldn't be able to handle the truth."

Jack stood up. "The intelligence world isn't for gentlemen, Peter. Things aren't discovered over tea and crumpets. The deaths of Sean's wife and child are only one of the many wounds your son endures on a daily basis. Just be thankful he has the ability to sift through the bullshit and keep his eye on the end game. I'm not calling him back, and neither is Charlie." Jack

*Blind Influence* | 33

walked to the door and waited for Peter to join him. Lord Adkins looked at Charlie. He stood slowly and started for the door. Charlie stood as well.

"If I may, sir, Sean has always said that if the Serpent was to be allowed to continue his killing, it would be because of you."

Jack turned and gave Charlie a stern look. Although Jack had the leeway to be so frank with a member of Parliament, he didn't want Charlie to think others would be afforded the same luxury.

"Forgive me and let me explain," Charlie said. "Sean's biggest fear isn't that he will fail. In fact, Sean's biggest fear is that you would pull him off the job. He has asked me time and time again to not allow that to happen. Sean may be obsessed, but we can't afford to have this madman continue to control the free world through his ruthlessness and terror. Let me finish by saying that Sean is our best agent. I know that doesn't mean a thing to a father whose son is putting his life on the line every day." Charlie paused. "When he checks in, I'll ask him to call you."

Lord Adkins did not look at Charlie. He moved to the door and stopped to look eye to eye with Jack Kensington. "You know I could have your job for this," he said through clenched teeth.

Jack smiled at his friend. "Yes. Who would you trust enough to replace me with? We work well together, Peter. Don't fuck that up." The two men stared into each other's eyes, some kind of challenge to see who would be the first to crack a smile and forgive the harsh but true statements that had been made. Jack knew it had to be Peter, and he waited, never blinking. Peter knew Jack was right. He finally broke into the smile that signaled all was well between them.

Peter extended his hand to Jack. "At least keep me informed. It is a father's obligation to worry about his son, you know." He looked at Charlie and gave a nod. "A call would be nice." And with that, Lord Peter Adkins left the room and returned to Parliament.

Jack closed the door and turned to Charlie. "It goes without saying … "

"Not a word, sir," Charlie finished.

"Have you heard from Sean?" Jack asked.

"No, sir. I expect that we'll hear something soon. As far as any of us know, he is still in France. I've not seen any intelligence to say that the Serpent has left France. As soon as I know something, I will let you know."

Jack paused a moment. "Yes, do that. The closer he gets, the quieter it will be, Charlie."

"Yes, sir," Charlie answered as he watched the director leave his office.

# Day Two

# Washington, DC

*I*t was probably the worst sleepless night that Norman Sipes had ever had. He stumbled to the kitchen and began to make coffee. It was early morning. The sun had not yet risen. Sipes had tossed and turned all night. The sleeping pill he had taken hadn't even made him drowsy. He had a full day in front of him—a day of meetings that required him to be at his best. He started making a list in his head of things he needed to do, while putting the filter and coffee into the coffee machine. First off was to call Tony to find out if the lawyer had thought of anything to keep him from appearing before Jenkins's committee. Then he had a meeting with Joseph Engle.

He moved to the sink to fill the coffeepot with water. Walking back to the coffee machine, he already had a full list of meetings to attend and phone calls to make. He poured the water from the coffeepot into the coffee machine, replaced the pot, and pressed the button.

"I apologize, sir." The butler was standing in his pajamas and robe, tying the belt to the robe as he spoke. "Did you leave a note saying you would be up this early? Did I miss that?"

"No, David. You are fine. I just couldn't sleep. It is a waste of time to lay in bed with your eyes wide open," Sipes answered. "There is no sense both of us being tired today. Why don't you go back to sleep?"

David walked over to the cabinet and grabbed a coffee mug. "I won't be able to get back to sleep, sir. Once up, I might as well get busy. What would you like for breakfast?"

"The usual will do. I didn't get to eat dinner last night, so if you could make a little extra bacon?"

"Yes, sir," David answered as he started gathering the pans, eggs, bacon, and potatoes. "I'll head out for the paper before I get started. I'll bring it to you in your study with the coffee when it is done brewing."

"Thank you, David." Sipes left the kitchen, heading for the study, turning lights on along his way. He reached the study and entered.

38 | *Linda Riesenberg Fisler*

His study was his sanctuary. The bookcases were full of his favorite books. He walked to his desk, which he had managed to procure from the Pentagon. It held a special meaning, and he recalled how proud he had been when he was appointed to the Joint Chiefs of Staff six years ago. His medals and stars were framed in a lit shadowbox hanging on the wall opposite the desk. The room was painted in a rich hunter green with burgundy accents that highlighted the woodgrain in his desk.

The big leather desk chair was calling his name. He moved to it and sat down. Sighing, he spun around and opened the blinds on the window behind his desk. It was still dark, but he wanted to catch the first rays of sunlight. As he turned back around, David was entering the room.

"Here you go, sir." David placed the coffee and paper on the cluttered desk. "I'll start your breakfast now. Would you like to eat it in here, sir?"

"Yes, please. I might as well get some of these bills paid and paperwork done."

"Yes, sir." David left to perform his duties.

Sipes got busy writing out checks to cover his personal expenses. Just as he was writing out the last check, David entered with his breakfast. Without a word, the butler placed the food on a cleared corner of the desk, filled Sipes's coffee cup, and then left the room.

With the morning sun rising, Sipes started looking over the financial report of his oil company. Sipes Oil Company had formerly been a little-known company on the verge of bankruptcy when Sipes had convinced a number of his highly successful friends to help him purchase the company after his forced retirement from the Pentagon. Joseph Engle was the financier behind the project. Mark Stevens was also an investor, but since he had become vice president, his participation had been suspended, even if on paper only. There were numerous other investors, most of them silent partners, and for the first three years, they were relatively happy with its operation. Contrary to popular public belief, Sipes Oil Company was not on the way to making itself known as one of the seven sisters. The media's constant reporting of the pending oil crisis had triggered a downward spiral in profits at Sipes Oil earlier than any of the other big seven companies. It was becoming apparent to the investors that Sipes was more hot air than hot prospector. The pressure was mounting on the young oil company to make the splash in the oil market that had been promised to its investors. Sipes had one last operation that was secretly being executed. This operation was known only by a few of Sipes's friends, who were also the most vocal investors in the company. These influential friends were determined to build their futures at the expense of Sipes, and Sipes had no idea that these friends thought of him as expendable.

The phone rang and shook Sipes out of his concentration. Looking up at the clock, he was surprised to see that it was already 8:30 in the morning. He was surprised that time had flown by so quickly. Just as he reached for the phone, the bell rang, indicating that someone was at the gate of his property. He picked up the phone, leaving the visitor at the gate for David to answer. "Hello," he growled into the phone.

"Norm, it is Joseph. What time are you coming over this morning?" Joseph Engle, a friend and one of the most vocal investors in Sipes Oil Company, was calling to firm up their meeting.

"What time is good for you?" Sipes answered the question with a question, trying to sound accommodating.

"I believe the sooner the better. I have been looking over your books, and it is worse than you think."

"I'll be over in about an hour, if that is good for you," Sipes snapped, trying to control his temper. Sipes was known for his quick temper and sharp tongue that barked commands that typically were followed flawlessly, lest the verbose leader deliver another tongue lashing.

"Perfect. See you then." Joseph slammed the phone down in Sipes's ear. Sipes followed suit and slammed the receiver down, mainly for his own satisfaction.

David entered the room just as the receiver was being slammed down and hesitated to enter his boss's sanctuary with an envelope. "I'm sorry, sir. I didn't see this one coming." He handed Sipes the envelope. Within it, as promised, was the subpoena to appear before Jenkins's committee.

Sipes took the envelope and threw it on his desk. "Not your fault, David." Sipes pointed to himself. "This big mouth did it all by himself." He stood up, stretching, then started out from behind his desk. "I'm heading up to

40 | *Linda Riesenberg Fisler*

get dressed. I'll be heading over to Joseph Engle's office before I head to the corporate offices, if anyone calls asking for me."

Sipes dressed quickly, got into his car, and was at Engle's office more quickly than he had expected. For some reason, the typical DC traffic wasn't as bad as it usually was. The elevator doors opened, and Sipes was greeted by Engle's secretary. If Sipes hadn't the weight of the world on his shoulders, he might have noticed just how beautiful the woman in her late thirties really was. Instead, he sauntered up to her desk and mumbled, "He's expecting me."

"One moment, Mr. Sipes, and I will let him know you are here." She gestured to a chair placed along the wall parallel to her desk. Sipes turned, walked over to the chair, and sat down. He placed his briefcase next to the chair. The lack of sleep was starting to take its toll. He was hoping to be offered some coffee. When he looked up to ask for it, the secretary was gone. He looked around the office but was met with disappointment: no coffeepot in sight. The secretary returned from Joseph Engle's office with a smile on her face. "Mr. Engle will see you now, Mr. Sipes."

Sipes stood and headed for the door now being held open by the secretary. She smiled as he passed her. "May I have some coffee, black; the stronger the better," Sipes demanded.

"I'll take care of that, Nancy. If you can just do what I asked," Engle said, standing to move over to his coffeepot.

"Thank you, sir. I'll get to that right away," Nancy said as she closed the door to his office.

Without wasting a moment, Engle took charge of the meeting. "Sit down, Sipes." Engle began pouring coffee for Sipes and then for himself. Taking a mug in each hand, he walked back to his desk, handing a mug to Sipes on his way. He sat down. "Do I need to tell you how fucking stupid you were last night?" Before Sipes could answer, Engle answered for him. "No, I don't think so. Your company is on the brink of bankruptcy, and you have no business acumen to stop it. What do you do? You pick a fight with one of the most powerful senators on Capitol Hill. Brilliant!" Engle stared at Sipes, who did not speak a word. "Did you get your subpoena?"

*Blind Influence* | 41

"It is on my desk in my study. I'm calling Tony right after I'm done getting my ass chewed out by you."

"I'm done chewing your ass out, because obviously, it doesn't help. In my estimation, you have about thirty days of operating money available before Sipes Oil is flat broke. I'm not financing you any longer. This little pet project of yours is costing a fortune. You better hope you can continue it. With Andrews changing his position on ANWR, I don't think your political connections will do you much good about getting a permit before the big oil companies like you've been touting to us."

"Joe, listen. I know you have no reason to believe me, but that special project is going to pay off, and things will look totally different in a few weeks. All I'm asking is for you to cover me for sixty days. If you want, wait for a week or two; hell, take the full thirty days before investing. But I'm telling you we are this close." Sipes raised his right hand with his thumb and index finger about an inch apart.

"Damn right I'm waiting for thirty days. I don't give a shit how close you are, and if Andrews does veto the ANWR act, I won't be subsidizing your company ever again. I just can't understand how you allowed yourself to get into this position. Jenkins's committee is going to tear you limb from limb." Before Sipes, who was now beginning to show the anger that was welling up inside him, could answer, Engle ended the meeting. "I'm done with you. If you'll excuse me, I've got other, more successful people waiting to meet with me." He reached over to his desk phone and depressed a button. "Nancy, get Donald Tipperman on the phone for me. Mr. Sipes is on his way out."

As angry as Sipes was, he said nothing. He stood and walked toward the door. He turned and was about to speak but thought the better of it. In one way, he felt like a beat puppy. In another way, he was harboring a secret that he couldn't share with anyone. All he knew was that if everything went as planned, he'd be giving some back to this pompous-ass financier in a few days.

# In Flight

$S$ean's Concorde flight was on time, and the passengers were boarded quickly. Although the Concorde flight was the fastest way to get to DC, he was hopeful to grab some sleep. The flight had been uneventful so far. He had been running on adrenaline for the past few days, being led to believe that he was closer to catching the Serpent than he had been. He hadn't realized just how exhausted he was until he was in the air, safe and sound, as the jet's engines began to lull him to sleep. By the time the flight attendant came around with the meal, Sean was sleeping.

Short sleep time was something Sean had gotten accustomed to, and not because of his line of work. Previous to his obsession with the Serpent, as his father would say, Sean had had no problem sleeping for eight hours. He could also fall asleep quicker than someone could count to ten. There were times when Sean would actually fight falling asleep. This wasn't one of those times. His body craved the rest.

It always started the same way. There before him was his beautiful brunette wife, Sarah, smiling, with her baby-blue eyes twinkling in the light. It was peaceful, and he could hear her soft mirth in his ear as she moved closer to him. By her side was their daughter. Sarah was holding the young girl by the hand. Both were bathed in golden light, and it felt real to Sean. Then he heard the cheerful calls of "Daddy!" from his beautiful daughter, all of five years old. The curls of her dark brown hair blowing in the gentle wind, her soft little voice beckoning him to come and play with her as she ran to the yard from the house, were within his reach. The stable lifestyle that made his hellish day job worth it was before his eyes, and his body ached at their absence.

Then it started. The siren was the first thing to warn him something was wrong. The golden light turned dark. The bittersweet taste of adrenaline began in his mouth, and he swallowed, trying to quell it. A red flashing light accosted his eyes, and he could see himself running to his home—their home. He ran into the house, unable to catch his breath. He tried to wake himself from the nightmare. He didn't want to live this again.

The red light flashed through the open door, and he entered the family room. There, on the floor, were Sarah and Kate, his daughter. They were lying in a puddle of blood, their blood. Sean saw himself fall to his knees,

*Blind Influence* | 43

weakened by the sight and feeling their souls, their energy bonds, leave his body. He cried out, but his voice cannot be heard. He crawled toward them but was thwarted by an agent who told him it was a crime scene. Sean forced his way to their sides. He gently touched his wife's cheek, caressing the line of her jaw. Her mouth opened as blood gushed from it. And then Sean saw what he didn't need to see to know who created this horrendous murder. Sarah's and Kate's tongue confirmed what Sean had already known. Their tongues had been mutilated to resemble the forked tongue of a snake: the Serpent's calling card. The Serpent had killed his wife and child. Only Sarah and Kate knew the torture that inhumane assassin made them suffer.

Sean forced himself to wake up with a sudden jerk that caught the eye of the flight attendant. He was sweating from the awful reality that visited him every time he tried to sleep. He was looking around, trying to bring himself back to the reality he was currently in. He was on the Concorde. He was on his way to Washington.

"Are you all right?" the flight attendant asked, placing a hand on his arm to get his attention. "Can I get you something? Some water?"

Sean sat up, turning his head to look at her. "Yes, please."

"Nightmare? I have them too. They always seem so real, but there aren't, you know." She was trying to reassure him.

Sean tried to smile. "Yes, well, they don't call them nightmares for nothing." When the flight attendant returned with his water, he asked, "How far out are we?"

"We have about an hour to go yet. You missed dinner. Would you like me to heat one up for you?"

"If it wouldn't be any trouble, I would appreciate that," Sean answered with a smile.

"No trouble at all. Hope you like salmon; it is all I have left."

"It will do fine. Thank you," Sean said, taking a sip of water. He wasn't all that hungry but wasn't sure when he'd get his next meal. It was time to turn his attention to determining the Serpent's next move.

*Linda Riesenberg Fisler*

# Washington, DC

"Kevin Thompson, FBI," he identified himself. Kevin Thompson was a man in his late thirties, solidly built, with tortoise-rimmed glasses that hid his brown eyes, thick dishwater-blonde hair and a moustache that made him look older than his age. His walk unveiled the years of drudgery he had endured working at the FBI. The battles with the superiors in which he implored his superiors to do the right thing had taken away the love he'd once had for his job. If it wasn't for the alimony payments, he would have found gainful employment elsewhere. The reality was that he had little motivation to get down to the details of any case, only to know that it was probably going to be covered up or the case completely dropped. All he knew was that working for the FBI was nothing like it was portrayed in the movies. "Is Chief Bailey around?" he asked the DC police officer at the front desk.

"Yeah," the officer said, not even looking up from the paper he was reading. "He is in his office."

"Thanks." Thompson walked to DC Police Chief Jerome Bailey's office. He had worked with the police chief numerous times in the past, and it was one of things he did enjoy about his job. This routine visit wouldn't prove to be exciting, but just to sit for a few minutes and chat with Jerome was a welcome change to his day. The reason for the visit was really something a flunky could do, but it dawned on Thompson that he was just that flunky. He reached the police chief's office door and knocked on it.

"Yeah, what is it now?!" A booming, deep bass voice barked from inside the office. Jerome Bailey was a stocky, handsome African American with an infectious laugh when he allowed himself to indulge in a moment of amusement. His bark was worse than his bite. He always gave the impression that he was so busy, he didn't have the time of day to give anyone. Although he gave the impression of being a micromanager, he really wasn't. When he gave his men an assignment, he was hands-off and fully expected it to be executed with perfection. He trusted the men and women of the DC police force in varying degrees, depending on their past performances. He knew whom he could trust with the different types of cases and who excelled at solving them. A rather personable commander, he was well liked by all he worked with both within the police force and externally with the many government agencies.

*Blind Influence* | 45

Thompson peered around the door to see that Jerome was on the phone. He waved at Bailey, who pointed to a chair. Just as Thompson sat down, Jerome let that infectious laugh escape his lips, which in turn made Thompson smile. "I would have loved to have been there. Girl, I swear I miss you. Wish you would come back on to our side." Bailey looked at Thompson and held up his index finger to indicate that he would only be a minute. He laughed again. "I might just hold you to that. I need to run. It was nice talking to you, Nikki. Bye." He hung up the phone. "Well, now, what brings the FBI to my office this lovely sunny morning?"

Thompson chuckled. "Nothing, exactly. My boss decided that I needed to check up on the DC coverage of Andrews's visit to the Russian embassy tomorrow."

Bailey looked at Thompson. "POTUS is going to the Russian embassy tomorrow?" He almost pulled it off, but he couldn't prevent his wry smile from slipping across his lips. He laughed again. "It's all taken care of, Kevin. Do you want the details?"

"Yeah. I'm sure I'll be asked where your men will be and all that."

"Are you on the detail?" Bailey asked.

"Yep. The FBI will have a handful of folks around. They aren't expecting much, but the Secret Service asked us to help secure the surrounding building since the parking garage is under construction. Somebody said something about it being condemned."

"I heard that too. So I'll have a detail check it out and post a few guards around the entrances. That starts tonight. Let me get you a copy of this." Bailey walked to the door of his office. "Matt—can you run a copy of this for Agent Thompson?" He handed the document to Matt, who went off to copy it. "It's routine, really. We'll block off the streets a few hours before his arrival, secure the buildings, and have patrols wandering around just like every other detail we've ever done."

"I know, but Secret Service seems a bit jumpy on this one. Not sure why except that it is the Russian embassy he is going to, I suppose."

"What's up with that? Usually they go to the White House."

46 | *Linda Riesenberg Fisler*

"I don't know. If you believe the news, it is some kind of outreach or something. I don't follow politics. I have enough of that shit on my day job just trying to keep my nose clean," Thompson answered with some disgust in his voice.

"Turned down again?" Bailey asked.

Thompson nodded in the affirmative. "Guess I don't kiss ass enough."

Bailey smiled. "Keep it that way. Something is going to break for you, Kevin. You are a really good agent. Trust me, one day soon, you'll be leading an investigation and you'll be wishing for these days. It isn't as glamorous as it seems."

"It isn't so much leading an investigation as it was working internationally with the CIA and others. Just a change of scenery was what I was hoping for. I lead investigations now, so it isn't that big a deal. Just really tired of the same political bullshit that keeps rearing its ugly head."

"It's everywhere," Bailey answered as Matt returned with the copied documents, handing them to him. "Thanks, Matt. Here you go, Kevin. Naturally, this is confidential stuff." Thompson nodded that he understood. "Anything else I can help you with?"

Thompson was looking over the document. "Nope, this should do it." He extended his hand to Bailey. "Thanks. It was good to see you again."

Bailey shook Thompson's hand. "I'm sure I'll see you tomorrow."

Thompson laughed. "It's a date."

Bailey returned the laughter. "Oh please! Not that!" Both men laughed as Bailey walked Thompson to the door. "Be safe."

"You too." Thompson walked out of Bailey's office into the bustle of DC headquarters. He was charged with writing up a report with recommendations and then briefing the five officers who would be working with the DC force to secure the area once the plan was approved. It was just another day on the job, with tons of preparation for something that would go off without a glitch. It was back to FBI headquarters and to his desk, where he would pull all the information together to present in a briefing later in the day.

*Blind Influence* | 47

Nicole spent the morning in court, and although she had proven the client was innocent through a random noting of reasonable doubt, it still made her sick that she had prevented someone guilty of a crime from serving his jail time. Granted, it was a white-collar crime, but it still hurt innocent people. It was after these types of cases that Nicole questioned just why she had left the DA's office. Though there had been cases during her tenure as a District Attorney in which an innocent person had been wrongly accused or sentenced, it seemed to Nicole that more often than not, the guilty were going unpunished. She felt she was contributing more to that as a defense attorney, and she wasn't sure that she liked it.

The doors of the elevator opened to the law firm's offices. She was jolted out of her concentration by the loud voices of two young men, appearing to be of Native American descent, and a young woman, who was sitting on the floor of the office and refusing to move. It seemed everyone was screaming, including one of the first-year associates and the receptionist. Nicole moved out of the elevator, totally ignored. She stood and watched for a moment. She looked through the glass doors to the inner offices. No one seemed interested in helping the receptionist out of her plight.

After a few minutes, Nicole decided she had heard enough. She shifted her briefcase to her left hand and placed the index finger and thumb of her right hand in her mouth, drew in a deep breath, and whistled at as high a pitch and as loudly as she could manage. This caught everyone's attention, mainly because of the length of the whistle. "What in the world is going on here?"

Everyone started talking at her all at once. She whistled again, and they stopped. She looked at the first-year associate, who was trying to get the young native woman off the floor. "Stand up," Nicole said to the bent over first year associate. He did so immediately. She turned to the receptionist. "Jean, what's going on?"

"These people would like a meeting with Mr. Shafer, but he is currently in a meeting. They don't believe me," Jean answered, exasperated. "I tried to explain that we have other lawyers they could meet with, but they won't listen."

"She is just trying to get rid of us," one of the native young men chimed in.

Nicole smiled. "Yes, well, there is nothing that will get you ejected from this law office faster than screaming and yelling at our receptionist." The

48 | *Linda Riesenberg Fisler*

two Native American males smiled at Nicole. She held out her hand. "My name is Nicole Charbonneau. I'm a lawyer here with this firm, and I'd be more than happy to talk with you."

The young woman on the floor looked up at her. "Are you a good lawyer?"

"Would any lawyer tell you they weren't?" Nicole asked.

The two men laughed. The young woman on the floor made a disapproving face. "We need the best lawyer we can get."

"And you think that is Tony Shafer," Nicole stated, finding it interesting that they did, as Tony hadn't tried a case in over a year.

"That is what we were told."

"By who?" Nicole asked, intrigued.

"There was a sign that said all inquiries should be made to this law firm on the side of the drilling equipment that they are moving onto our lands. We tried calling several times, but we could never talk to anyone."

"What?" Nicole asked in shock. "Wait … " She turned to Jean. "Buzz us in. If the three of you will follow me, I'd like to hear your story, and if there is anything I can do to help, I'd be more than honored to do so."

"We don't have a lot of money," one of the young men said, bowing his head.

"We do pro bono work," Nicole said as she motioned to the door. She had discerned that these three were from Alaska. She wanted to hear the rest of their story in the privacy of her office.

"Shall I buzz Mr. Shafer?" Jean asked.

"I thought he was in a meeting," Nicole answered, smiling. She winked at Jean and her blunder.

Nicole led the three natives to her office. Although not as nice as the partners' offices, Nicole's office was roomy enough, decorated with comfortable furniture in the conversation area, two chairs and a couch, a wooden

*Blind Influence* | 49

bookcase filled with law books, and a wooden desk. "Please sit down." She motioned to the conversation area. "I'm sure you'll find the couch much more comfortable," she said to the young woman. She walked over to her desk and placed her briefcase upon it. She grabbed a pen and pad of paper, then walked over to the chair closest to her desk and sat down. "Now, tell me, one at time, your names and where you live."

The young lady—Nicole guessed she was in her early twenties—spoke first. "My name is Ahnah, A-H-N-A-H, Nertornartok." She spelled the name out for Nicole. "These are my brothers, Annakpok," who acknowledged himself when Ahnah said his name, "and my older brother, Nagojut. We live in Alaska, being of Inuit descent. Our land is part of what your government calls the ANWR."

Nicole smiled at the *your government* comment. "It is nice to meet you. You mentioned that someone is drilling for oil on your lands?"

Nagojut, the oldest of the three and a very handsome man of what Nicole guessed was his late twenties, possibly early thirties, pulled a manila enveloped out of his coat and placed it on the table between them. "Yes. We brought proof." He looked at the envelope. "They have been there for about three months, building their rig. They have not started drilling yet as of when we left to come down here to Washington."

"May I?" Nicole pointed to the envelope.

"Yes, please," Nagojut responded.

"When did you leave?" Nicole asked as she opened the envelope.

"We left two weeks ago. We had to drive all this way. The car barely made it. There were repairs to it that we had to make along the way."

Nicole looked up at Nagojut when he spoke. She removed the enlarged photographs from the envelope.

"We barely had enough money to get the film processed," Nagojut added.

"When was the last time you had anything to eat?" Nicole asked. The three looked at each other. Nicole was looking at the evidence of drilling rig construction before her eyes. The Inuit were telling the truth. An oil company

50 | *Linda Riesenberg Fisler*

was setting up shop to drill for oil on ANWR, in violation of law and prior to the Alaska National Interest Lands Conservation Act. She quickly moved through the photographs. "I'm sorry, when did you say?"

"It was yesterday," Ahnah responded. "That isn't important. What is important is the damage that this company is causing to our lands and environment."

Nicole stood up. "Well, I think getting something to eat is just as important as this information." She walked back to her desk with the photographs, then opened her briefcase and placed the photographs in it before closing it again.

"We need those back," Annakpok said, pointing to the briefcase.

Nicole smiled. "No, I don't think you do." She picked up her briefcase and walked to her door, then opened the door. "Let's go get something to eat. I'll buy."

Ahnah stood up, about to launch into another loud protest, when Nicole stopped her by raising her hand. "I don't think you understand. I'm taking your case. I'm hungry, and it is lunchtime. Let's go get something to eat, and we'll talk over lunch." Nicole started out of her office, turned to see that the Inuit were not following. She walked back into her office, bent over to Nagojut, and whispered, "It is better if we talk somewhere else, for reasons I can't address here. I ask that you follow my lead." She stood up again and said, "You do eat lunch, don't you?"

Nagojut stood and started to follow her. He motioned for his brother and sister to follow, which they did. They retraced their steps out to the reception lobby. "Jean, if anyone is looking for me, I'll be at lunch." Nicole pressed the elevator button.

"Mr. Shafer did inquire about you. He wanted you to stop in his office as soon as possible."

"I'll stop in after lunch. I shouldn't be too long. Thanks, Jean." The elevator doors opened, and the four disappeared inside. When the doors opened again, they were in the parking garage. "My car is right over here," Nicole said. They moved to her car, got in, and were off to a restaurant for lunch.

*Blind Influence* | 51

Nicole decided that the Old Ebbitt Grill would be the best spot to grab a bite. She also liked the fact that the restaurant had valet parking, making it easy for her to get in and out quickly. They arrived at the old saloon and restaurant just around noon. Although its clientele included some of the most prominent people in DC, she knew that those people tended to eat a little later than the lunch hour between twelve and one. She asked for a booth so their conversation would be a bit more private.

They were shown to their booth, and the waitress arrived to take their drink orders, all opting for nonalcoholic beverages. Nicole encouraged her new clients to order whatever they wanted. She knew they had to be starving. After the waitress took their orders, she opened her briefcase. "Now, tell me again. This oil company showed up about three months ago?"

"Yes," confirmed Ahnah.

Nicole began looking more closely at the three photographs. While it was clear that the photos were of drilling equipment, there were no signs of which company was preparing to do the drilling. "Were there any company logos on the equipment, or did any of the employees tell you who is responsible?"

"There are no company logos, and the men simply won't talk to us. As you can see in this photograph, they are carrying weapons." Annakpok pointed to one of the photographs.

"Yes, I see that now. Have they threatened you?"

"Yes," Ahnah said. "We went down there to ask who authorized this." Nicole looked at the feisty young woman, who anticipated her next question. "We approached them peacefully. We thought that they may have just gotten lost. From the minute we approached them, they trained their guns on us."

"Then what happened?"

Nagojut took over the conversation. "There was a man, who we assume is in charge of this operation; he came out of one of the trailers. Ahnah and I were there with two others. The place that they are proposing to drill on is where our land joins with two other members of our tribe; however, the state government deems it to be a right-of-way or easement of some kind.

So when this man came toward us, he told us that they were on state property and that we should go about our business. We asked if he was lost, and he said no. We asked what he was going to be doing, and all he would say is to contact your law firm."

The waitress arrived with their food, and Nicole quickly gathered the photographs. She put them away in her briefcase and set the briefcase next to her on the bench of the booth. After being served, they started their conversation again.

"I'm going to have to do some research here," Nicole started. She watched her new clients devour their food. "I don't know why they would tell you to contact us. We don't typically handle these kinds of cases."

"So you won't help us?" Nagojut asked, almost defeated.

"I didn't say that," Nicole answered. "These photos don't make a case, especially when I don't know who to charge. But it is enough evidence to say that further investigation is warranted." She took a bit or two of her salad.

"You don't know anything about this, then?" Ahnah asked.

"No, I don't. But I am good friends with Tony Shafer, and I can certainly ask him. And believe me, you will get more answers from me than you would from him. So, if you work with me, we should be able to make enough noise to get this shut down."

The three siblings smiled. Nagojut turned to his brother and sister. "It is worth our long journey." They nodded in agreement.

Nicole smiled. "I need to keep the photographs, and I need you to go back home and collect as many photographs as you can over the next few weeks."

"What will you be doing?" Ahnah asked.

"I'll be doing a lot of research and fact finding. It would be really nice to find out who is behind this and which company this is. That's what I'll be trying to find out."

*Blind Influence* | 53

"We can continue to ask," Nagojut added.

"No. It is clear these guys mean business. I know it is your land and it is hard for you not to stand up for what you own, but don't put yourselves in harm's way," Nicole said. "When we are done here, we are going to head over to a camera shop, where I'll get some very powerful cameras and lenses for you to use in gathering your intelligence from afar. Then I'm going to take you to the airport, where you'll start your journey home. Is there any way for you to get the word to someone to pick you up at the nearest airport?"

"Yes. We do have electricity and phones, Nicole," Nagojut said, smiling at her.

Nicole almost blushed. "I'm sorry." Nagojut acknowledged her apology with a smile. "Well, let's finish up and get started," she said.

There was a little more to their conversation about what sort of photos would be best and how to send the film. Nicole took her legal pad out of her briefcase as they were finishing their meal. She wrote down an address and phone number. "Here is my home address and phone number." She handed it to Nagojut. "Until I know what the firm's involvement in this is, send everything to this address and only call my home phone number."

Ahnah seemed almost embarrassed to ask her next question. "Nicole, I'm sorry, but I have to ask this. What if your firm is representing this oil company?"

"Don't apologize. I've been asking myself that question for the last hour now." Nicole looked at her clients. "What is going on here is wrong and it needs to be stopped. I firmly believe that. I'm against drilling on your land. If my firm is involved in this, then I would have to welcome you as my first clients to my new law firm. I am a bit short-staffed, so I hope you'll be patient as we ramp up the firm's capability." She smiled.

"Thank you," Nagojut said, as Annakpok and Ahnah nodded in agreement.

Nicole paid their bill, and they all began walking out to Nicole's car. Just before they quit the restaurant, Senator Jenkins walked in with two other senators.

---

54 | *Linda Riesenberg Fisler*

"Ms. Charbonneau," Senator Jenkins acknowledged as he held the door to the restaurant open for her to walk out. "We meet again. I was going to call you later. I hope the ride home after the dinner last night wasn't too unpleasant."

"Hello, Senator." Nicole gestured for her clients to go on to the car. "No, it wasn't unpleasant at all. Tony gave the usual team-player speech, and I reminded him of the terms of my employment with his law firm." Nicole smiled.

Jenkins gave a little laugh. "Remind me to never cross you." The senators who were with him called to him, pointing to their watches. "If you'll excuse me, we have a short break before we have to be back for a vote. May I call you sometime?"

Nicole smiled. "Of course, Senator."

He extended his hand for her to shake. "Then I shall make that a priority and a pleasure." Nicole shook his hand. "And please call me Bobby."

"I look forward to it, Bobby."

"Bobby, c'mon, we don't have all day," one of his fellow senators called.

"Until then," Jenkins said as he entered the restaurant with a smile on his face.

Nicole returned the smile while she reminded herself why he was the most eligible bachelor on Capitol Hill. She shook her head to clear it as she began to walk to her car. Next, she did what she had promised to do for her new clients, visiting the camera shop, purchasing the camera equipment, and then taking them to the airport. There, she purchased three tickets, which sent her clients on their way back to Alaska. She arrived back at the office at about 4:30.

"Where have you been?" Jean greeted her as the elevator doors opened. "Tony's been screaming for you every half hour."

Nicole smiled. "He'll live. Do I have any other messages?"

*Blind Influence* | 55

Jean handed her a few pieces of paper, notes that contained phone numbers, messages, and client names. "Thanks. Isn't it about time for you to head home?" Nicole asked as she started for her office.

"Good night, Nikki," Jean said.

"Good night, Jean," Nicole called back as she walked through the door.

She was walking, looking over her messages, when she was intercepted by her friend and colleague Carol Gartner. Carol, upon first impression, seemed to be the complete opposite of Nicole. Carol had been the first person, besides Tony, to befriend Nicole when Nicole had arrived at Rosen, Shafer, and Pruett. She called Nicole her special project. Nicole, in Carol's estimation, was a workaholic and needed to let her hair down desperately. And Carol felt she was just the person to help. Carol was a lawyer by day and party girl by night. She was petite, always in heels, and had black curly hair. Her hazel eyes were a mirror to the world, and she was a caring soul. She wanted desperately to be married to just the right millionaire so she could quit being a lawyer and begin working on the causes she loved. She was a walking contradiction, and that was what made her so interesting to Nicole. They were best of friends, and each brought out qualities in the other that most didn't see. Although Carol was a couple of years older than Nicole, it was Nicole who felt and played the role of older sister.

"Hey, Nikki," Carol called, walking up to give her a hug. "Where have you been all day?"

"Courting new clients," Nicole answered. "What have you been up to?" she asked as she kept walking to her office.

Carol stopped and turned back for her office cube. "Hey—I want to show you something, I'll be right in." She disappeared around the corner. Nicole went into her office and moved behind her desk. She put everything she had been carrying on her desk and sat down in her desk chair.

"Look at this!" Carol exclaimed as she walked into Nicole's office and up to her desk.

Nicole swung her office chair around, sitting up and taking the brochure from Carol. "What's this, another get-rich-quick scheme?" she asked.

Carol sat down, somewhat dejected by Nicole's comment. "I was actually thinking it would be a nice place to go on vacation," Carol answered.

Nicole looked up. "I'm sorry, Carol. It's been a long day. It does look peaceful." Nicole started flipping through the brochure.

"It's in France, along the Mediterranean Sea. I thought it would be a great jumping-off point to other places," Carol responded, hoping to sway Nicole away from her first impression of the get-rich-quick scheme. It was just that, of course.

Nicole looked at the prices located at the back of the brochure. She looked at Carol and smiled. "At these prices, I won't be jumping off to anywhere. Are you kidding me?"

"Oh, come on, Nicole, live a little," Carol begged her.

Nicole's phone rang. "Carol, that's almost a year's salary! How can you even afford a place like this?" She picked up her phone. "Hello?" It was Tony, and he wasn't at all amused by Nicole's absence all afternoon. "Yes, Tony, I'll be right there." She hung up the phone and looked at Carol. "I have to go see the boss man." She got up from her desk.

"Well, keep the brochure and look it over. We can talk about it Friday night," Carol answered, getting up and starting for the door of the office with Nicole.

"Friday night?" Nicole asked.

"Don't tell me you forgot about it?" Carol said, stopping and looking at her. "You did! You did forget!"

Nicole rolled her eyes. "OK, we have established that I forgot. Now, tell me what I've forgotten."

"You promised to go to Conversations with me."

"And just what is Conversations?"

"Jeez—do you live here? It's only the hottest new nightclub in town. Everybody who is anybody belongs there."

*Blind Influence* | 57

"Belongs there? And how did you get to belong?" Nicole asked, making quotation marks to emphasize the word *belong*.

"A certain representative with a bad habit"—Carol pointed to her nose—"gave me two passes. You said you would go, Nikki, and I'm not letting you back out of this one." Carol was usually the go-to girl for cases like these. Nicole had suspected how Carol made the cases disappear before they became public, but she had never really asked. She did know that it was a high-stakes game and one day, Carol was going to get hurt. "I told you to stop handling those cases," Nicole scolded her.

"Tony gave me this one. What was I supposed to do?"

"I'll talk to Tony about that. Carol, you can be a great lawyer. You don't need to do this shit."

"Just tell me you will go to Conversations with me," Carol begged.

"Why can't you go alone?"

"Nikki! Seriously, you don't go alone to Conversations. Come on, we will drink and dance, maybe meet a few fun-loving guys. What do you say?"

"I'd rather go see a movie," Nicole shot back. Carol looked at her, and Nicole could see she had wounded her friend with her last remark. "Oh, OK, I'll go. But promise me this is the last time you handle this type of case."

"I promise as long as it doesn't get me fired for not doing them!" Carol said as she left Nicole's office. Nicole smiled as she followed Carol out into the hallway. She turned to go to Tony's office and heard Carol say, "I'll meet you there at nine on Friday."

"Wait!" Nicole called back. "Meet me there? Can't we drive together? I have no idea where this place is located."

"C Street," Carol called as she started to clean off her desk.

"The hottest new nightclub is on C Street?"

Carol stopped and looked over the cubicle at Nicole, who was outside Tony's office door. "Well, yeah, where else would it be?"

Nicole again rolled her eyes. "Alright, I'll meet you there at nine on Friday," she said, opening the door to Tony's office. "Talk with you tomorrow." She turned and entered the office.

The minute Nicole walked into Tony's office, she could almost forget she was in a lawyer's office. Grandly decorated with wool rugs and hardwood floors, and with a view of the Capitol out the windows behind his wooden desk, his office was noticeably different from the others. Tony was at his bar, which was centered between two large bookcases filled with law books and reference books that Nicole guessed got used only when she came in to borrow them.

She waited for Tony to address her. She could not tell from his actions if she was about to receive another lecture or if he was celebrating something. "Would you like something?" he asked.

"No thanks. I still have some work to do," she answered.

"Where were you all day?" Tony asked.

"I'm sure you heard about our Inuit visitors."

Tony headed back to his desk, taking a drink of the scotch he had just poured himself. He sat down, nodding his head as he swallowed.

Nicole continued. "I wanted to hear what they had to say. They came a long way to not be heard, and there might have been something we could do to help, as in represent them."

"Was there?"

"I'm not sure. There are some things I want to look into, and I'll let you know," Nicole said, sitting across from Tony. "Was there something you wanted?"

"Just a congratulations on winning the case this morning. That was a tricky one and your client wasn't the best at covering his tracks." Tony reached for a stack of manila folders on his desk. "I have a few more cases for you."

Nicole looked at the folders. "Are these more friends of yours?"

"Not all of them. Most are cases I know you can win and will bring you some recognition."

"Tony, don't do this today. I'm not real proud of myself for winning that case. He was guilty and he hurt a lot of innocent people." Nicole continued to look at Tony, her eyes pleading with him.

"They obviously didn't have enough evidence," Tony corrected her. "And obviously, he wasn't guilty, or you wouldn't have gotten him off."

"That is semantics," Nicole answered. She was getting tired of fighting Tony. She knew these new cases were her punishment for not protecting Sipes the night before. "I think I need some time off."

"Why don't you join me sailing this weekend?"

"Thanks, but I've got plans this weekend." Other than Friday night with Carol, she really did not have anything planned except for time alone in her condo, just trying to relax. She stood to leave, but Tony called her name and lifted the folders from his desk. "Tony, I really don't want those," she said.

"That's too bad. You work for me," he reminded her.

Nicole was reaching her breaking point. She walked toward his desk, trying to control her anger. When she got to the desk, she took the folders from his hands and placed them on his desk. She leaned over just far enough for Tony to have the ability to look down her shirt at her breasts. She smiled seductively at him and said, "You don't own me, so don't think for one moment that I won't walk out that door for good at any time. Don't be a fool."

Tony moved his gaze from Nicole's breasts to her eyes. "You'll take these cases."

Nicole stood up. "No, I think I'll take a vacation." She turned and walked to his office door. She opened the door.

"Nicole, you will take these cases, or you can pack your things and take as long a vacation as you desire," Tony said with only a hint of the anger he felt coming through in his voice.

"Really, Tony? You really want to push me into that corner?" She closed the door and seductively walked back to him, hiding the anger that was growing inside her. She knew whenever she accompanied him to dinners like the one the previous night or to any little affair that he wanted his friends' envy, that he used her. She tolerated all the put-downs and whispers around the beltway because she was making those connections and she knew one day she would walk out that door to start her own firm. "I'm the best lawyer you got in this firm, and you know it. Without me, you wouldn't be able to afford that yacht you endlessly sail around on while I bring in the money for you, and you know it. So I'll ask you again, do you really want to push me into that corner?"

Tony knew she was right. She was the best attorney at the firm. More importantly, he didn't want to think that she would walk out of his life, which would happen if he pushed this issue. "Nikki, I have got people asking for you to represent them. They know how good you are. Can we strike a deal? Look through these and only take the ones you are comfortable with taking."

Nicole knew that Tony had already promised these clients that she would represent them. "And if I don't find one in there that I'm comfortable with, then what happens?"

"We'll cross that bridge when we get to it." Tony pushed the folders toward her.

It came down to whether Nicole was ready to make the break from the firm at that very second. She stood there, contemplating her options. She folded her arms, looking at the files. Then she looked up from the files at Tony. The sheepish grin on his face told her that he thought he had won this fight, something Nicole couldn't accept on this day, for some reason.

"I'll think about it," she said as she turned and walked back to the door. Without another word, she walked out of his office. She smiled when she heard Tony screaming her name. It was late, and no one else was in the office. When she got back to her office, she locked her desk.

She had picked up her briefcase and started to leave when Tony appeared at her door with the files. As she started to walk past him, Tony shoved the files into her arms.

*Blind Influence* | 61

Without saying a word, Nicole walked over to a first-year associate's desk and dropped the folders on it, then continued walking out the door of the office to the elevator without looking back. Maybe it was fate, but when she depressed the call elevator button, the elevator was there waiting. The doors opened, and Nicole walked into the elevator, pressing the button to close the elevator doors as quickly as she could. Before Tony could confront her again, the doors closed and she was on her way to the parking garage. After a few minutes, she was in her car, and then she allowed a little smile to cross her lips.

# Day Three

# Washington, DC

*I*t was only Wednesday, and Nicole was exhausted. In a trance, dreaming about where she would go on that vacation that she had threatened Tony with, she walked back to her car from the courthouse. She started to notice an almost panicked behavior by the people around her. She heard the sirens of police cars and possibly fire and rescue trucks. There seemed to be the sirens of many emergency vehicles echoing among the downtown buildings. Catching only bits and pieces of information from the conversations that were quickly being spoken by people passing her on the street, she could only surmise that someone important had been injured. In DC, scores of people fit that bill.

She continued on to her car. Knowing she was going back to an office with more cases involving guilty clients who became rich at their clients' expense, just as this client had done, weighed heavily on her.

She had just gotten another criminal off the hook, although she had never asked the client if he were guilty. It was another white-collar crime that had hurt thousands of middle-class people who wouldn't be receiving any of their money back from unfortunately investing in her client's schemes. She smiled as she thought about justice being blind. It was more than blind. Maybe justice was deaf, dumb, and blind. Her job at Rosen, Shafer, and Pruett was pretty clear: find the reasonable doubt that would make her client go free. She questioned why she had left the DA's office. At least when working there, she really had felt she was on the right side of the equation, trying to do some good and put these crooks in jail. Then she remembered that she hadn't been trying white-collar crime when she was in the DA's office. All the gruesome murder cases for which she had pieced together the events, working with forensics and visiting the autopsy doctors in the morgue came back to her. Not having witnessed the murders as they had occurred, she had the burden of proof to make the jury believe she had indeed witnessed it. All that blood and sorrow had gotten to her, and she had needed a break. Yes, she remembered now why she had been enticed by Tony's offer.

She reached her car, placed her briefcase behind the driver's seat, and got in, closing the door. She rested her head on the steering wheel for a minute before starting the car. She turned on the radio and selected the NPR station because she felt a need for some soothing symphonic music. Instead, she received news that jolted her out of her self-pitying mood and back into reality. She wasn't sure she'd heard the disc jockey right, sitting in her idling car, staring at the radio.

"Repeating the latest in this … " The disc jockey paused, looking for the right words. "Horrible, horrible event. The President of the United States, President George Andrews, has been assassinated. It has just been confirmed that he was pronounced dead on arrival at Walter Reed." There was another pause. "The streets are a mess, naturally, with law enforcement locking down the city the best they can in hopes of catching the person or persons who committed this heinous crime. There are no words to describe this cold-blooded murder."

Nicole blinked as the disc jockey finished his sentence. She was stunned. The same question kept spinning around in her head. *Why would anyone want to kill this president?* He was very middle of the road. He never really offended anyone, and history would probably forget him, like the rest of the mediocre presidents. She put her car in reverse and started to back out of her parking spot, knowing it would take some time to get back to her office, which was located just a few blocks away from the Capitol. Everything the disc jockey had said was repeated several times on her drive back. There was really no new information being given from either law enforcement or the so-called experts on the panel who were speculating on possibilities that were better left unsaid.

After an hour or so, Nicole arrived back at her office. The elevator doors opened to the reception area, where she found Jean sitting at her desk with teary eyes and a tissue in her hand. "Hi, Nikki," Jean greeted her. "Have you heard?" She barely got that out before she started to cry yet again.

"Yes. Are you all right?" Nicole asked, concerned. She could understand being upset about the president's assassination, but for someone who didn't know him and never had met him, Jean's seemingly uncontrollable crying was hard for her to comprehend. After all, Nicole had met the president numerous times at different parties and dinners. This presented another conundrum for Nicole. Just why wasn't she more upset?

"Yes, it is just awful. Have you seen it, the assassination, I mean?" Jean asked.

"No, I've not seen it yet. Has Tony seen it?" Nicole asked as she headed to the door to the offices.

"Yes, he is in his office."

"Thanks. Jean, if you need to take a break, ask Carrie to cover for you."

Jean nodded to Nicole as she buzzed the door for Nicole to enter the office area. Nicole walked through the door to a virtually empty office area. It was eerily quiet as she walked to her office. Just as she reached her office door, a familiar voice called to her.

"Nikki," Carol called as she was walking from the conference room. "Where the hell have you been?"

"I was in court this morning, and then it took forever to get here."

"So you've heard," Carol said, following Nicole into her office. "Jeez—it was gruesome."

"I keep hearing that word."

"You haven't seen it yet?" Carol asked.

"No, I just got here, and I don't have a TV in my car," Nicole answered sarcastically. "Where is everyone?" She asked as she sat down behind her desk. Carol sat down across from her.

"In the conference room, glued to the TV and listening to the '*finest team of experts*,'" Carol did her best imitation of Walter Cronkite. "It is really sick."

"What is, the assassination or the fact they are all glued to the TV?"

"Both." Carol chuckled. "They keep playing it over and over. It is just awful."

Nicole stood up and headed for the door. "Not you too!" Carol exclaimed as she stood to follow Nicole. "I guess it was just a matter of time," Carol muttered to herself as she gave in to the fact that Nicole would succumb to watching the video over and over like the rest of America.

"How many shots were fired?" Nicole asked as she walked into the conference room. The experts were speculating on the motive for the assassination.

"Kenny said four, the experts say three. I defer to you, former DA," David, a third-year associate, chided.

"I haven't seen it yet."

Carol plopped down in a chair despondently. "Don't worry, they will show it again."

After a few minutes, as Carol predicted, they showed the assassination again in real time. Of course, there had been numerous news agencies capturing the president's exit from his car as he had walked up to the Russian embassy. The president was guarded by the Secret Service, who tried to move him to the door as quickly as possible. The openness of the plaza area clearly was the weakest protection point. Everything seemed to be going as planned. Suddenly, the president grabbed his throat with both hands, falling to his knees, at which point the Secret Service sprang into action. Two agents grabbed the president's upper arms, noticing the blood that had begun flowing from his neck wound. The two agents seemed to be assessing the president's condition while the others began visual scans, reaching for their guns, and talking on radios. In all the madness, one agent grabbed his knee less than a millisecond of the president being shot. The agent fell down. The two holding the president tried to stand him upright as a noticeable amount of blood was soaking the president's white shirt. Totally unaware of what was coming next, the cameraman had caught yet another strike. This one was to the back of the president's head, and exiting his frontal lobe. This caught Nicole by surprise, as she felt the first shot had basically killed the president, given the amount of blood he had lost in such a short period of time.

"Oh my God," Nicole whispered in horror. It reminded her of Kennedy's fatal shot. It was just as brutal and shocking. It took Nicole several minutes to regain her senses. Even though she continued to watch the remaining minute of the video, there was one thing that didn't make sense to her. "Wait a minute," she said a little more loudly as she moved toward the television. As she reached it, the video concluded. The experts gave some additional comments, but Nicole wasn't listening. "Come on, play it again," Nicole pleaded.

*Blind Influence* | 67

"Geez, Nikki!" Carol responded in disgust.

Nicole ignored her friend. The experts decided it was time to play the video in slow motion so they could provide their observations and document the support for their arguments. It didn't matter to Nicole what these experts were saying. She was, from her own experience in the DA's office, making her own observations—and something just didn't seem right. With every paused frame, her eyes were darting about and her brain cataloging every move and position. "Give me a piece of paper, napkin—something with a straight edge," Nicole demanded, throwing her hand behind her, toward the table where her fellow lawyers were sitting. She snapped her fingers until finally she was handed what she wanted. She quickly used the straight edge to align the first bullet to the downed Secret Service agent. It wasn't perfect, but given the angle of the video that was presented, it was possible that the bullet exited the president's throat and struck the agent's knee. The exit angle depended on if the bullet had hit any bone, which would have changed the angle or if the killer wanted to shoot the agent to distract the rest of the agents just long enough for the fatal shot. The video started again and showed once more the fatal shot to the back of the head, exiting the front. When the bullet exited, it took with it a portion of the president's skull, exposing all that lay beneath. The Secret Service agents in close vicinity were sprayed with blood, skull fragments, and brain tissue.

Nicole blinked a couple of times and swallowed back the urge to get sick. Something didn't quite fit, but she couldn't figure it out. She laid the paper down on the table and turned to walk out of the room, mumbling, "I need to call Jerome."

"What?" A third-year associate asked.

Nicole came out of her trance. "Nothing," she said as she walked toward the door.

Kenny, who said there were three shots, couldn't stand it any longer. "How many do you think?"

"Two shots; there were two shots," Nicole answered as she began to leave the room. "And that is one hell of a sniper." She left the room and quickened her pace to her office. Carol had started down the hall after Nicole but was met with Nicole's office door slamming in her face. Carol tried to open it, but it was locked. "Nikki?"

"Not now, Carol," Nicole called back as she picked up the phone receiver and began dialing. "I'll stop by in few minutes."

Carol walked away from Nicole's door, somewhat confused by her friend's actions. She returned to her desk, having seen enough of the assassination and knowing she had some important work to do for a deposition the following morning.

Nicole sat down in her desk chair and began to tap a pencil on her desk. Her mind was racing a mile a minute. She had forgotten how this felt. She felt as if she were back in her old job. "Chief Bailey, please."

"He's rather busy at the moment," a distracted and harried officer answered on the other end.

"Tell him it's Nicole Charbonneau," Nicole answered. She smiled, as she knew Bailey would take the call.

After what seemed like an eternity to Nicole, Bailey finally picked up the phone. "Bailey." The booming bass voice shouted. It was gruff and intended to be that way, his deep bass voice making sure that anyone who didn't have business, or the courage, talking to him would quickly be hanging up the phone.

"Jerome, it is Nikki. It's about time," she started.

"I'm a little busy here, Nikki," he shot back. "You don't work with us anymore, remember?"

"Yeah, yeah," Nicole answered sarcastically. "Look, something is not right here."

"No shit!" Bailey almost yelled back.

"Two shots," Nicole stated flatly.

"Well thank you, Ms. Attorney General. You know I wasn't really sure." He was intentionally being sarcastic.

"Jerome, you and I both know this is going to be covered up. We need to make sure—"

*Blind Influence* | 69

"Just who are *we*?" Bailey questioned. "Nicole, I'm serious. You don't work here anymore. Besides, the announcement hasn't been made yet, but the FBI believes they have got their man."

Nicole was surprised and sat up in her chair. "Really? How did that happen?"

Bailey almost laughed at her surprise. "The usual way, I guess. I don't have all the information. In the meantime, I'm handling a lot of things that— *Noooo*!" Bailey yelled as he read a memo that had just been handed him. "Ah fuck! Nikki, I got to go!"

Nicole could hear him yelling as he slammed the receiver down.

# FBI Headquarters

The florescent lights washed out any hint of color in the linoleum floor, gray walls, or the metal table that sported a fake marble top. There were three chairs in the room. One was occupied by a man in blue pants and a blue and white striped shirt. Across from him was a wall with a mirror that started about four feet above the floor. He was in an interrogation room, so the man knew it was a two-way mirror. The man knew he was being watched. He balanced his chair on the back two legs as he rested his head and shoulders against the opposite wall from the mirror. His head was tilted a little to the left as he stared at the mirror. He squinted to see if that helped reduce the glare and provide a hint as to who was on the other side. He was trying his best not to lose his temper. Actually, he had been trying not to lose his temper for the last four hours.

The chair came forward, the two front legs hitting the floor with a loud thud. He sprang from the chair and started pacing. His mind was racing with every possible foul word he could think of. As he paced, he kept staring at the mirror. He then stopped, gave a chuckle because he could, after all, see himself in the mirror. *I look like the crazed man that I am*, he thought. He slowly walked up to the mirror and cupped his hands on both sides of his face and looked through the mirror. "Let's get this started, shall we?" he said to the people on the other side of the mirror. "I'm not the man you are after, and you are wasting valuable time." Sean could see that two of the three men behind the glass were not amused. He walked back away from the mirror and sat down. He rocked the chair on its back legs again and rested his head and shoulders against the wall. He closed his eyes and waited.

After a few minutes, two men came into the room. One of them was the only one of the three who had smiled when Sean had looked through the mirror. The other man looked like he was going to bust out of the clothes he was wearing. He wasn't overweight; he was all muscle. He wore his shoulder holster into the room, although there was no gun in the holster. When Sean looked the musclebound man he wanted to laugh. He didn't, however. He just looked at them both, hoping to hear he was allowed to leave.

"Kevin Thompson, FBI," the man who had smiled behind the mirror said as he extended his hand. "This is Max."

*Blind Influence* | 71

"Is he the muscle who is going to rough me up if I don't cooperate?" Sean asked as he shook Thompson's hand.

Thompson laughed at Sean's accusation. "No, Mr. Adkins. We typically don't rough up agents who are allies with us." Thompson flipped one of the chairs around so that when he sat down, he could rest his forearms on the back of the chair. "We'd just like to ask a few questions."

Sean brought the front legs of the chair back to the floor again with a thud. He looked at Thompson to ask his first question.

"MI-6?"

"Yes," Sean answered.

"What were you doing in the building that was closed off and secure?"

"I was tracking the man that killed your president," Sean answered.

Thompson took a deep breath and exhaled. "There are some, Mr. Adkins, who believe you shot the president." Thompson really hated this, wasting time interrogating someone he knew wasn't guilty. His superiors in the dark room behind the mirror really wanted to know why and how Sean had gotten into the United States without their knowledge. They wanted to know about his mission.

"Well, I can't help it if the FBI is stupid, now can I?" Sean answered.

Thompson tried not to smile. Though the remark had been made to irritate him, he actually agreed with the observation.

"Can we cut the crap here, Thompson? What is it you want to know?" Sean asked.

"Why are you here, and how did you get here without anyone's knowledge?"

Sean smiled. "Neither are really any of your concern, but obviously, I'm tracking the assassin that killed your president. He's killed before, and he is going to kill again. The more we dick around here, the colder the trail is getting," he answered. "If you must know everything, then call Charlie

Dawson at SIS headquarters. He'll give you what you need to know, based on your clearance, of course." When Thompson stood up and started for the door, Sean added, "And please hurry. I'd really like to get out of here."

Thompson smiled as he walked out of the room. He had walked to his desk and picked up the phone when one of his superiors walked out of the observation room. "What are you doing?"

"I'm calling Charlie Dawson at SIS," Thompson answered. "He isn't our man, and he isn't going to tell us anything. It's a waste of time. We'd learn more tailing him than we are sitting here." His supervisor was about to answer him when he was interrupted by someone answering the call on the other end. "May I speak with Charlie Dawson? This is Kevin Thompson of the FBI. Thank you." Thompson had looked down at his desk when the phone was answered, and he wasn't about to look up. "Mr. Dawson? This is Lieutenant Kevin Thompson of the FBI."

Suddenly, Thompson pulled the phone from his ear, as Charlie was screaming. The only part that Thompson understood was the part asking for his superior. "I believe he wants to talk to you." Thompson handed the phone to his boss. "Can we let him go now?"

His superior nodded and motioned to the interrogation room where Sean was sitting. Thompson picked up a small box that contained Sean's gun and holster and a manila folder that contained his personal information and badge. "But have him tailed," Thompson's superior said with a hand over the receiver.

Thompson acknowledged the statement before leaving his desk for the interrogation room. He motioned for his partner to stay at his desk and see to other details. Thompson opened the door to the interrogation room, trying really hard not to laugh. "Here you go." He placed the box on the table.

Sean immediately began to put his holster on and gather his things. "What are you laughing about?" he finally asked.

"I don't know who you are or what you are into, but my boss is getting his ass chewed out by your boss." Thompson tried to stop smiling. "And that makes my day, since he is always riding my ass."

*Blind Influence* | 73

Sean looked at Thompson very seriously and then gave a short laugh. "Something tells me we are cut from the same cloth." Sean finished collecting his gear, then extended his hand. "Thanks, and can you tell me how to get out of here?"

"I'll walk you down," Thompson answered as he opened the door. His superiors were gone, and Max was at his desk, deploying the agents to tail Sean. When they got to the elevator and the doors closed, Thompson turned to Sean. "You know we are going to be tailing you."

"Now why would you want to do that?" Sean asked, feigning surprise.

"It is a condition of letting you go free," Thompson answered. He shrugged his shoulders.

"You know I'm just going to call Charlie to have that changed," Sean countered.

"I know that, they know that, but they don't seem to understand that," Thompson answered. "I just wanted you to know."

Sean looked at Thompson. "May I ask why are you telling me all this?"

"I want the son of a bitch caught. I couldn't care less which of us catches him."

"More people should have your attitude," Sean answered. The elevator reached its appointed floor. Thompson and Sean walked to the door of the FBI building. Sean extended his hand again. "Thank you again. I'm staying at the Washington Hilton, if you should come across any information that you think I could use."

Thompson shook his hand. "And you know where I'm at if you need my help." Thompson wasn't entirely sure why Sean had been so free with that information. Besides, he had seen the key in Sean's personal belongings. Thompson didn't expect to hear or see Sean again, but he couldn't have been more wrong.

# Capitol Hill

"**S**enator," Chris, the young man who was Senator Robert Jenkins's chief of staff, called from the senator's outer office, "Senator Mercer is on line one."

"Thank you, Chris." Jenkins picked up the receiver. "Senator, how can I help you?"

Mercer was the Democratic Party Whip and Majority Leader in the Senate. He represented the great state of Maine and had many, many years of experience, but never in any of his terms had he witnessed the cold-blooded murder of the leader of the free world. His voice broke as he answered Jenkins's question. "I wanted to check with you, since you are the Intelligence Committee chairperson, if you had any information that I could share at this point?"

"I have nothing yet, Senator," Jenkins answered. "I've been told by the FBI and the CIA that they have leads. They told me that they are actively pursuing those leads. Honestly, Daniel, with the noise in the background when I was talking to these people, I get the impression we aren't anywhere near having the culprit. With that in mind, I wouldn't want to embarrass our law enforcement branch with a statement at this time."

"Yes … yes, of course," Daniel Mercer answered. "I'm going to address the chamber in five minutes. My staff is calling everyone personally, requesting them to be in the chamber. Vice President Stevens—President Stevens," he corrected himself, which led to the awkwardness of the moment, "was in New York City and has been rushed to *Executive One*—or is it *Air Force One* now?" Mercer wondered.

Jenkins smiled at the senator's predicament. "For now and for the reassurance of the American people, let's call it *Air Force One*."

"Kelly is finishing up my speech now, so I'll pass that on if he didn't think of it himself," Mercer replied. "I suppose I don't need to tell you to keep me informed."

"As soon as I know something, Senator, I will pass it on to you," Jenkins answered and then hung up the phone. "Chris," he called to his aide, "can you come in here, please, and close the door."

*Blind Influence* | 75

Chris did as instructed. "Yes, Senator?" he asked, standing in front of the senator's desk.

"The next few days are going to be unsettling and a bit confusing. There is going to be a lot of information that this office is privy to that others in Congress will not be privy to. Some of that information is better to die in this office then make its way to others who feel they could benefit from such knowledge."

"Yes, sir."

"I ask that you be the only one in this office besides me to handle any information coming from the FBI or CIA. Any information passed to me is passed in sealed envelopes between us or in the confidence of this office only. Is that clear?"

"Yes, sir."

"We wouldn't want this information falling in the wrong hands, so to speak." Jenkins smiled at his chief of staff and winked. "That's all. Thank you, Chris."

Chris gave another acknowledgment before turning and heading back to his desk just outside the senator's office door. Jenkins checked his watch and headed for the Senate floor.

All the senators had heard the call by the majority leader to be in the Senate chamber within five minutes and were walking around, engaging each other in conversation before Senator Mercer was to enter the Senate. Jenkins was just entering the chamber when he was stopped by Senator Barker.

"Is there any news from our enforcement and intelligence agencies?" Barker asked Jenkins.

"There is nothing substantial to report at this time," Jenkins patiently answered as he entered the chamber behind Barker. "They are hard at work and as anxious as we are to capture the murderer."

Jenkins was asked the same question several times as he walked to his desk in the Senate, and the answer was patiently given each time as it had been to Senator Barker. He looked around the room at all the senators erratically

76 | *Linda Riesenberg Fisler*

standing throughout the chamber. He looked at his watch. Then, in a rather commanding voice, he called out, "Gentleman and ladies of the Senate." He waited a second as the conversations came to the end. "Gentleman and ladies of the Senate, may I have your attention for a brief second?" The senator was not speaking into the microphone, so C-Span was not picking up his voice. It probably looked very strange on camera that all the senators were turning to look at Senator Jenkins. "Thank you. I would like to suggest that we present a dignified and orderly appearance to the people of the United States at this time of crisis. May I ask each of you to move to your seats here in this chamber? Senator Mercer should be arriving shortly to give us and the nation the sad news."

The senators all began to move to their seats. There were times when Jenkins's military background was extremely useful in regaining order in a sometimes unorderly Senate. It also didn't hurt that he was considered by most to be the third most powerful senator in the chamber. "Thank you," he told them all.

Within a minute, Senator Mercer entered the Senate. Those who were not standing got to their feet as he approached the front of the chamber. The senator stood at one of the two podiums located at the front of the room and waited to be acknowledged by the president pro tem. "The chair recognizes the honorable senator from Maine, Mr. Mercer, for as long a time as needed."

"Thank you, Mr. President," Mercer said, then turned to the Senate to give his speech. "Mr. President, fellow esteemed members of this United States Senate, and to our esteemed citizens of this country, it is with a heavy heart and much sorrow that I address our nation at this time. As you may be aware, President George Andrews was unmercifully assassinated this morning. His passing leaves many of his policies unanswered, but his legacy and service to this country will long be remembered. Although we may not have agreed with all of his policies, we knew we could discuss and negotiate until a fair and balanced decision was created to the benefit of all the American people. Long live his legacy. Long live the story of his military career and the legacy of being a father, grandfather, uncle, and brother to those who loved him unconditionally and whose hearts, like ours, have broken on this day."

Mercer paused for a brief moment before going on. "The nation has lost its leader, but it must go on. It would be what the president would have wanted, and it is decreed that it should happen by our Constitution. We here in Congress would like to reassure the American people that those provisions stated in the Constitution are being enacted as I speak. The speaker of the house will elaborate further, but the vice president is aboard *Air Force One*, returning from New York City. He has been sworn in as president. As we have lost one great leader, a new leader assumes the reins of his presidency. I, as well as every member of the Senate, extend my deepest sympathy to Mrs. Andrews, the Andrews family, friends, colleagues, and the American people in this hour of President Andrews's death. I ask that we have a moment of silence for President Andrews."

Senator Mercer bowed his head, as did all in the Senate, out of respect for the slain president. After he had finished his prayer, Senator Mercer looked at the president pro tem. "Thank you, Mr. President. I yield the floor back to you." With that, Mercer left the podium and started for the door with the intention of heading back to his office. The Senate returned to its duties. Many senators, including Jenkins, followed Senator Mercer's lead, returning to their offices or committees that were in session.

# New York City

"**W**hat the fuck is going on!" Vice President Stevens yelled as the Secret Service whisked him out of the United Nations building lobby and back into his bulletproof limousine. Once inside the limousine, Mark was still angry with the agents for what he considered was rough handling. "Will someone please tell me what the fuck is going on?"

The special agent in charge of the Secret Service detailed to protect Vice President Stevens finally acknowledged his question. "Mr. Vice President, the president has been assassinated in Washington, DC. He was shot and killed as he walked from his car to the Russian embassy. Our orders are to secure your position back onboard *Air Force One*, where you will be sworn in as president and returned to Washington, DC, immediately."

"What? He was assassinated?" Mark looked at the agent. "He's dead?"

"Yes, sir," the agent answered. "I apologize for our rough handling of you, sir. It is imperative that we get you to the safety of *Air Force One*. We do not have the assassin in custody, and quite frankly, sir, at this time, we don't know if there is a larger plot at work or the motives for the assassination. We ask for your cooperation."

"Yes … yes, of course. How are my wife and family?" Mark asked.

"They are secured at Blair House, Mr. President. Mrs. Andrews and her family are in lockdown at the White House."

"Thank you," Mark answered as he turned his head to look out the window of the limousine. It was anything but quiet inside the limousine. The agents were barking commands, making sure something hadn't been missed. The limousine drove directly up to *Air Force One*, which was surrounded by more Secret Service agents. Mark Stevens was again whisked out of the limousine and up the stairs to the safety of the plane. Inside, he adjusted his suit and stood in the aisle. The door to the plane shut, and the engines whined into life.

"We need to get this plane in the air, *now*." One of the agents yelled into the cockpit. "You better sit down and buckle up, Mr. President." Mark did what he was told to do. "Why isn't this fucking plane moving?"

*Blind Influence* | 79

"We are getting demands from the press—" another agent began.

"Fuck the press! Get this plane in the air right now!" The agent who had been interrupted continued in a calm voice. "They are stating that someone should be present to get a picture of the swearing-in of President Stevens. They said it would be reassuring to the American people to see this."

"I think it is reassuring to the American people that this man is safely on his way back to Washington, DC," Stevens's head of security answered rather impatiently. "Oh, for Christ's sake, does anyone have a fucking camera?!"

"Here's one," another agent answered.

Sarcastically, the head of Stevens's security detail asked, "Now can we get this damn plane off the fucking ground?"

"Yes, sir." The agent turned and headed to the cockpit to give the order. The rest of the men sat down and buckled up as the plane began to move.

"Once we are in the air, Mr. President, we will swear you in officially. There is a judge waiting to do just that." The agent nodded his head toward the unknown person sitting in the first row where the press typically sat.

Mark acknowledged that he had heard the agent. Everything seemed to be moving in slow motion for Mark Stevens. Although it was only a few minutes, it felt like an eternity before they were ready to swear him in as president of the United States. He had been waiting for this moment ever since he had entered into politics. Everything he had done in his political and sometimes in his private life had been calculated and executed with the end result of being president someday. Although most men would be feeling a bit threatened by what could turn out to be a plot to kill not only the president but also the vice president as the Secret Service agents speculated, Mark Stevens was unusually calm. He began making a list of things he wanted to accomplish in the remaining year of President Andrews's term.

There was so much commotion on the plane that no one seemed to notice the absence of emotion in President Stevens. But then President Andrews and his vice president had not been the best of friends either. To every person on that plane, the sole objective was to get Mark

Stevens back to Washington alive and sworn in as president so that one of the most powerful nations in the world didn't appear vulnerable.

"It's time, Mr. President," an agent said to Mark, who stood and followed him to the place where the swearing-in would be held. One agent took photos while others flanked the judge and Stevens. The photographs were the public witness to the event and would be published upon arrival of *Air Force One* at Andrews Air Force Base.

"I, Mark Stevens, do solemnly swear that I will faithfully execute the Office of President of the United States." He paused as the judge read the next passage. "And will, to the best of my ability, preserve, protect, and defend the Constitution of the United States," he finished. A few congratulations were murmured, though it somehow didn't seem proper to congratulate someone achieving the office of the presidency under these conditions.

Mark noticed the uneasiness in everyone. "Thank you all for your service at this time when it is most needed. Let's get back to Washington and work." Mark thanked the judge and assured him that they would get him back to New York as quickly as possible.

The rest of the flight was uneventful now that the swearing-in had occurred. Mark sat in the president's office, writing a speech that he would deliver later that evening or even upon arrival in Washington. He wanted to be prepared.

# Capitol Hill

*I*t was now evening, and Jenkins had just told Chris to go home. It had been a long day, a day in which his country had awakened to the continuing service of President Andrews and ended in the midst of a crisis and with a new president. Little had been accomplished in terms of law making. There had been continual interruptions, with everyone wanting to know the latest information. Jenkins had even made a plea to his fellow congressmen to allow the process to take its course and to stop calling the law enforcement agency for updates. It wasn't as if the law enforcement agencies hadn't enough to do.

It was well after 10:00 p.m. when Jenkins's phone rang. It was Michael Jefferies, director of the FBI, on the other end. "Yes, Mr. Jefferies, how can I help you?" Jenkins asked.

"We have a break in the case, sir. I was wondering, if you aren't too tired, if you could swing by here and we'll fill you in on the details," Jefferies answered.

"That is good news. I'll be leaving in five minutes, so I'll see you shortly," Jenkins answered before hanging up the phone. He quickly cleared his desk, placing some documents in his safe and locking it. Others, he shoved into his top drawer and then locked his desk. He had to admit to himself that he was anxious to hear what the FBI had come up with so quickly, given the pandemonium he had heard throughout the day whenever he had spoken with the various heads of the different security agencies. He grabbed his coat and headed to his car.

The eerie silence of the Capitol echoed the uneasiness of the nation, but this heightened fear was felt nowhere near the level as in Washington, where at this moment, an assassin was still on the loose.

There was little traffic on the roads, and Jenkins made it to FBI headquarters in record time. He entered the lobby, where he was greeted by an agent.

"Senator Jenkins, I'm Lieutenant Kevin Thompson. Director Jefferies asked that I meet you and escort you to his office." Thompson seemed a bit nervous.

"He did?" Jenkins answered. "I suppose, Lieutenant, that the director thinks I forgot my way to his office?" Thompson wasn't sure if he was to answer that question and if so, what exactly to say, which was evident to Jenkins. "Relax, Lieutenant. I'll take that up with him."

"Yes, sir," Thompson answered as they walked to the elevators.

"Tell me, Lieutenant, how do you think this investigation of the president's assassination is going?"

"I'm not at liberty to discuss—"

"I'll remind you that I am chairman of the Intelligence Committee, Lieutenant Thompson. I believe that is your name, correct?" Jenkins was removing his coat as he was speaking.

"Yes, sir," Thompson answered as the doors on the elevator opened. Thompson could have sworn that Senator Jenkins heard him breathe a sigh of relief when on the other side of the doors stood Director Jefferies.

"It's good to see you can get this assignment correct, Thompson," Jefferies snapped at him. "Senator, it is good to see you again." He stuck out his hand for the senator to shake. The man with the obnoxious habits then cleared his throat and pushed his glasses back up his nose with his other hand as he waited.

"Director Jefferies," Jenkins acknowledged, shaking his hand. It was almost comical to Jenkins that Jefferies was even attempting to make Thompson shudder by trying to be authoritative.

"We'll meet in my office," the director snapped as if marking his territory.

"I assumed so, as you instructed on your call inviting me here, Director," Jenkins replied rather sharply. He didn't care if he was in Jefferies's office or standing on the street. He wanted Jefferies to understand who was in charge. "The escort wasn't necessary."

"Yes, well, we wanted to make sure you got here safely."

"Keeping me safe in your own building, Director? Is there something you aren't telling me?" Jenkins inquired.

"No, it has just been a strange day," Jefferies answered as the three men entered Jefferies's office. Jefferies motioned to the chair in front of his desk as he walked past it. Jenkins noticed little beads of sweat start to appear over Jefferies's brow. "Today has been a long day," Jefferies started but was interrupted by Jenkins.

"Excuse me, Director. Lieutenant Thompson, if you would kindly not stand behind me. I would like for you to either grab a chair to sit beside me or move where I can see you. It isn't that I don't trust you; it is just that the office is rather small and I have a feeling of someone breathing down my neck." While he was not ill at ease with Thompson behind him, his real motive was to watch Thompson's reactions to what the director presented.

"Yes, sir." Thompson moved and stood in front of the filing cabinet, in view of the senator and the director.

"Thank you, Lieutenant. Continue, Director," Jenkins commanded, asserting his authority once again.

Jefferies cleared his throat and patted the tiny beads of sweat from his forehead with a handkerchief he produced from his suit coat pocket. "As I was saying, it has been a long day and the FBI is proud to say we have found our man."

Thompson's head snapped over to look at Jefferies. This was the first he had heard of this.

Jefferies took a photograph out of a folder, the very folder that Thompson had given him a few hours earlier. "Here he is."

Thompson peered over to see the photograph that Jefferies had thrown across the table to Jenkins. He couldn't believe what he was seeing.

Jenkins looked out of the corner of his eye at Thompson's reaction, which Thompson was trying desperately to suppress. Jenkins picked up the photograph. He showed no emotions. He set the photograph back on the director's desk. "Where is this man now? I assume you have him in custody," Jenkins said.

"Well, no. Lieutenant Thompson released him earlier today," Jefferies answered.

84 | *Linda Riesenberg Fisler*

"Why was that?" Jenkins asked, looking first at Thompson and then at Jefferies.

"Let's just say we thought we might want to tail him a while to see if he was acting on his own," Jefferies answered. "I wanted to fill you in on what is happening, and then we'll send some agents over to arrest him formerly."

"Including Lieutenant Thompson?" Jenkins asked.

"I haven't decided yet."

"I see." Jenkins sat for a second, looking at the photograph on the desk. He knew that the man in the photograph had not committed this crime. He knew he had to tread lightly, as something else was going on here and he was on the outside of whatever it was. "What makes you think he committed this crime? What evidence do you have?"

"He was arrested in the very building, almost the exact spot, where the fatal shots were fired. When Thompson discovered him, he tried to flee, which was a desperate attempt to escape."

"Do you have any ballistics or other evidence? Did he have in his possession a gun that matches the bullets that hit the president—excuse me, killed the president?"

"Yes," Jefferies answered.

Thompson's head snapped again to look at Jefferies.

"I see." Jenkins stood up. "Well, I guess your next move is obvious. I'd like to be present when you have this man in your custody. I assume you are going to question him again." Jenkins put on his coat and started for the door. "I only have two requests, Director." He turned back to face Jefferies. "First and foremost, no mention of any of this to the press until we know for sure this man did it."

"But ... " Jefferies interrupted.

"Let me say this again. You are getting a direct order from me to not talk to the press about this person until I approve it. Do you understand, Director?"

"Yes, sir."

"You understand that I have the power to make your life miserable if you go against that order?' Jenkins asked sternly.

"Yes, Senator, I do," Jefferies answered, irritated. "What's your second request?"

"I would ask that Lieutenant Thompson escort me to my car. Obviously, Washington isn't as safe as it used to be."

"Yes, of course. Thompson ... " Jefferies answered, waving his hand as a way of finishing his command. "And then go arrest Adkins."

"Yes, sir," Thompson answered as he headed toward the door, following Jenkins out of the room.

They reached the elevator, neither man speaking.

When they were inside the elevator, Jenkins could tell by Thompson's body language that he was not feeling at ease with the task assigned to him. "Lieutenant, I'd like you to walk me all the way to my car, if you don't mind." Jenkins tilted his head in the direction of the speaker located above the elevator buttons. This motion indicated that he knew the conversations inside the elevator could be listened to.

"Yes, sir," Thompson answered.

As the two men exited the building, an agent caught up to them. "Thompson!" the agent yelled from the door leading outside. Both men stopped and turned. "Chief Bailey wants to talk to you. He said it is urgent."

"Tell him I'll call him back in a few minutes. I need to escort the senator to his car."

"He doesn't want to hear that ... "

"Tell him I'll be right there after I walk the senator to his car," Thompson answered with a bit more authority to his voice.

The senator and Thompson turned to continue walking to Jenkins's car. "It is becoming an interesting night. Lieutenant, I saw your reactions to the director's assertions. Am I correct in assuming that this Adkins fellow didn't kill the president?"

"Answering that puts me in a rather awkward position, Senator."

"I understand. Then let me say this. I would welcome your assistance in this investigation if you feel it necessary to talk with someone in the event that something doesn't appear quite what it should be." Jenkins unlocked his car door and opened it. "If I were you, Lieutenant, I would be very careful with your actions over the next twenty-four hours. Tell Chief Bailey I said hello and apologize that I kept you from him."

With that, Jenkins got in his car and started it. He gave one final look at Thompson before he drove away from the bewildered FBI agent.

Thompson wasn't sure what had just happened. He knew only one thing. He wasn't holding the winning hand in this game of poker and could easily be dealt with if the need arose. He turned and trotted back into the building. He quickly returned to his desk. "What line?" he shouted over to the other agent in the room.

"Line two," the officer answered.

"Thompson," he said after he pressed the button.

"It's about fucking time," Bailey said, annoyed. "Get over to the alley behind the Air and Space Museum as quick as you can."

"Why?"

"Just get here!" Bailey yelled.

Thompson put the phone down and shook his head. "What an unbelievable day!" He grabbed his coat and started for the door. "I'm out of here," he said as he left the office area. He got to his car, got in, and started it. He was heading over to the Air and Space Museum when he spotted a phone booth. He pulled the car over, moved to the phone, took out a quarter from his pocket, and inserted it into the phone. He depressed the 0. "Yes, operator, can you connect me to the Washington Hilton, please? Thank you." Thompson looked around while he waited for the front desk to answer the call. "Yes, connect me to Sean Adkins's room, please. This is Lieutenant

*Blind Influence* | 87

Kevin Thompson of the FBI." Waiting for Sean to answer the phone, he nervously looked around to make sure he wasn't being watched.

"Yes?" Adkins answered.

"Sean, this is Kevin Thompson from the—"

"Yes, I remember you. What can I do for you, Lieutenant?"

"I'm not sure," Thompson answered.

"Where are you?" Sean asked.

"I'm in the dark," Thompson answered rather obscurely, but somewhat truthfully. "Listen, I have to run an errand. Think you can meet me on Independence Ave.? You will know where when you get there."

"Sure." Sean knew they were being listened to and that the lieutenant was being evasive on purpose. He hung up the phone and started to think about how to get out of the hotel without attracting too much attention.

Thompson hung up, got back in his car, and headed to the Air and Space Museum. When he arrived, he walked past the Washington, DC, police who were guarding the entrance to the alley by showing them his credentials. "Hey, I'm expecting a guy to meet me here. He's with British Intelligence, so let him back."

"If Chief Bailey says it's OK."

"He will," Thompson said as he started to walk by the guard. "Just let him and no one else back here." Thompson walked up to Chief Bailey, noticing the two bodies covered in white sheets. "What do you have?"

"I have two dead Secret Service agents," Bailey answered quietly, walking out of earshot of his officers working on the crime scene.

"What?" Thompson asked. "What makes you think they are Secret Service?"

"Their badges that I took from them and that are now in my back pocket," Bailey answered. He pulled the badges out to show Thompson.

---

88 | *Linda Riesenberg Fisler*

"What the fuck?" Thompson answered, confused. "Well, this doesn't happen every day. Have you notified the Secret Service?"

"Not yet. I wanted to talk to you first," Bailey said. "There is something bigger going on here. They were shot execution style about thirty minutes apart." Bailey turned, walking back toward the bodies. "And one of them was dragged to this spot." He pointed to the blood trail created by the murderer as he had dragged the bodies to one location.

Thompson looked at the bodies and the trail of blood and scratched his head. Just as he was about to ask a question, one of the DC police officers walked up to Chief Bailey. "There's a guy out here who says that Lieutenant Thompson asked him to come here."

"Is he British?" Thompson asked, turning to look back at the police barricade back down the alley. "Yeah, that's him. He's clear, Chief."

"Let him in." The chief looked at Thompson. "Who is this guy?"

"MI-6. His name is Sean Adkins. There is some weird shit going on here," Thompson stated, turning to greet Sean. He extended his hand for Sean to shake. "Sean, did you have any trouble getting away from our friends?"

Sean shook Thompson's hand. "No. It helps when you really don't know where you are going."

Thompson smiled at Sean's comment. "Chief Bailey with the Washington, DC, police, I'd like you to meet Sean Adkins, MI-6."

The two men shook hands. "What happened here?" Sean asked as he surveyed the scene.

"Two Secret Service agents were murdered," Bailey answered.

"Were these two men on the president's detail this morning?" Sean asked.

"I don't know, but we can check. That would require us to contact the Secret—"

"Don't bother," Sean answered. "May I examine them?"

*Blind Influence* | 89

"Sure," Bailey answered.

Sean walked up to one of the bodies and pulled the sheet back. The agent's hands were tied behind his back. There was a handkerchief tying the jaw shut. Sean could feel the adrenaline starting to surge through him, the bittersweet taste of it in his mouth as his saliva glands excreted with the rush. He tried hard to push back the vision that was flashing in his mind's eye. He blinked out the vision of his wife lying in the same position as the agent before him now, with hands bound behind his back and his feet tied together.

Sean blinked again and shook his head.

"You okay?" Thompson asked, standing over him.

"Yes," Sean answered. Thompson's voice had pulled him back from the brink of reliving yet again the night of his wife's and daughter's murder. "Chief, may I?"

Bailey and Thompson moved closer as the chief gave his approval. Adkins pulled the handkerchief off the agent's head. The agent's jaw fell open as a massive amount of blood streamed from it.

"Oh shit!" Thompson exclaimed as he watched the blood rapidly flow from the agent's mouth to the ground.

"Jesus!" Chief Bailey said at the same time in disgust. Both men tried hard not to turn their heads but were unsuccessful.

Sean moved the head slightly, causing the tongue to dislodge from the roof of the mouth where it had been stuffed. It was the Serpent's calling card. Just as he had done with Sean's wife and child, the Serpent had forked the tongue. The Serpent wanted Sean to know that he knew Sean was here. He also wanted Sean to know he was cleaning up loose ends. Sean stood up. "Without a doubt, these two men were a part of your president's detail this morning."

"Are you saying these two men were working with the assassin?" Bailey asked in disbelief. "Mr. Adkins, the Secret Service is beyond reproach. They—"

90 | *Linda Riesenberg Fisler*

"I understand that, Chief, and it pains me just as much to say this. These two men were recruited by the Serpent." He turned to Thompson. "Your assassin is the Serpent. I knew this earlier today. I've been tracking this cold-blooded bastard since he was involved with the IRA. This"—he pointed to the tongue of the agent—"is his calling card. Don't believe me, check it out. Sergio Serpiente, aka Sergio the Serpent."

Thompson looked up from the agent and at Sean. "That's the project, your project, to track this assassin down and kill him?"

Sean chuckled. "Now I know who has been trying to get information on my project."

"Label anything super-classified, and we get nosey," Thompson answered. "That, and we don't even trust our own CIA. The Serpent has never been here before. Why now?"

"The payoff must be huge," Sean answered, his thoughts trailing away from their discussion.

"Must be? You mean he hasn't been paid yet?" Bailey asked.

"I don't think so. These two were his first victims. He couldn't afford to have their involvement discovered. If you are unlucky enough to see his face, you won't be alive for very long. He probably promised them money. When they came to collect it, he killed them."

"How come you are still alive?" Thompson asked.

Sean stared at Thompson. He wasn't sure how he wanted to answer that. "It's part of the thrill. He has had his opportunities to kill me. He took more from me by keeping me alive." Sean started to walk away.

"Wait," Thompson said. "We have a small problem. The director of the FBI wants me to arrest you for the murder of the president. I am supposed to be on my way to do that right now."

"That is a predicament," Sean said flatly. "How do you suppose we fix this?"

*Blind Influence* | 91

"I think we can with the chief's help," Thompson said, taking his coat off. "We'll throw my coat over your head, and the chief here will cuff you. We'll get you in the back of my car, and we'll get the hell out of here to someplace where we can talk freely without being overheard."

"Fuck," the chief said. "How the fuck did I get right smack in the middle of another damn cover-up?!"

Sean looked at Bailey, then at Thompson. "He's right."

"It's going to be covered up, either way." Thompson looked at Bailey. "But I'm not elected. Act like your hands are cuffed. Chief, I'll be in touch when I can."

Thompson threw his coat over Sean's head. He acted like he was cuffing Sean's hands, and then he led Sean out of the alley to his car. To his amazement, Bailey was right behind him. When he reached his car, Thompson put Sean in the back.

The chief walked over to his own car, barking out commands to his officers to secure the scene until the forensic unit arrived for the bodies. He put the IDs of the Secret Service men in his pocket. For now, they would be body A and body B.

Thompson's car pulled out, and Bailey got in his own car, following Thompson away from the scene. Thompson turned right when they reached the next light, and Bailey turned the opposite way.

Thompson drove to the Jefferson Memorial and exited the car. Sean followed him to the memorial, where they met Chief Bailey again. Sean was a bit confused, given the good-bye in the alley. "Was that some kind of secret code between the two of you?" he inquired.

"You might say that. It isn't our first cover-up," Bailey answered.

"How did I become the assassin?" Sean asked Thompson.

"I really don't know. One minute, I'm escorting Senator Jenkins—" Thompson started.

"Jenkins? Are you referring to Bobby Jenkins from North Carolina?" Sean asked.

---

92 | *Linda Riesenberg Fisler*

"Yes. Do you know him?" Thompson asked.

"Yes. I know him very well, actually," Sean answered. "Go ahead. You were escorting Jenkins to where?"

"I was escorting Jenkins from the lobby to the director's office. He asked me to stay, and before I knew it, Jefferies pulled out a photo of you, saying you were responsible for the president's death. I literally was in shock, since earlier in the day, I had told the director you worked for MI-6."

"Did Jenkins see your reaction?" Sean asked.

"Yes. He didn't indicate that he knew you, though. He made some comment that if I didn't like how this was playing out that I should contact him. I suppose that you are being set up, Sean. Someone wants you out of the way and charged with the murder."

"Yes, it does appear that way." Sean looked at Thompson. "Am I under arrest?"

"Not by me," Thompson answered. "We need to catch the real assassin." When Sean started to turn to leave, he asked, "How can we help you?"

Sean paused. "You can't, really. You might want to talk to Jenkins, though."

Thompson looked at Sean, puzzled by his answer. "Wait a minute! If you are escaping, the least you could do is give me a punch to make it look good!" he said jokingly. Before he knew it, he had received a punch to his mouth from Chief Bailey. Thompson grabbed his jaw while Sean laughed.

"That's for getting me involved in yet another cover up!" Bailey answered the confused Thompson before he even had a chance to ask the question.

Sean turned and disappeared into the night. "I hope he finds that assassin," Thompson stated, still rubbing his jaw.

"What are you going to do?" Bailey asked.

"He got away. Guess I have to go look for him," Thompson said. "And I think I'm going to be unemployed rather soon. Right now, I'm going home, going to ice down my jaw, and in the morning, I think I'm going to pay a visit to a certain senator from North Carolina."

*Blind Influence* | 93

# Day Four

# Washington, DC

"Chief Bailey, please. Nicole Charbonneau." Nicole had the front cover of the *Washington Post* splayed across her desk. "I'll hold," she answered the question the police officer had asked. She was reading the article's sketchy details.

"Nicole, you know I love to hear from you, but sweetheart, I'm really busy right now," Chief Bailey said as he answered the phone. "Please stop bothering me!"

"Good morning to you too." Nicole was very use to the chief's booming bass voice. It didn't intimidate her in the least. After all, she had worked with him for three and half years. "Who are these guys?"

"You know I can't answer that."

"Chief—"

"You are not a DA anymore."

"You're just aiding the cover-up," Nicole tossed out.

"Nikki, I am dead serious here. Keep your nose out of this. The less you know, the better."

Nicole's interest went from a casual to piqued interest now. "So there is going to be a cover-up."

"I didn't say that," Bailey answered.

"Yes you did, in a roundabout way. Jerome, we've worked together for years. I know you." Nicole looked over the photos in the paper again. Her eyes caught the shoe of one of the covered bodies. "Oh my God," she murmured.

"What?" Bailey asked.

"These men in the alley, they were, no way—they couldn't be," Nicole said to herself. She held the paper closer to her eyes. "They are in some kind of service. Marines?"

---

96 | *Linda Riesenberg Fisler*

"Nikki, stop it!" Bailey yelled. "I can't tell you one way or the other. Now stop it!"

"Not Marines. Those shoes, though; there something about them. I've seen them before."

"I'm hanging up now, Nikki."

"Another cover-up is coming. Is a cover-up happening, Jerome?"

"Stay out of it, Nikki." Bailey was almost pleading now.

"There is. I'll give you a call back later with some scenarios," Nicole said as her mind started piecing things together.

"What part of stay out of this don't you understand?" Bailey answered, annoyed with Nicole's persistence. "This goes higher than you think, and you are not privy to this information. Now, go back to your private-citizen life and let us law-enforcement types deal with this."

"I know where I've seen those shoes!"

"I'm hanging up now, Nikki. Have a great day!"

Nicole heard a click on the other end. "Jerome?" she called into the phone. "They are Secret Service agents. Those are Jeff's shoes," Nicole murmured to herself. Jeff was Nicole's ex-fiancé. Although she hadn't seen him in a little over a year, she had always chided him about the shoes he wore. He went for comfort, especially because he was on his feet most the day and had to be able to move quickly. He didn't like the really dressy shoes that others in his line of duty chose. "It can't be."

Nicole looked through her Rolodex and found Jeff's number. She picked up the phone and dialed the number. There was no answer. Did she dare to call Jeff's boss? Why not? She could just casually ask about Jeff, saying that she had discovered something of his that she wanted to return. It was innocent enough. She gathered the courage to call Jeff's boss. "Hello, I'm looking for James McLaren, please." Nicole waited a few minutes on the line. "Hi, James, it is Nicole Charbonneau. I'm fine, thank you. I'm looking for Jeff."

*Blind Influence* | 97

"You are not the only one. He didn't report this morning. Are you two back together?" James asked.

"No, no. I stumbled across an old family heirloom that he had given me when we were together. I don't feel right keeping it. I was going to ask him if he wanted it back," Nicole answered.

"Well, if he doesn't get here soon and if it is worth anything, he may need to hock it," James answered. He was very annoyed. "It's not like him to not call in or to be late. You know that. There is no answer at his apartment, and to make things worse, another guy hasn't shown up this morning either. It's not like we aren't at some heightened crisis level, you know, with the assassination and all." James was venting a bit, and he realized it. "I'm sorry, Nikki. It's just bad timing."

Nicole was in shock. She couldn't believe what she was hearing. Two men from the Secret Service missing this morning, and two unidentified men in an alley murdered. In a calm voice, she responded, "No problem, James. I hope they show up soon. If you remember, tell Jeff to give me a call when he gets a chance." She knew that call would never come. "You take care of yourself, James. Bye." She hung up the phone and sat back in her chair in shock. Her face was pale and she was still in shock when Carol walked into her office.

Carol was shocked to see Nicole the way she was. "Hey, are you OK?"

Nicole snapped out of it. "Yeah, I'm sorry. I just got some really bad news." Nicole began to fold up the paper to set it aside.

"Sorry. Anything you want to talk about?" Carol asked, sitting down across from Nicole's desk.

"No. Thanks," Nicole answered, still trying to gain her balance. "So, what's on your agenda today?"

Carol laughed. "That sounds so formal. I have to be in court this afternoon. What about you?" Carol was unaware that Tony Shafer had just walked into Nicole's office.

"I'll be doing some research on a case most the day. Hi, Tony, can I help you with something?" Nicole addressed him.

Carol stood to leave. "Well, I'll talk with you later. Need to get my documents together for this afternoon. Good morning, Mr. Shafer."

"Morning, Carol. Good luck in court today," Tony answered as she walked past him. Carol acknowledged his wish with a thank you. "Morning, Nikki," Tony said as he walked up to the chair that Carol had vacated. He sat down. "Any plans this evening?" He asked. Even though he was still upset with how their last conversation had ended, Tony wanted Nicole by his side.

"No, not really. Why?"

"Mark is giving a little party at Blair House," Tony blurted, not realizing how disrespectful it sounded.

"*What?*" Nicole exclaimed with disdain and disbelief in her voice.

"Now wait, it is only a small party. Party isn't the right word. That was a bad choice on my part. It is a small gathering meant to get the cabinet and important members of Congress together to remember President Andrews," Tony said quickly.

"Who is going to be there?" Nicole asked with a smirk on her face.

"I told you, most the cabinet, Senators Jenkins, Barker, a few others that are on key committees. You know the usual list of suspects." Tony gave a short laugh. In light of what Nicole had just been thinking, the choice of words almost seemed appropriate. "Look, Mark just wants to honor President Andrews and have some informal talks about which policies would honor him appropriately. It would be a good opportunity for you to get your two cents in," Tony added, hoping to entice her.

Nicole sat for a moment. She wasn't sure how much information Senator Jenkins was being given, but it might give her the opportunity to present her theory. Although the theory was not totally thought out, maybe she could pass on a small bit that would help him. She decided she couldn't pass up the opportunity. "All right, Tony. What time should I meet you there?"

Tony, being the old-school gentleman he was, answered, "I'll pick you up at 7:30. There will be food and drink, so no need to go to dinner first."

*Blind Influence* | 99

"I just want to say that having this meeting prior to the president being buried is just unconceivable to me," Nicole answered. "And don't be surprised if I tell Mark that."

"Just add 'Mr. President' before you lay into him, Nikki," Tony reminded her as he walk out of her office.

# Jenkins's Home

**W**hereas Nicole and Tony always prided themselves on getting to the office early, it was usually midmorning before most senators got to their offices on Capitol Hill. Most usually arranged breakfast meetings at various establishments around town or took the time to read upcoming legislation in the comfort of their home offices. This happened to be one of those mornings that Senator Jenkins had scheduled to do just that. There were some votes coming up on some legislation that he wanted to read before heading into the office. When his alarm went off at six, he was very tempted to roll over and catch another hour of sleep. His missing lower right leg was throbbing with the phantom pain that had haunted him ever since his injury in the line of duty. He sat up and reached for his prosthesis.

Securing his fake lower leg, he stood and reached for his robe. Walking out of the bedroom, he headed to the kitchen to start some coffee. He needed to brew it strong this morning. He hadn't slept well. The conversation at FBI headquarters with the director had kept him tossing and turning all night.

After pouring the water into the coffeemaker, Jenkins walked to the front door to get the morning paper. He had opened the door and stooped down to pick the paper up when a pair of shoes appeared in front of his eyes from nowhere. Senator Jenkins picked up the paper, beginning to stand upright as his eyes scanned the legs that were attached to those shoes. He continued his motion upward. When he saw the face of the man standing in front of him, he smiled. "I was wondering when I would have the honor of your presence. Come on in."

Jenkins opened the door further and moved aside to let his visitor enter his condo. As the visitor passed, the senator stood for a moment and looked around the outside. He wanted to make sure that his visitor hadn't been followed, although he knew that the visitor would have taken great strides to make sure that hadn't occurred. When confident that the man had not been followed, the senator went inside, shutting the door behind him.

It was in the early afternoon when Nicole was told that Senator Jenkins was going to go in front of the press and make an announcement. One of the junior associates poked a head in her office and told her the junior associates were going to head to the conference room to watch it. Nicole had not accomplished much on her normal work but instead was making a list of her possible suspects and their possible motives. She gathered her papers and put them in a folder that she placed in the top drawer of her desk for now. She stood up and followed her colleague to the conference room.

They entered the room just as Senator Jenkins arrived at the podium. He looked uncommonly nervous, fidgeting with his tie and buttoning his coat. He placed a leather-bound folder on the podium and opened it. His normally calm, authoritative voice seemed to waver as he began his announcement. "Good morning." He paused and took a quick drink of water. "I won't be taking any questions after this announcement. Today I stand before you, the press and the American people, to announce the formation of a special investigation into the assassination of the president. The investigation will be handled out of my office, and when appropriate, the findings of the investigation will be presented to a special commission that I will be forming this afternoon. Why am I forming this special investigation and commission? I am not at liberty to say at this point except to say that information which has been forwarded to me from the FBI and others in the intelligence community has prompted me to this action. It is, in my opinion, which has been formed and guided by my love of this country, that it is of utmost importance to ensure that President Andrews's brutal assassination not be met with years of conspiracy theories and speculation. That is all I have to say at this time."

Jenkins closed the leather-bound folder that contained his statement, lowered his head, and walked quickly out of the room as the press shouted questions at him. He never once paused to answer any question, nor did he make any eye contact with the press.

"Holy shit!" one of the associates said out loud. "Unbelievable!"

"What?" another associate asked.

"Well, I never would have thought that Jenkins would be involved in the assassination."

Nicole's head snapped to look at the associate who had made the comment. She didn't have to ask the question. Most of the room did for her. "What are you talking about? Jenkins is beyond reproach."

"He is power-hungry and greedy, just like all the rest of them. What better way to cover up your involvement than to take over the investigation? There is none. This way, he can control what gets told to the American public. He can also point fingers at those who would be running against him for the presidency." The associate stood up to leave the room. "I wouldn't put it past him, and it is politics as usual."

"When did you get so cynical?" Nicole asked him as he approached her to walk out the door.

"I'm not cynical, Nikki. I'm a realist. Who has the most to gain from launching this investigation? And who is the senator that leads the Intelligence Committee and sits on the Financial Committee and Foreign Relations Committee? He has maneuvered himself very well. This is the next step to secure his run for president, and he'll make sure that we all fall in love with him and with his quaint Southern accent by the time his election campaign is announced. I wouldn't be surprised if we all aren't begging him to run, and in all that hustle and bustle, we, the American public, will be so deliriously happy to have what appears to be a real leader again, we won't even notice that nothing has been reported on Andrews's assassination." He turned around to see everyone's scornful looks. "Just watch. You can chide me all you want *if* it doesn't happen." With that final remark, the associate left the room.

Nicole smiled as he left—a smile that slowly faded when she realized that one comment she could agree with was that the American public may not ever know the truth of President Andrews's assassination. Her thoughts went back to her list of suspects and motives. She hadn't considered Jenkins.

She headed back to her office. She had more thinking to do before this evening.

## *Blair House*

*B*y the time Tony arrived to pick her up for the gathering at Blair House, Nicole was pretty confident that Senator Jenkins had nothing to do with the assassination. If the opportunity presented itself, she was going to present the information to the senator that the two bodies in the alley behind the Air and Space Museum were the bodies of two Secret Service agents. That should impress the senator enough to get her some kind of appointment to his commission, she hoped. She wanted to be a part of the investigation, and having an ordinary citizen on the committee might calm the talk of Jenkins's involvement in the assassination. Her skills from her days working in the District Attorney's office wouldn't hurt, either.

When Tony and Nicole arrived at Blair House, Nicole honestly couldn't remember a thing Tony had been rambling on about as they had driven to the gathering. Her mind was racing, going over all the facts, her facts, as she started for the door with Tony at her side. "Nikki," Tony asked, "are you feeling all right?"

"Yes. Why?" Nicole asked.

"You just seem really distant."

"Oh, I'm sorry. It's a case I'm working on, and you know me, until I get all the facts correct, I can't stop thinking about it."

"Well, try and relax tonight. Sometimes you worry me that you work entirely too hard," Tony said as the door to Blair House was opened by the new first lady. "Hello, Katherine," Tony greeted the visibly upset first lady. He hugged her. "I'm so sorry, Katherine," he whispered in her ear.

"Thank you, Tony. Sorry to have to greet you this way. I just got off the phone with Barbara Andrews. It is just heart-wrenching." Katherine turned her attention to Nicole. "Welcome, Ms. Charbonneau."

Nicole was surprised that Katherine knew her by name. Although Nicole had attended many functions with Tony where Katherine and the now president were in attendance, Nicole had never really talked with Katherine. To Nicole's knowledge, this was the first time that Nicole had actually talked to the first lady in person, which in itself was a strange predicament.

Maybe Katherine knew more than Nicole thought regarding Mark's many indiscretions. That thought made Nicole wonder if Katherine even suspected that Mark had desired her; the idea of Mark and her in an affair made Nicole feel sick. "Mrs. Stevens, I am so sorry for your loss. If you could express my sympathies to Mrs. Andrews the next time you talk ... "

Katherine smiled at Nicole, whose gracious comment caught her off guard. "I certainly will, Ms. Charbonneau. Thank you." She turned to point in the direction of the gathering. "Mark and the others are down the hallway to the left. I will be there shortly. I need to freshen up a bit." She closed the door behind them. "If you will excuse me—" she started as she took their coats.

"Of course we will," Tony interrupted as he motioned for Nicole to begin down the hallway.

Nicole reached the room with Tony at her side. Tony had been correct. It was a relatively small gathering. Mostly members of President Andrews's cabinet, heads of the various powerful committees in Congress were in attendance. For a brief second, she almost gave Mark Stevens the benefit of the doubt and thought that he really was interested in honoring the president.

As they entered the room, all eyes turned to see them. Mark rose from a chair where he had been in conversation with the secretary of defense. "Hi, Tony and Nikki, thanks for coming."

"Our pleasure. I mean ... " Tony answered, shaking his hand and furrowing his brow at the odd way his answer sounded. "I didn't mean ... I meant it is our honor, Mr. President." He wasn't satisfied with that answer, either.

Mark smiled. "I know it is awkward," he answered, letting go of Tony's hand. "Continue to call me Mark, Tony. We have been friends for such a long time, I'm not sure I'd answer you if you called me anything else but Mark."

"I think it is appropriate for me to call you Mr. President, regardless of that. It will take some getting used to, though," Tony answered.

"Ms. Charbonneau. Thank you for coming, as well." Mark extended his hand. Nicole took his hand and resisted the motion that Mark was trying

*Blind Influence* | 105

to undertake. He wanted to kiss her hand, but Nicole withdrew it before he was able to do so.

"Thank you, Mr. President," she answered.

"Would you like something to drink, Ms. Charbonneau?" Katherine asked as she came up behind Nicole, a strict-sounding disapproval of her husband's apparent action in her voice.

"Yes, please," Nicole answered, so very happy that her rejection had possibly been seen by the first lady.

"Tony?" Katherine asked.

"I'll have the usual, Katherine. Thank you."

"I'll help you, Mrs. Stevens," Nicole said as she followed Katherine to the bar in the room.

"Thank you," Katherine said as they walked. "The staff has been working so hard to pack us up that I didn't have the heart for them to work this evening, so if you need anything, don't hesitate to ask or even help yourself."

"That was very sweet of you. I imagine this is a hardship on so many people. One doesn't stop to think," Nicole answered.

"Yes. You know, in some ways, our staff knows us so much better than most of the American public. They see all the intimate details of our daily lives," Katherine said, beginning to pour Tony's scotch. She looked up at Nicole when she said "intimate." Nicole caught her meaning.

"This is my first visit to Blair House during your and President Stevens's stay here," Nicole started. "I like what you've done with this room." Nicole was trying to work out a nice way to let Katherine know that she had no interest in Mark Stevens.

"Thank you. What would you like to drink, dear?" Katherine asked.

"I'll have a gin and tonic, please," Nicole answered. She paused but then decided she needed to put Katherine's suspicions to rest. "Mrs. Stevens, this may be a bit forward of me."

106 | *Linda Riesenberg Fisler*

"Be as forward as you like," Katherine answered, the tone of her voice sending the signal that she was preparing for the worst.

"Thank you," Nicole answered as she took her drink and started in a low voice. "I'd like to put your mind at ease concerning, well, let's say some possible speculation you may have observed or heard about your husband and possibly myself." She cleared her throat, trying to muster the courage. She continued in a low voice, stepping a bit closer to Katherine. "Am I right in my assumption of your speculation?"

"Yes. I know how Mark feels about you. You have a lot of spunk to show up here this evening, Ms. Charbonneau," Katherine said sharply.

Nicole looked down and almost smiled. "Mrs. Stevens, I have no romantic or even casual interest in your husband." She looked at Katherine, who had a surprised look on her face. "I don't know who told you otherwise, but it is of great importance to me that you know I don't know your husband in an intimate way."

Katherine almost seemed relieved, and she smiled at Nicole. "Ms. Charbonneau, of all the things I have heard about you, there is one quality that is true that I can attest to this very minute."

"I'm not sure I want to know what that is," Nicole said, again looking down at her feet.

"Your honesty is admirable," Katherine said, extending her hand and taking Nicole's into hers. She continued in a low voice. "Thank you for telling me what you did. You are aware of the rumors, then?"

"Painfully aware, and I am not the one spreading them," Nicole answered.

"Part of the reason I was so upset earlier was because of the call from Barbara, but also the thought of having this president's mistress"—Nicole's eyes shot up to meet Katherine's—"right here under the same roof as I am was almost too much to bear this evening." She squeezed Nicole's hand to keep her from talking. "I thank you, Nicole, for being so direct, and now I can hold my head high this evening."

"Mrs. Stevens, I don't know what you have heard or from whom, but you have every reason to hold your head high when I am in the room with you now, and especially in the future." Nicole went on, "If you would be more comfortable with me leaving, just say the word."

"No. Please stay. But know that I will have the upper hand the next time Mark threatens replacing me with you," Katherine answered. "I must get this drink to Tony. Thank you again." With that, Katherine left Nicole standing alone at the bar in shock.

Nicole watched Katherine walk over to Mark and Tony. She took a drink of her gin and tonic, suppressing the urge to down the whole drink in one swallow. She had known Mark Stevens was scum, but she hadn't realized how much of a scumbag he really was until this moment. And yet in some way, she wished she could be a fly in the room when Katherine got her chance to throw it back at Mark.

So deep in thought, Nicole didn't notice that Senator Jenkins was approaching. "Good evening, Nikki," he said as he reached her. Nicole jumped back to the reality of the room at his greeting. "I really must find some way of saying hello to you that doesn't scare you half to death," he chuckled.

Nicole smiled. "It isn't you, Senator. I just need to clear my mind of a number of things and stay in the moment." Senator Jenkins poured himself another drink. "How are you this evening?" Nicole asked.

"As well as can be expected, I suppose. Like you, I'm in a contemplative mood." The senator lifted his glass of scotch to toast with Nicole's glass. Their glasses clinked, their eyes met, and they both took a drink.

"Senator, I was surprised by your announcement today."

Jenkins looked at Nicole. "Really, why is that?"

"I'm not sure. Perhaps part of it is because it is so quick after the incident to form a special investigation."

"It seems most are surprised by it, but rest assured I have my reasons." Jenkins took another drink. "Besides, when you look back at most of the assassinations, commissions have been formed to look over the findings."

"Yes, that is true. Senator," Nicole started, unsure of how she wanted to proceed. "I know something, and I'm not sure how to start the discussion."

108 | *Linda Riesenberg Fisler*

"I've told you before, Nikki, to call me Bobby. Perhaps that will help."

Nicole smiled. "It's about the double murder in the alley behind—"

Jenkins reached out and took Nicole's elbow. He led her away from the others and into the hallway. "The Air and Space Museum," she finished as they reached the hallway. She had a confused look on her face but continued, actually relieved that they could talk more privately. "I know they are Secret Service agents."

Jenkins looked at her with a look of confusion first and then with an intense look which Nicole mistook for anger. "I suggest that you keep any speculation, and that is all that it is on your part, to yourself."

"But—" Nicole started.

"If you would like to remain alive, I would stop your meddling and leave the investigation up to my staff and the FBI."

"Are you threatening me, Senator?"

"Whichever answer gets you to stop," the senator answered sternly and coldly as he deliberately brushed past her and back into the room.

Nicole felt her breath leave her body. She felt like she was being suffocated. The fear the senator had instilled in her with the tone of his voice and the deliberate brush with her body was causing her heart to palpitate. Her flight-or-fight response was beginning to raise her body temperature. Could it be that Senator Jenkins could be the greedy, power-hungry, cold-blooded conspirator behind the assassination, as her colleague had suggested earlier in the day? She started for the door, where Katherine intercepted her.

"Nicole, are you feeling all right?" Katherine asked.

Nicole tried to gather her composure, but it wasn't going to happen. "I'm sorry. I just need some air." She walked to the front door as Katherine grabbed her coat from the closet. Nicole took it and opened the door. "Thank you. Good night." She slipped to the other side of what she felt was the safety of the night air. She hurriedly threw on her coat and began to walk to the gatehouse. "Open it, please," she said in a stern voice.

*Blind Influence* | 109

"You shouldn't be out walking alone, ma'am."

"I'll be fine. Thank you," Nicole said as she almost ran through the gate. She turned down the street, looking for a telephone to call Carol. She needed her faithful friend and her experience of getting out of any tight situation. She picked up her pace, her heels clicking on the sidewalk echoing in the dark winter night. She rounded the corner, which placed her in a business district where she could find a phone. She entered a restaurant and went directly to the pay phones. "I need you to come and get me," she said as soon as Carol answered the phone. She gave Carol the details where she could be found and then hung up. She had to get control of the adrenaline that was pulsing through her body.

Carol didn't ask any questions or resist the thought of showing up later. She had never heard Nicole's voice that scared. It was only a matter of ten minutes before Carol entered the restaurant. "Nikki," she said as she entered, "what's the matter?"

"Let's go," Nicole said as she exited the restaurant. They quickly moved to Carol's double-parked car. As soon as they were in the vehicle, Carol pulled away. The traffic she pulled into didn't waste any time honking their horns and yelling expletives out of hastily wound-down windows.

"What the hell is going on, Nikki?" Carol demanded.

Nicole sat for a moment, trying to gather her thoughts. "I'm not sure, Carol, but I think Senator Jenkins just threatened me."

"What? You're insane!" Carol answered with a little chuckle. She looked over at Nicole and realized that she was serious. "What happened that made you think he threatened you, and in what way?"

"In the conference room at work when you were in court, Jenkins announced his special investigation into the assassination of President Andrews. One of the associates said that Jenkins was involved in the assassination."

"That's crazy. What would he have to gain from assassinating the president?"

"Power and the investigation would put him in the news for the next year or so, strengthening his image to the American people, and the world, for that matter, to run for president himself. Anyway, I went through a hundred scenarios at least, and none led me to his involvement, so this evening, I thought I would share with him my theory on the two dead people who were found in the alley behind the Air and Space Museum."

"You what?" Carol was getting confused. "What bodies?"

"There were two men murdered behind the Air and Space Museum. It was in the paper this morning."

"Oh, OK," Carol said, remembering she had hastily read the story. "You developed a theory on that murder?"

"Yes. One of the men was Jeff."

"Your ex?"

"Yes."

"And you know this how?" Carol asked.

"The shoes of one of the men were the shoes Jeff wore."

Carol laughed. Nicole, however, wasn't amused.

"Come on, Nikki! Do you know how many shoes look alike in the world? You are basing your whole theory on a pair of shoes that happen to be on the body of a person murdered in the alley, who happens to be your ex-fiancé."

"I thought the same thing, but I called Jeff's condo and no answer. So I called his boss, and Jeff hadn't reported to work. He was never late."

"So one day he is late. It happens to all of us."

"Don't you get it, Carol? The men in the alley were two Secret Service agents. James said that Jeff and one other man had not reported for duty. That is just too much of a coincidence."

"OK, fine. But what does all this have to do with Jenkins threatening you?"

"I started to give this information to Jenkins, and he rushed me out of the room, into the empty hallway, and told me if I wanted to remain alive that I would stop snooping around and never speak about this to anyone."

*Blind Influence* | 111

"Sounds like good advice to me. Nikki, you are making some pretty serious accusations, and not to mention you are not exactly a part of the club, so to speak. You are not privy to all the things that are happening in Washington. You are always warning me that these people are ruthless. I think you need to take your own advice on this one."

Nicole sat in the car, looking out the window as Carol pulled up to her condo. "I can't help but think I'm on to something here, Carol. You should have seen his reaction."

"Even if you are on to something here, Nikki, and even if Jenkins is a part of it, what are you going to do about it? Tell Bailey and have the DC cops arrest Jenkins? You do understand that Jenkins is head of the Intelligence Committee. Talk about someone who could make you disappear! Let it go, Nikki." Carol sat for a moment before adding, "And I don't believe he threatened you. I think he was just giving you some friendly advice to keep your mouth shut and nose out of it." Nicole looked at Carol. "Whoever ordered the assassination of the president has lots of money and lots of power," Carol explained. "In either case, they hold the trump card over you and me. If you want to form theories and motives because it is something you like doing, then go for it. But I wouldn't be sharing those with some of the most powerful men on this planet. Do you know what I mean?"

"You don't believe me."

"It is not a matter of believing you or not. I'm just saying it's not a game and you are not in the position to do anything about it." Carol motioned to the door of Nicole's condo. "Now, go get some sleep, and I'll see you in the office in the morning. Tomorrow night, we'll go out and blow off some steam at Conversations."

Nicole smiled. "I had forgotten about that. I'll see you tomorrow." Nicole got out of the car and walked to her condo. Carol didn't drive away until Nicole was safely inside.

Nicole was very tired and went right up to her bedroom. Maybe Carol was right. She certainly didn't have all the facts of the case. Within a few minutes after climbing into her bed, she was fast asleep.

Meanwhile, Kevin Thompson had been having probably the worst day at the agency in his twelve-year career. It ended with the director calling him

112 | *Linda Riesenberg Fisler*

into the office to voice his displeasure at Thompson letting Sean Adkins escape. Although Thompson knew that Sean was not the assassin, he'd had to endure the hour-long tongue lashing.

At home, he sat down on the chair in front of his television to catch the news before he headed off to bed. He popped open a can of beer and settled in for a rest. He was only half listening until a story caught his attention.

"Senator Robert Jenkins announced today that he will be forming a special investigation ... " The announcer went on reading his copy. Well, this wasn't getting any better. More bureaucracy wasn't what this case needed. In disgust, Thompson flipped the television off and set his half-empty can of beer on the end table. He sighed as he realized that yet another conspiracy was being played out before his eyes. He smirked as he realized just how powerless he was at the agency.

"I am just a puppet, trying to keep people from cutting my strings," he said out loud. He made movements with his arms like he was a puppet. He shook his head in disgust. "What is the use?" he questioned as he stood up and headed for his bed.

*Blind Influence*

# Day Five

# Washington, DC

Nicole was seated at her desk the next morning, working on a case that was due to be in front of the judge on the following Wednesday. She had a couple of law books open to important cases that her brief was using to establish precedence. There was a knock on her door, and it opened to reveal Tony. At that moment, she realized she had not told Tony she was leaving Mark's gathering. "Tony—"

"How are you feeling this morning?" he asked.

"I'm fine. I'm sorry about last night."

"Senator Jenkins and Katherine said that you suddenly weren't feeling well. Jenkins said that you had gotten a cab home," Tony started. Nicole didn't say anything. She wanted to hear what else Senator Jenkins had said. "I'm sorry that you didn't tell me. I would have been glad to have taken you home, Nikki."

Nicole smiled. "I know. It just suddenly came upon me."

"That was obvious. I saw Senator Jenkins hurriedly escorting you from the room. I was wondering what was going on. By the time I got free from the secretary, you were gone and Jenkins had said that you had gotten sick."

"It must have been something I ate at lunch. I'm fine now. Thank you for your concern. I am sorry I wasn't able to tell you," Nicole added.

"Well, Senator Jenkins seems to be really interested in you. He was asking questions about your background."

"What kind of questions?" Nicole asked.

"He just wanted to know about your work background. What kind of cases you handle within our firm and what cases you may have worked on with the DA's office. He was really impressed with your background. He may be interested in you being on his special investigation."

"He said that?"

116 | *Linda Riesenberg Fisler*

"No, I'm just guessing based on his questions." Tony started back for the door. "I put in a good word for you, and of course, your involvement would help the firm as well." He smiled. "I need to get back. I'm glad you are feeling better."

Nicole suddenly wasn't feeling as well as she thought. "Thanks," she murmured as her mind started racing in a million different directions. Was Jenkins really considering her for a position on the committee, or was he trying to determine if she had the skills to put the pieces together that led to Jenkins's possible involvement in the assassination?

She looked out the window as she contemplated the many answers to the many questions that kept racing through her head. Then she heard Carol's voice in her head with her advice given the night before. Was Nicole just a pawn in a game that was getting more and more complicated? *Maybe I should sit this dance out*, she thought.

She returned her attention to the case that was in front of her. After all, it wasn't as if this case wasn't going to be hard enough to win without her being distracted by something that she had little power to influence.

Before she knew it, it was five o'clock and time for her to call it a day. Carol had stopped in earlier to finalize the arrangements for their evening at Conversations. They had decided that they would meet at the club because Carol wasn't sure what time she would be out of court. This was fine with Nicole. Past excursions to places like this usually resulted with Carol leaving with someone whom Carol hoped would be her future, rich husband. Nicole really didn't like the nightclub scene, so driving separately allowed her to leave whenever Carol hooked up with the next man of her dreams. She never put much faith in finding anyone to have a serious relationship with in a nightclub. She actually was looking forward to an early evening and sleeping in on Saturday.

She packed up her work for the day, replacing the law books in the bookcase and placing her briefs in her briefcase to review in the warmth and security of her home sometime during the weekend. She headed out the door to grab something to eat before getting ready for the night on the town.

She arrived at Conversations a few minutes early, finding a parking space close to the doors of what Carol described as the hottest new nightclub in

DC. There wasn't much to the outside of the place. In fact, you wouldn't even know it existed if you didn't have the address—but then, the line of people waiting to get in might be the first clue. There was a rather large gentleman stationed at the door. She walked up to him and inquired if this place was indeed Conversations. He nodded and stuck out his hand, wanting something to indicate that she could enter. Nicole smiled and said that she was waiting for a friend who had the passes. The gentleman nodded and pointed to where she should stand. Nicole moved there and patiently waited for Carol on what was turning out to be a bitterly cold November night.

After a short wait, Carol arrived and greeted Nicole with a hug. Nicole could smell that Carol had already started her weekend party a bit early. When she questioned Carol about it, Carol explained that she had unexpectedly won the case and stopped off for a drink and dinner with her client. She'd had only a couple drinks and was fine. The party was already on, Carol informed Nicole as they entered the building. Carol wanted to party and celebrate the victory that she was sure Tony would be ecstatic about as well. Nicole just shook her head and followed Carol into the nightclub. Carol rarely needed an excuse to party. Even though Carol was a few years older than Nicole, Nicole thought of Carol as the little sister she had always wanted. Nicole was an only child and her parents had passed in an unfortunate car accident only a few short years ago. She remembered Carol not leaving her side during that awful time in her life. Carol was alone as well and had comforted Nicole that night by saying that they could be each other's family now.

Carol's life was very different than Nicole's. While Nicole had had a loving home in an affluent neighborhood, Carol had been in foster homes. Her father had been abusive, and her mother, unable to deal with Carol's father, had been drunk most the time. It had gotten so bad that the mother had called Social Services to have her daughter removed. That call had cost Carol's mother her life the evening Carol had been removed from the home. Carol had moved around from foster home to foster home, yet in all the upheaval, Carol had never lost sight of what she wanted to do. She had worked hard and put herself through school.

Nicole smiled. She thought of the memory of paying off Carol's school loans when Nicole received the first bonus she had earned at Rosen, Shafer, and Pruett. This was shortly after Nicole's parents had died. Those two kindnesses had created a bond between the two of them. It was more than a friendship. They helped each other in good times and bad. They were sisters.

118 | *Linda Riesenberg Fisler*

No matter what, Nicole was glad that Carol was someone she could count on, love, and enjoy life with. She'd do anything for her sister.

They entered the nightclub and were instantly accosted by the loud music and flashing strobe lights. The dance floor was packed, and so was just about every nook and cranny of the place. Nicole and Carol made their way to the bar for a drink.

"They call this place Conversations? I can barely hear myself think!" Nicole yelled over to Carol, even though her friend was standing right beside her.

"Aw, Nikki, I'm surprised at you. There is more than one way to communicate!" Carol said as she raised a provocative eyebrow. She then threw her head back in laughter. This was Carol's usual behavior whenever she was being watched by someone she wanted to get to know better. The bartender returned with their drinks, and they paid for them.

"Sheesh, Carol, we just arrived!" Nicole shook her head. "At least share one drink with me."

"Relax, he disappeared in the crowd. Come on, let's find a table." Carol started off in the direction of a quieter area where tables were arranged. Nicole followed and then stopped with Carol to survey the room. There was a glass partition between the tables and the dance floor; however, open doorways still allowed the loud music to filter into the room. Nicole was scanning the area for an open table when her eyes caught the site of Norman Sipes, who appeared to be in a heated conversation with Congressman Davis. She assumed it was heated, because Sipes was leaning over the table and pointing a finger at Davis. *He could just be talking loud enough to be heard*, Nicole reminded herself.

"There's one," Carol said and pointed in the direction of a vacated table. There was only one problem. The table was adjacent to the table Sipes was sitting at, and there was no way that Nicole wanted to spend the evening dodging Norman Sipes.

It was too late. Carol was on her way to claim the table. Nicole began walking behind Carol, her eyes fixed on Sipes, hoping that his conversation would keep him engaged so she could slip by him. She kept her eyes on him, trying to plan out a path to avoid the meeting if she could.

Sipes continued to talk with the congressman, and then, something strange seemed to happen. Sipes sat back and glared at the congressman. A few seconds later, the congressman removed a white envelop from his breast pocket and set it on the table in front of him. The congressman then began to talk, using gestures implying that he was upset with Sipes, or at least not very happy about something. Nicole wished that she could read lips.

The congressman picked up the envelope again, but just as the envelope looked as if it were being exchanged between the two men, someone stepped in front of Nicole. She moved to try to see around the person and caught a quick glimpse of Sipes putting the envelope into his breast pocket of his suit. He then abruptly quitted the table and disappeared into the crowd.

"Oh, excuse me!" Nicole said loudly as she walked into a nicely dressed man she didn't know. "Did I spill anything on you? I'm so sorry."

"It is quite all right," the man with a British accent answered. "It is my fault entirely. I need to look where I'm going." He and Nicole held their gaze for a brief second. The man smiled at her, but the smile didn't last. "I'm sorry, I need to be somewhere." With that, the man disappeared into the crowd. Nicole, although she thought the man was very attractive, shrugged off the encounter and started again for her table.

She gave a sigh of relief that she had not had to walk past Sipes and endure his advances, but yet, there was a side of her that wondered what had just occurred. She was very sure that it was some kind of payoff, but for what? She chuckled to herself that sometime in the very near future, she or Carol would end up trying to defend Sipes for whatever had just occurred. She took a drink and arrived at the table. Carol was already seated and looked at Nicole as she sat down.

"What?" Nicole asked.

"Took you long enough to get here," Carol answered.

"I was trying to avoid Norman Sipes. He was at the table with Congressman Davis over there. I just didn't want him to see me."

"Sipes Oil Company? You didn't want him to see you?" Carol asked. "Nikki, aren't you being a bit callous?" She then added a laugh and said, "He must really get you going!"

---

120 | *Linda Riesenberg Fisler*

"I would just like to avoid him if possible," Nicole said, trying to end the conversation. Then she noticed that Carol had gotten the attention of a handsome man who had just exited a table in the distance. The man had a smile on his face and looked like he had just walked out of the pages of *Gentleman's Quarterly*. His Armani suit was neatly pressed, his black hair a striking contrast to his blue eyes. Those blue eyes; there was something about them. He started over to their table. Nicole looked at Carol, whose gaze did not move from the man's. Their eyes were locked on each other, but there was something about the man that made Nicole uneasy. He arrived at the table.

"Good evening, ladies," he greeted them with a heavy accent that Nicole could not place. Carol answered with a seductive hello. It was clear to Nicole that she wasn't needed, so she stood up. The motion caught the man's attention. "Pardon me, did I interrupt something?" His accent was detectable in the midst of the loud music, but Nicole just couldn't place it.

"No, I just need to visit the ladies' room," Nicole answered. A slow song started to play.

"Dance with me?" Carol asked, extending her hand to the man, whose attention was back on her. He took her hand, helping her out of her chair.

Carol looked quickly over at Nicole and raised her eyebrows, giving a little smile. Nicole mouthed, "Be careful," as the man led Carol to the dance floor.

Just as Nicole was about to turn from the table, the man she had literally run into earlier appeared, and he grabbed her by the wrist, beginning to manhandle her to the dance floor. She barely had time to put her drink on a rapidly passing table. "Quickly, what is your friend's name?" the man demanded.

"Excuse me!" Nicole said loudly and in a rather irritated tone. "Let go of me!"

"Tell me your friend's name!" the man demanded again. They reached the dance floor, and the British man took Nicole in his arms to dance the same slow song that Carol and the man with the icy blue eyes were swaying to. That man's attention was still fixed on Carol. "Her life is in danger. Please, tell me her name quickly. I might be able to help her."

*Blind Influence* | 121

"Her life? If you release your death grip on me, maybe I would be more obliged to cooperate with you," Nicole answered.

The man realized that his actions and his firm hold on the woman in his arms was nothing short of brutal. "I apologize." He relaxed his grip on Nicole. "Your friend's life is in danger. I would like to help her. To do so, I need to know her name. Please believe me."

"Her name is Carol. But how—"

"I'm going to move toward them, and when I release you, get away from me as quickly as possible. I know exactly how the man will react, and you don't want to be near us. Leave quickly! Do not dance with him or let him grab you. Do you understand?"

"Yes," Nicole answered, still confused. "How do I know that she is going to be—"

"No more questions. Just do as I say."

Nicole looked around and noticed they were closer to Carol and her dance partner. She continued to look around to get her bearings.

"Shit!" the British man said, suddenly letting her go. "Get out of here!"

At that precise moment, Nicole heard gunshots, two of them. She turned to see Carol's lifeless body falling to the dance floor. There were screams as the people around her began to panic, but Nicole wanted to get to her friend. It was like swimming upstream in a wildly rushing river. "Carol!" Nicole screamed. The music had stopped, and more gunshots could be heard. Nicole didn't care. Her friend was lying on the dance floor, motionless. "Carol!" Nicole screamed again, trying to get to her friend's side.

"Nicole! Get out of here!" Sipes yelled as he rushed past her.

A few more gunshots rang out, and suddenly, the crowd changed directions. The gunshots had come from the direction the crowd had been running to, in the direction of the back exit. This enabled Nicole to get to Carol. She moved to Carol's side and knelt down. Carol was already lying in a puddle of blood. "Noooo!" Nicole screamed in anguish. She placed one of her hands behind Carol's head and the other around Carol's waist, bending over her friend and bringing her lifeless body to hers. "Carol, stay with me!" Nicole pleaded. She was oblivious to the chaos around her. She felt the warm blood from Carol's head wound on her hand, then laid Carol down, knowing that her friend was dead. She looked at Carol's blood covering her hand and clasped it to her breaking heart.

Two more gunshots echoed in her ears and pulled her back to the moment. She looked around, hearing another gunshot. She needed to seek shelter and found to her right some toppled tables. She crawled to the protection of those tables.

More shots ringing out brought Nicole back to the reality before her. They again came from the direction the panicked crowd was heading: the front door of the nightclub. Turning away from the shots again, the crowd headed for the other exits. Screams and chaos ensued, but Nicole sat quietly in her shelter of tables, staring in shock at Carol's lifeless body. A few tears ran down Nicole's cheeks as her mind recalled the two men she didn't know by name but who obviously had a hand in killing her friend. She could see the man with the icy blue eyes vividly in front of her as, for the first time, Nicole began to feel anger and hatred fill the spot in her heart that had been filled with love for Carol. She knew that she would not be able to forgive that man until justice could be carried out. In that moment, Nicole vowed to do everything she could to avenge the pointless killing of her friend whom she loved like a sister.

The crowd ran out of the exits, and the nightclub became eerily quiet for a few minutes. In those few minutes, Nicole pulled the tables closer to her to ensure that she was not visible, just in case one of those two men she would never forget were still in the club. Soon, she heard sirens get closer and closer to the club. Nicole's eyes never lost sight of her lifeless friend lying in her own blood on the cold, lonely dance floor.

The house lights went on, causing Nicole to blink. She could hear the voices of the arriving police officers. Although the officers were surprised and shocked at the sight, Nicole was shaking from the shock of witnessing the cruel way in which her friend had been killed. She knew the officers were talking, but it didn't register in her mind, nor did she care what they were saying. One officer went over and grabbed a couple of white tablecloths from nearby tables to cover Carol, as if that would give her back some kind of dignity. The police went about their duty, collecting statements from the few remaining employees, and Nicole sat there, hidden, staring.

For what seemed like an eternity, Nicole sat in her fortress of tables, safe and secure. Then she heard a familiar voice. Another old friend had entered the scene, and his voice began to bring her back to the living. "All right," the booming voice of Chief Bailey rang out as he walked toward the dance floor. "What the hell happened here, and why was it so important that I be here?" For the first time, Nicole looked away from Carol's body and at Chief Bailey. She heard her mind calling to Bailey, but voice formed no sound. Nothing was coming out of her mouth. One of the officers pulled the tablecloth back from Carol's head, revealing it to the chief.

"Oh Jesus!" Bailey exclaimed. He turned his back and motioned for the officer to cover Carol again. Jerome tried to gather the rushing emotions that were running through his body. He stood there for a few minutes, trying to collect all the emotions that were coursing through him.

Another voice came from the distance and addressed the chief. "Looks like I get to work with you again, Chief." Kevin Thompson walked up to the chief and choked back the joke he had been about to say when he saw how visibly upset Bailey was. "Did you know the victim?" Thompson asked.

"Yes, I did. Good friend of a good friend of mine." Bailey gathered his wits and took a deep breath. "I don't know if she was here or not, but for her sake, I hope she wasn't."

Thompson moved to the body, putting on a pair of gloves, and pulled the tablecloth back, beginning to examine the body for the wounds. He stood up, looking down at the body. "Wow! That was a pretty cold-blooded murder." Thompson started to scan the nightclub, trying to imagine the scene.

"What brings the FBI into this investigation?" Bailey asked.

"I got a call from our friend," Thompson whispered as he continued to scan the club. His eyes came to rest on the tables toppled directly across from him and the small bloody prints on the dance floor that led to the carpet and ultimately the tables. He bent down to get a better look. He could swear that someone was huddle in them. He started to move slowly to them, motioning to Bailey to stay where he was.

Just before getting to the tables, Thompson got down on his knees and peered in to see Nicole, who had tears on her face, her blood-soaked hand to her heart. "Hello," Thompson started as he slowly moved one of the

124 | *Linda Riesenberg Fisler*

tables away to reveal her. "My name is Kevin Thompson. Can I help you?" Thompson asked quietly.

Nicole's eyes began to fill with tears again as she moved her blood-soaked hand from her heart and extend it to Thompson. She couldn't speak, but she pointed to Carol with it. Her mind said, *That was my sister, my best friend. I want that bastard caught!* but nothing came out of her mouth.

"A good friend of yours, no doubt," Thompson said as he reached for her arm. "Let's get you cleaned up." He started to gently pull her from the tables, but Nicole resisted. "It's OK, I am with the FBI, and nothing is going to happen to you. I promise." Thompson tried again to help her from the tables, still meeting some resistance.

Bailey had become interested in what was unfolding in that huddle of tables and began to walk toward it. He caught a glimpse of the cinnamon-colored hair of his friend. "Nikki," he said quietly. "Oh, Nikki!" He cursed the fact that Nicole had witnessed the cold-blooded murder of her best friend. He walked closer to the tables as Thompson turned his head to address him.

"Chief, don't say any names, please. I'll explain later," Thompson said quietly. Turning back to Nicole, Thompson said, "Will you please come out of there? Chief Bailey and I want to get you cleaned up."

Nicole allowed the stranger to help her out of the tables now that Chief Bailey was close by. Thompson turned to Bailey. "Get your men out of here." It was a bit like an order, but Bailey didn't hesitate to have his men move outside to secure the unguarded doors. "And get rid of the nightclub staff," Thompson said when he noticed that a few had taken interest in the person emerging from the table.

Bailey called to one of his men to escort the staff to the manager's office and stay there. "What's going on, Kev?" Bailey asked.

"Later. Right now, let's get her cleaned up a bit." Thompson added, "and then away from here."

They helped Nicole to a chair a little farther away from Carol. She sat down as the chief left to get some wet cloths to wash Carol's blood from Nicole's arm and hand. Thompson grabbed one of the cameras that had been left behind by the police. He apologized to Nicole for having to take

*Blind Influence* | 125

pictures of her like this. Nicole shook her head and said, "I understand." Thompson had her stand as he tried his best to keep her head out of the shots. Her arms and dress were covered in blood. There was even some blood on her cheek where she had pressed her cheek to Carol's. Thompson helped Nicole back into the chair as Bailey came back with the wet cloths.

Bailey saw that Thompson had taken the photos and thanked him for his thoroughness. "I get a copy," Thompson answered, and Bailey agreed. Thompson pulled a chair up to Nicole and began to clean her arms and hands. Tears began to run down Nicole's cheeks again. "I'm sorry," Thompson said to her. "Can you tell me what happened here?"

"Some jackass hot-shot foreigner killed my best friend," Nicole answered. Nicole was coming out of her shock, and her anger was again welling up inside her. Her anger was motivating her to speak. Bailey's lips curled as he thought to himself that he would have heard nothing less from her. Nicole looked at Bailey and then at Thompson. "And the minute you have that son of bitch in custody, I want to know. I want the case," Nicole said.

"You don't work for the—" Bailey started.

"I will by Monday," Nicole answered. "I want that son of bitch to fry for this."

"Nikki … " Bailey said her name softly.

Thompson looked at Bailey and interceded. "Can you describe the son of a bitch? There are so many here in DC," Thompson said.

Nicole looked at him to see a little smile on his face. Thompson looked Nicole in the eye, a look they held for a few seconds. "Yes, he was about six feet and had these icy blue eyes … " Nicole shivered when she saw those eyes in her mind. Thompson noted the shiver.

"OK … that's good for now," Thompson interrupted as he put the cloths down, done cleaning her arms. He turned to Bailey and led him a little way from Nicole. "I need to get her out of here and somewhere safe. That's on the advice of our friend."

"Why?" Bailey asked. "She can stay with me and my wife."

"No. Sean gave me explicit instruction if she mentioned his eye color. It was a clue from Sean and very important. Jerome, this is between you and me. She can identify the Serpent. He'll be back for her, and Sean is the only one who can keep her safe. We have no idea what this guy looks like, and we know how cold-blooded he can be. Right now, I'm for giving MI-6 all the help they need."

"Promise me that she'll be safe," Bailey said.

"I promise as much as I can promise." Thompson turned back to Nicole as he spoke to Bailey. "Give me a few minutes, and then get your men away from the front entrance and my car." He walked back to Nicole and brought his chair closer to her before sitting down. Nicole looked at him once he was sitting. "Nikki, I'm working with the British government on a case, and I need you to trust me." Nicole started to say something, her mind recalling the other foreigner, with whom she had danced. He had had a British accent. She stopped, mainly because Thompson held up his hand. "I know it is really difficult to do, but I do ask that you come with me and we'll make sure you are safe."

"Why wouldn't I be safe?" Nicole asked, shaking her head.

"You are in danger, and we want to protect you." Thompson stood up. "Let's get you out of here."

"Where are you taking me?"

"You'll see," Thompson said as he took her by the arm to lead her to his car. "No more questions until we get to where I'm taking you. Is that a deal?" Thompson looked at Nicole, who agreed with some reservation.

Bailey returned and met them as they reached the front doors of the nightclub. Nicole gave Bailey a hug. "Take good care of her, Jerome," she said as tears filled her eyes again.

"I will, Nikki. You take care of you. I trust this guy with my life, so you do too, OK?" Bailey said as he let her go. Nicole could only nod in agreement as she wiped the tears from her eyes.

Thompson slipped his coat around Nicole, sliding his arm around her waist, and began to lead her to his car. It was dark outside, and Thompson

*Blind Influence* | 127

moved as quickly as he could to his car, opening one of the back doors. Then he asked Nicole to lie down across the back seat as she got in, a request that Nicole found very odd. She did as she was instructed, and Thompson moved quickly to the driver's seat, started the car, and peeled out from the scene, determined to get Nicole to safety.

# Jenkins's Home

*I*t was late, and the phantom pain was excruciating for Senator Jenkins. He sat down in the great room of his condo and removed the prosthesis to provide a much-needed massage. He had been standing a lot lately, and the long hours he had been putting in were taking their toll. He knew he would be receiving visitors soon, so as much as he wanted to take his tired, aching body to bed, he knew there would be no point. He put his prosthesis back on and walked to his bar. He grabbed his bottle of Glenmorangie, pouring some in a glass, and walked back to the chair to wait. After a few drinks from his glass and about fifteen minutes later, there was a knock on his door. The senator stood and walked over to answer it. He was shocked to see who was standing on the other side.

"Nikki?" he asked in confusion.

Nicole, who was wearing Thompson's trench coat that was a number of sizes too big for her, looked at Thompson. She took his arm, not quite sure what was about to happen.

Thompson looked down at Nicole's hand on his arm. He wasn't sure why she had put it there, but he wasn't about to do anything about it. Jenkins noticed Nicole's reaction and her bloodstained hand.

"Sorry to bother you so late, Senator Jenkins. A mutual friend asked that I bring—"

"I see. Come in please," the senator said as he opened the door wider for them to enter. "Have a seat in the great room." He raised his arm in the direction of the room as they entered. Thompson led Nicole to the couch, where they both sat down. The senator closed the door and followed them into the room. "Can I get you anything to drink?"

Nicole realized how dehydrated she was and asked for a glass of water. Thompson declined. The senator retrieved a glass of water and then sat down, taking another drink of his scotch before he spoke. "I have to say that I am very surprised to see you here." He was looking at Nicole.

"Had I realized that this is where Mr. Thompson of the FBI was taking me, I would not have come," Nicole answered.

The comment puzzled Jenkins. Then he thought back to Blair House, where he had commented to her to stay out of the investigation. He realized now that his warning may have been taken as a threat to her life. "Why are you here?"

Thompson felt a need to correct something Nicole had said. "I'm not with the FBI." He gave a little chuckle. "Well, not since this morning."

"But you identified yourself as—" Nicole started.

"I know," Thompson said. "I was fired this morning."

"You were fired," Jenkins repeated. "May I ask for what?"

"I let Adkins escape, for one thing," Thompson answered. "Insubordination was the other reason given."

"I see," Jenkins answered. He sighed. "Well, I'll see if I can do something about that. You never know what else might be waiting around the corner."

Nicole wasn't sure what was going on but was beginning to wish that she had stayed with Chief Bailey back at Conversations. She was beginning to think that she may never see the light of day. Nothing was making sense, and she couldn't help but wonder if she was in a bad dream. She took a drink of her water, as she was starting to feel lightheaded. She placed the water glass down and started to take off Thompson's coat. In doing so, she revealed her blood-soaked dress. Jenkins looked at the blood stains and realized that Nicole was now caught up in the affair.

"Are you feeling all right, Nicole?" the senator asked.

That was when Nicole realized that her bloodstained dress was in plain sight. She found it odd that Jenkins didn't comment on it or that he wasn't sickened by its appearance. "Yes. It's not my blood," she answered rather coldly. She also wasn't about to say more than she needed to until she could figure out what was at hand. She had to admit, everything about this situation was odd. She had been a witness to the murder of her best friend by a foreigner, and now she was seated in the great room of the senator who was chairman of the Intelligence Committee, escorted there by an ex-FBI agent.

The senator smiled as Nicole's eyes darted back and forth and her brow furrowed in thought. "Kevin, I think it would be best if you worked for my investigation starting now. Do you think you would be interested?" Jenkins asked while watching Nicole's reaction.

Before Thompson could answer, there was another knock at the door. "Excuse me. This is probably the person I was expecting." Jenkins moved to the front door and opened it. It was the party he had been expecting, and he ushered his guest in without saying a word, leading him to the great room.

Upon entering, the visitor's head turned to see Thompson and Nicole. He breathed a sigh of relief. "Thank God you are all right," Sean said as he faced Nicole. "Thank you, Kevin, for doing me this favor."

Nicole's mouth dropped. She shook her head in disbelief. She had a feeling she had landed smack-dab in the middle of a nightmare. She wasn't sure what was going on, but she knew everything was happening way too fast. After Jenkins's threat, she was sure he was involved in the assassination, but what did these other two have to do with that? "Who are you?" This was all Nicole could utter.

Sean smiled. "I am sure you are utterly confused by all that has happened this evening."

"No shit," Nicole responded. "That is a great observation." Her sarcasm was an indication that she was running out of patience.

"Nikki, your safety is our number-one concern," Jenkins assured her.

"Forgive me, Senator, if I don't believe you," Nicole answered. "I mean, you only threatened my life last night at Blair House. This English chap damn near wrestled me to the dance floor this evening, where I could now be lying next to my best friend, just as dead. Someone who identifies himself to me as an FBI agent asks me to trust him, then tells me later he's not an FBI agent." Nicole stood up. "Clearly, there is some kind of cover-up going on. I haven't figured it out yet, but obviously when I do, if I do, I won't be around to tell anyone."

Sean looked at the senator. Then he looked at Thompson. "You aren't with the FBI any longer?" he asked Thompson.

*Blind Influence* | 131

"I have asked Kevin to join our investigation, Sean," Jenkins stated.

"That depends on what you are going to do with the answers you find," Thompson stated, as he was quite sure he didn't want to be involved in any cover-up.

"Seems like a fair statement," Jenkins said as he stood and moved to his bar. "Can I get anyone something to drink?"

"This isn't a damn cocktail party. What the hell is going on here?" Nicole demanded.

A silence seemed to hang in the air. Jenkins tilted his head in thought. He wasn't sure what was really going on, either, but clearly, the other gentlemen in the room knew more than he did. He turned back to the bar and refilled his scotch glass. "The bar is open to anyone who will need a drink at any time. Sean, I suggest you get comfortable, because we have a long night ahead of us."

"Hello?" Nicole said. "Did anyone hear me?"

Jenkins moved back to his chair. "Yes, Nikki. We heard you. Please sit down."

Sean moved to a chair over by the bar. Jenkins sat back down in his favorite chair. Thompson was still sitting on the couch. Finally, after an exasperating moment or two, Nicole sat back down on the couch. She brushed the hair out of her eyes and thought how wonderful a shower sounded. *That will have to wait*, she told herself.

Jenkins started the conversation. "First, before we get into the heart of this, I want to address Nikki's comment about my misinterpreted threat." He looked directly into Nicole's eyes. "I did not threaten your life. I know you think that I did, and I apologize, but I wanted you to realize that you were sticking your pretty little neck into a rather complicated situation. There were only four people who knew that those bodies in the alley were Secret Service, and to this day, there are only five who know that." Jenkins took a drink of his scotch. "I was trying to keep you out of this before your wonderful detective work and intelligence got you in trouble. I thought if I warned you appropriately, you wouldn't be brought into this. As it turns out, you are meant to be involved, I suppose."

132 | *Linda Riesenberg Fisler*

"So it *was* Jeff," Nicole said, realizing she had now lost two people she had cared for deeply.

"Jeff?" Jenkins asked.

"One of the Secret Servicemen was named Jeff Brotherton," Thompson informed Jenkins, who acknowledged his comment with a nod of his head.

"Jeff was my ex-fiancé." Nicole volunteered. "I recognized his shoes, which weren't covered up in the photograph in the paper. I made a few calls and found out he hadn't reported to work, and I figured it had to be him. I wanted to tell you that, Senator, because I wasn't sure that information was being given to you."

"While I wasn't aware of his name, I was aware that the murdered men were Secret Service agents," Jenkins informed her.

"So there *is* a cover-up," Nicole concluded.

Jenkins smiled. "There is an investigation—more than one, actually. As for a cover-up, I can't answer that," Jenkins said, taking another drink. "Right now, it is imperative that at least one person's identity be kept secret."

"Two," Sean corrected.

Nicole turned her head to look at Sean. Exasperated, Nicole asked, "And I'll ask one more time, who are you?"

Sean sat for a moment, his eyes locked on Nicole's, as he formulated his answer. "One of three people who can identify the assassin who murdered your president," Sean paused to let that comment hang in the air a moment. Nicole's breathing started to quicken. "And he also murdered your friend Carol."

Jenkins's head snapped to look at Sean. "He was there tonight?"

"Yes. The payment happened at the nightclub," Sean confirmed.

"Wait a minute!" Nicole said in disbelief.

"I didn't see the payoff," Jenkins stated flatly.

*Blind Influence* | 133

Sean took his eyes off of Nicole for the first time since making his statement to look at Jenkins. "Begging your pardon, sir, you didn't know who to look for. He was there. He now has his money. And the person that paid him off will be killed within forty-eight hours. It depends on how badly I wounded the assassin this evening as to the method he will use to kill that person."

Thompson and Jenkins almost jumped out of their seats as they said together, "You wounded him?!" Thompson looked at the senator. "We need to get his description to the hospitals."

"He won't go to hospital. It's not that bad, I'm afraid. Considering he was still able to fire his gun at me, I think I only grazed his firing hand with a bullet," Sean said, disappointed. "Besides, if he goes to the hospital, he would alter his identity before he went there. For now, there is no reason to put what he looks like out to the general public. Doing so would only cause more deaths."

Sean noticed that Nicole had not stopped looking at him. He acknowledged her stare by looking at her but not speaking.

"You said three people: you, me, and who else?" Nicole asked.

"I don't know his name, but if I saw a picture of him, I could identify him," Sean answered.

"I'm so confused," Nicole started. She looked at Jenkins. "Bobby, why are you starting your own investigation? You already admitted that there are several occurring."

"I started my own investigation for a very good reason, Nikki. The night of the president's assassination, I was called to FBI headquarters by the director. I was escorted up to his office by Lieutenant Thompson here, who stood quietly in the office while the director threw a photograph across his desk at me and declared the person in the photograph to be the assassin. Kevin walked me out of the office building and was instructed to bring that person back into custody and charge him with the assassination of the president. There was only one thing wrong. I knew the person in the photograph personally, and I knew he had not killed the president."

134 | *Linda Riesenberg Fisler*

"I knew it, too," Thompson added. "Although I admitted that to the director, I was ordered to arrest him anyway."

"But you didn't do that, did you?" Nicole asked.

"No, I didn't," Thompson answered. "That is why I was fired."

"And why I think you need to join me in my investigation, Kevin," Jenkins stated again.

"Who is this person?" Nicole asked.

"Me," Sean answered.

"OK. For the third time, who *are* you?!" Nicole asked again, frustrated by not receiving an answer.

"He is Sean Adkins. He is an MI-6 agent," Jenkins answered. "The next morning, he came here. He told me about the Secret Service men who were killed by the assassin for their help in the assassination of our president. The FBI is trying to cover up who assassinated the president. I just don't know why." Jenkins took a drink of his scotch. "I launched the investigation to find the truth, which I obviously was not getting from our intelligence community."

"Now I see why you were warning me," Nicole said with a frown on her face that her own investigation had not nearly come close to this complexity.

Sean spoke up. "That warning meant nothing. You could have not said a word about those Secret Service agents to Bobby. As long as you went to the nightclub this evening, you would still be right here."

Nicole looked at Sean. "You said only three people can identify him: you, me and the person who paid him off this evening. I can only surmise that this man is highly skilled, by the precision of his marksmanship. How come only three people can identify him? He was in a nightclub. Surely he talked to others before he chose Carol to dance with this evening? The place was packed."

*Blind Influence* | 135

"He wasn't there for that long. He arrived probably five minutes before his appointed time for the payoff. Right after that, he wanted to find someone to spend the night with, shall we say." He looked sympathetically at Nicole. "She would not have survived the night either way."

"You knew he was going to kill her?" Nicole asked, hearing a crack in her voice as she spoke.

"Nicole, if Carol would have left with him, she would have been tortured and killed. He is an animal. It would have been a hellish night for Carol. I was hopeful in the crowded nightclub that he would just let her go and come after me. I am so sorry," Sean said. He had seen many women over the years who had suffered at the hands of the Serpent. The Serpent celebrated an assassination from afar by killing in a slow ritual that ran the gamut from seduction to torture and mutilation to death. Sean swallowed as he suppressed the memory of finding his own beloved Sarah after she had suffered at the hands of the Serpent. He broke his gaze with Nicole to try to suppress the images flashing in his mind's eye. He cleared his throat and said, "Senator, if you don't mind, I'd like to help myself—"

"Help yourself." Jenkins cut him off as if he knew what Sean was experiencing. This caught Nicole's attention as she looked at the two men.

"Mr. Adkins," Nicole's low, cracking voice broke the silence in the room. "Would Carol have suffered a worst fate than she did this evening if she had left with him?"

"Yes. As cold-blooded as Carol's death was this evening, it was much swifter than if she had left with him," Sean answered without turning around to face her. "I am sorry that I could not save her." For a moment, he wasn't sure if he was talking about Carol or Sarah.

Jenkins looked at Sean and had the same thought. "You tried, Sean."

A silence hung over the room for a few minutes. Nicole wasn't sure if it was out of respect for Carol or perhaps because no one else knew what to say. She cleared her throat to speak. "So, what happens next?"

Sean turned with his drink, which he took a sip of, and sat back down. "A lot depends on the Serpent."

136 | *Linda Riesenberg Fisler*

"Who is the Serpent?" Nicole asked.

"That is the assassin's code name," Sean answered. "He'll need some bandages, antibiotics possibly, stitches depending on how deep the wound is. My feeling is that he'll knock over a pharmacy, get what he needs, including painkillers, and lay low for a couple days. He probably is not even in DC proper right now. In a few days, he will find the person that paid him off and kill him. He'll also be trying to find you. He won't consider leaving until he has killed you."

Nicole looked up at Sean. "What?" Nicole couldn't believe what she just heard. "I don't even know his name!" she protested.

"Nicole," Sean started, "I gave Kevin strict instructions. There were but two things you had to say that told me you could identify the Serpent again. If you said those two things, he was instructed to bring you here because your life is in danger."

"He could not possibly know my name."

"You think so?"

Nicole nodded in the affirmative, very confident of herself.

"How long did it take me to find out Carol's name?" He watched as that confidence drained from Nicole's face.

"He could have shot me from any vantage point as Kevin brought me here. He could have shot me outside of Conversations," Nicole pointed out.

"No." Sean shook his head. "I made sure to drive him further away from the nightclub on the off chance that you could identify him." Sean took another drink. "He would not have killed the person that paid him off this evening. He would have done that after his little celebration." He took another drink. "To maintain his ability to roam free, no one can be left behind that can identify him."

"What happens if some of the other patrons or workers at the nightclub can identify him?" Kevin asked. "Nikki is right, Sean. That place is usually packed to the gills."

*Blind Influence* | 137

"Nikki," Jenkins started, "who else did you see there tonight?"

"There were a number of senators, congressmen, and countless presidents and CEOs of different corporations. I really didn't pay that much attention. I did see Norman Sipes and tried my best to avoid him." Senator Jenkins smiled at this remark. "I saw Congressman Davis."

"You didn't see me there?" Jenkins asked.

"No. Were you there?"

"Yes, sitting in the back and trying to remain hidden," Jenkins said. "Thank you for confirming that I did a reasonably good job of that." Sean gave a little chuckle at Jenkins's remark, as the senator's remark had been meant for Sean, who had noticed Jenkins was there and had wanted him to leave.

"So we have established that I'm on the Serpent's—is that what you called him?" Nicole looked at Sean, who nodded an affirmative. "—list to kill. Excuse me for being a little selfish about this, but what are we going to do about that?"

Sean smiled. "Hopefully avoid that outcome if we can." He leaned forward in his chair. "We have an opportunity to catch this man when he comes after the person who paid him off."

"But you don't know him, and there were so many people there this evening," Nicole answered.

"Maybe if I describe him, you will know who he is. He really is an oddball character. He would really be the kind of person that sticks out in a crowd." Sean looked at the three people sitting in the room with him.

"It's worth a try," Nicole said. "Describe him."

"Well, he was a little short of two meters tall." He looked at his American counterparts. He could see them looking at him, wondering just how many feet and inches he was talking about. Sean stood up and said, "He is a little shorter than me." He laughed. "He was a bit overweight. His belly"—Sean extended his arms in front of his stomach—"protruded out in front of him about so far. He has a burr haircut—"

138 | *Linda Riesenberg Fisler*

"Oh my God!" Nicole interrupted. "Norman Sipes?!" She looked at Jenkins.

"So far, Nikki, he described a number of people." Jenkins addressed her. "I know Sipes can be a bit obnoxious, but he is a former three-star general, and I would find it difficult to believe that he was involved in the killing of a president. Go on, Sean."

"Nicole," Sean said, "remember the first time I ran into you tonight?"

"Yes, kind of, it was very short exchange," Nicole answered.

"Well, this person was in a conversation with another man at a table in front of us. He was yelling at the other gentleman. Or I assume he was yelling. Actually, everyone was yelling in that awfully noisy place."

Nicole smiled as she agreed with Sean's last comment. "Bobby, I know you won't believe me, but it was Norman Sipes who was engaged in a heated conversation with Congressman Davis."

Jenkins sat for a moment. "I remember taking notice of that conversation. Sean, are you sure it was one of those two people?"

"Get me a photograph of those two people, and I can confirm which one it was," Sean answered.

"I have a photo of Davis. Wait here." Jenkins got up, walked out of the room, and returned with a book that included a directory, complete with a photo, of all the Congress members. He opened the book and pointed to Davis. "This is Congressman Davis."

"And he did not pay off the Serpent," Sean said. "But he did pass a white envelope to Sipes during their discussion."

"I saw Sipes put that envelope in his pocket," Nicole confirmed.

Jenkins closed the book and returned to his seat. Being a veteran himself, part of him didn't want to believe that a fellow veteran could conspire to kill a president. "We've established that Sipes delivered the payment. We have not established a motive," Jenkins started. "Could he have just been the messenger?"

*Blind Influence* | 139

"Does it make him any less guilty?" Nicole asked bluntly.

"No," Sean replied flatly.

"Well, he has been subpoenaed to appear before my finance subcommittee on Monday. Maybe that will supply a motive. Desperate people do desperate things." Jenkins still did not want to believe that a former three-star general could even think of committing such a horrendous act.

Sean drew in a breath and let it go slowly. "I can only hope he is still alive on Monday morning."

Nicole turned her head toward the window and noticed the first rays of morning sunlight. "The sun is coming up." She stood up. "I would really like to get a shower and a change of clothes. Can someone drive me home or call a cab?"

"You aren't going home, Nicole," Sean answered. "We'll go get some things from your home and bring them here, but you can't go home as long as the Serpent is here and trying to find you."

"I just can't disappear. I have responsibilities to clients, and especially to a group of Inuit people in Alaska for which I am conducting research." All three gentlemen looked at Nicole, and she knew she wasn't going to win that argument. "Well, can someone at least go with me to my condo?"

"Let me know what you need, and I will go retrieve it for you. It's just too dangerous to let you go back to your condo," Sean said firmly. He saw Nicole slowly come to a realization that he had been living for some time now.

"My life is not going to be the same from this moment on, is it?" Her eyes were fixed on Sean, the only person in the room with whom she had something in common. They began to fill with tears as Sean could only manage to shake his head in the negative. Nicole put her hand, still slightly stained with Carol's blood, to her mouth, biting her lip to keep from crying. She was exhausted, physically and emotionally. She was quickly coming to her wits' end, and she didn't want anyone to see her this way. She longed for the sanctity of her condo, where she could be truly alone.

"Nikki," Jenkins said as he stood up, "I have an old robe around here somewhere. How about we go upstairs and look for it. I have a general idea where it is. You can at least get a shower and out of those clothes."

140 | *Linda Riesenberg Fisler*

Nicole blinked back the tears and nodded in agreement. She stood up. "The most important thing is my briefcase. It is in the foyer of my condo." She reached for her purse and realized for the first time that she didn't have it. "My purse … " She looked at Thompson and then at Sean.

"Now I know for sure you aren't going back to your flat," Sean said. "Kevin, feel like stretching your legs?"

Thompson stood up, stretched, and said, "Absolutely."

"Bobby, do you have a piece of paper that I could jot down the address and what I will need?" Nicole asked.

Sean spoke up. "Just tell us the address."

"It's 3408 O St Northwest," Nicole answered. Sean looked at Thompson, who nodded, confirming that he knew how to get to Nicole's condo. "You'll find a suitcase in my closet in the master bedroom. A pair of jeans, some t-shirts, the typical necessities can all be found in the walk-in closet. Grab what you think I'll need, but please don't forget my briefcase."

"We'll be back shortly," Sean said as he moved to the front door, with Thompson walking behind him.

A trail of destruction that followed the Serpent could be recognized if one were close enough to put the pieces together. That was the key to his success as an assassin: not to let anyone alive too close to put the pieces together. The only exception to the rule was Sean Adkins. He liked playing with Sean's emotions, letting Sean just close enough to think the Serpent could be captured. The Serpent began to wonder if it was time to end this game. He knew on the day he had murdered the president that Jacques had failed to keep his location in Washington from Sean. His anger placated only by the fact that Jacques was now dead in the alley of that filthy saloon.

He had crisscrossed Washington during the night after he had managed to shake Sean off his trail. In his mind's eye, the Serpent started to recall that horrendous attempt to capture him at the putrid nightclub. His lip curled in disgust as he recalled how Sean had pathetically tried to save the woman from the demonic pleasure that the Serpent would have been enjoying this very evening.

*Blind Influence* | 141

He threw a bag he had been holding onto the bed and closed the door of the hotel room. He had driven hours outside of Washington to ensure his safety so he could again gain the upper hand.

The contents of the bag revealed just what the Serpent had been doing in the waning hours of the night. Inside the bag were the ingredients that would allow him to alter his identity. He didn't dare return to his hotel room in the city. He didn't know how much information Sean had acquired. He took his .357 Magnum from its holster, and also the smaller MP-25, which was the gun he had concealed in his pocket and had used to shoot point blank in the back of the beautiful woman's head. He snarled again as the thought of Sean keeping him from his pleasures and inflicting the wound that was now throbbing. From another pocket, he withdrew a pint bottle of whiskey. From the chest pocket of his dress suit, he removed his payoff for assassinating the free world's president.

He examined his blood-soaked makeshift bandage, made from a shirt sleeve that he had ripped to tie up the injury. He walked over to the bed, where the bag was lying. He dumped the bag's contents out and found the bottle of painkillers he had stolen from the pharmacy that he had ransacked and robbed in the early morning. The bag also contained hair dye, bandages, hydrogen peroxide, small scissors, and various other sundries to take care of his wound and his identity. Perhaps the most important prop to change his identity was in his pocket. He removed a small container and set it on the nightstand. He would need to change his most memorable feature, his eyes. He walked to the sink and retrieved a glass of water, then walked back to the bed and sat down. He opened the bottle of painkillers and swallowed two pills. It was time to tend to his wound.

He grabbed what he needed to perform the surgery on his hand. Although the bullet had only grazed his hand, it had caused significant damage— enough damage that the Serpent cussed again for letting Sean get too close to him. He removed the makeshift bandage and cursed again as blood started to pour from the wound. He turned on the water in the sink and opened the bottle of peroxide. He had been through this before and knew what he had to do.

Pouring peroxide over the wound and wiping it clean, he was able to get a better feel for what he would do next. He worked on the wound for fifteen minutes to get it to stop bleeding. Luckily, the wound was on the fleshiest area near the palm, and this allowed him to glue the wound to itself. He wrapped his hand in a sterile bandage and walked back to where he had set the bottle of whiskey. He opened the bottle and took a drink. The painkillers were starting to take effect, and he crawled into bed for a long sleep, safe in his knowledge that he would again have the upper hand on his nemesis. He also knew that the two people who could place him here in the United States at the time of the president's assassination would soon be dead. He drifted off to sleep with thoughts of taking his pleasure with a woman he knew by the name of Nicole Charbonneau, thanks to Carol. He sighed as he imagined her, and softly, as he drifted off to sleep, "Nicole … " escaped his lips.

# Day Six

# London, England

*I*t was early afternoon when Charlie Dawson finally made it to his office. He had spent the morning in Lord Peter Adkins's office with Jack Kensington, explaining why Sean had been permitted to journey to the United States when the Joint Intelligence Committee had strictly forbidden it. It was the thorough ass-chewing that Jack had expected and that Charlie had been ordered to endure with the director. Charlie walked slowly to his office. The two-hour-long session had zapped his energy, and he wasn't in any hurry to jump into the reports and other duties that might surprise him on this hectic day.

"Sir," his secretary said, already on her way to him, "there is something here that needs your immediate attention. I've shut it down as best I could. I knew you would not want the intelligence committee to see this. It has to be a mistake." They continued to walk to Charlie's office. She handed him a paper right before his door.

"Thank you." He opened his door and walked in. "I'll have a look … "

"Please do so right away, sir." She returned to her desk.

Charlie ruffled his brow as he took note of his secretary's deep concern with what was written on this paper. It was very unusual for her to get so emotional over any news, really. He placed the paper down on the desk as he took his raincoat off and draped it over a chair. He got his eyeglasses out and sat down behind his desk, reaching for the paper. "Well now, let's see what you are all about," he said as he sat back in his chair.

Within two seconds, he was standing again, the paper in his hand, and his jaw dropped open. "What in the world!" he exclaimed. "Oh, this certainly won't do." He depressed the button that called his secretary. "Tell Elliot I want to see him immediately!" He demanded. He then picked up the receiver and began to dial an overseas number.

He was about to finish the number when Elliot, known as Mole to Sean, entered the office. "You wanted to see me immediately, sir?" Elliot questioned. Elliot was Sean's direct contact and responsible for tracking Sean's location through a series of communications they sent in code to one another.

146 | *Linda Riesenberg Fisler*

"Yes. Any contact from Sean?"

"There is none," Mole answered, "but given the random acts of violence scattered around the DC area, I'd say he is hot on the trail of the Serpent."

"What are you talking about, random acts of violence?" Charlie was confused. "There is always a lot of violence in DC."

"Well, sir, over the years that Sean and I have been tracking the Serpent, we have been able to determine the assassin's habits after his kill. We know he was hired to kill the president now. Why else would he have gone there? Any other job would have been too lowly for him to even risk going there."

"Yes, yes, I'll concede that," Charlie said, rather impatient and angry. He wanted answers, and this wasn't what he wanted to know. "Get on with it, man."

"Well, as I said, we've been following the patterns the Serpent engaged in after the assassinations that he has committed over the years—all the way back to his involvement with the IRA when Sean first encountered him. Based on that data, and some low intelligence that includes a couple murders and a break-in at a couple pharmacies that crisscross in a snakelike manner, I'd say Sean came close to apprehending if not killing him."

"Oh," Charlie said, not out of surprise, but in a more sarcastic tone. "Well then, can you tell me why the FBI is saying that Sean is wanted for the murder of President Andrews?" Charlie was almost yelling by the end of the sentence, and he was trying his best to throw the flimsy piece of paper at Elliot. If Charlie hadn't been so mad, Elliot would have almost found his attempts comical.

Elliot tried to retrieve the paper a couple of times. "What?" He finally grabbed the paper and began reading its content. "Who ... What ... " Elliot couldn't find the words to express his surprise. "Is there nothing these Yanks won't do to protect a conspiracy?"

"Where the hell did that question come from?" Charlie demanded.

"Sir, Sean would not have killed the president. You know that and I know that. This is some kind of cover-up. It has to be."

*Blind Influence* | 147

"Well, we have to find out before I end up back in front of Lord Adkins for another ass-chewing." Charlie sat down. "I didn't enjoy the first one, thank you very much. If this gets to him before I can explain it fully, we'll both be out of a job!"

"I can put a message in to Sean, but it might be better for you to call this Jefferies directly," Elliot said as he turned to go to his office.

"I'll do better than that!" Charlie said as he picked up the phone again and began to dial the overseas number for a second time.

# Jenkins's Home

$\mathcal{B}$obby Jenkins was headed back down the stairs. He had located the old robe promised to Nicole, who was now in the shower. In his hands, he held a sealed plastic bag, which contained Nicole's blood-soaked clothes. He paused at the bottom of the stairs as he pondered what to do with them. Were they evidence? Should they go to the DC police? If so, how would he explain that he had them without revealing where Nicole was located? He scratched his head and then decided the garage for now would be the best place to secure the items.

As he opened the door to walk back into his condo from the garage, he heard the phone ringing. He sat down in his favorite chair and picked up the phone. "Hello." From the receiver came a familiar British voice yelling his name. It was so loud that even after Jenkins removed the phone from his ear, he could still hear the gentleman's angry voice. He held the receiver away from his ear and waited for the opportune time to speak. "Charlie, will you calm down enough for me to enter this conversation?" He waited a few more moments, as Charlie wasn't through with his incoherent rant.

Finally, Charlie realized that the conversation was one-sided, he doing all the talking and, ashamedly, threatening. He realized that he was taking out some of what he had gotten from Lord Adkins this morning on Senator Jenkins. "I'm sorry, Bobby. I was in Lord Adkins's office all morning getting my ass chewed out only to come back to this crock of shit."

Jenkins laughed. "I understand. But what exactly did you come back to?"

"I have a communique from the FBI director alerting the intelligence community that Sean Adkins is wanted for the assassination of President Andrews."

Jenkins sat up in his chair at the words spoken by Charlie. A range of emotions ran through him. "What!?" Jenkins screamed into the phone. "Sean didn't kill the president."

"It's signed by Matthew Jefferies." Charlie stated, adding a little salt to the wound so to speak.

"Well, it will be retracted by him as well. I assure you, Charlie, we are not pursuing Sean Adkins for the murder of our president."

Charlie waited for a second and then asked. "I was going to call Jefferies, but decided to talk to you. I don't know what is going on over there, Bobby, but blaming it on Sean is not the answer. I have no idea who to trust." Charlie explained. "Is Sean all right, Bobby?"

"Yes, Charlie. He is hot on the trail of the Serpent. It has its costs associated with this, but Sean is performing admirably and has conducted himself in a very professional manner. There is a lot of collateral damage, especially last night, but nothing that could have been avoided."

"When was the last time you saw him?"

Jenkins looked at his watch. "It was about an hour ago."

"It sounds like he checks in with you more than those for whom he works," Charlie said, almost laughing.

"I am very much aware that the FBI for some reason wants to quickly blame this on Sean as a rogue agent from England, but I won't let that happen, Charlie." Jenkins paused. "Sean was arrested by an agent who used to work for the FBI and is now working with us. Sean came directly to me after his arrest. He has the full backing of the government, and I'll am going to make sure that Jefferies knows this."

"Thank you, Bobby. I'll wait to hear from you or Sean," Charlie answered.

"I will have him call you when he gets back. Good-bye, Charlie." Jenkins hung up the phone and started to plan out his next steps. Why would Jefferies issue that communique without his knowledge? Was it better to let Jefferies continue to incriminate himself or to tell Jefferies information that might interfere with what Sean needed to do next? He knew Jefferies and the intelligence agencies were under a lot of pressure to produce the assassin, but why would Jefferies want to claim that MI-6 was behind the assassination? These were all good questions that Jenkins couldn't answer.

Jenkins's attention was brought back to the present when he heard the water stop running in the shower. It was time for some coffee and breakfast. He decided that Sean and Thompson would be returning shortly and the two would be quite hungry. There was a lot of planning that needed to occur. There was no use in creating those plans on an empty stomach. Jenkins looked at his watch again and realized that the funeral for President Andrews was about to start. With that thought, he headed to his kitchen, stopping on the way to turn on the television.

The quiet room began to fill with the commentary of the funeral. Jenkins picked up the phone in the kitchen to call his aide, Chris. He asked Chris to issue a short statement expressing his sympathy to the Andrews family and the nation for the loss of a great man and leader, also that he regretted that the flu prevented him from attending the ceremony. After hanging up the phone, he walked to the refrigerator and began to pull out what he needed to fix breakfast.


Sean and Thompson pulled up to Nicole's condo in Sean's rental car. Each was ready with his weapon as they walked up to Nicole's front door. Sean started examining the door for any sign of forced entry. He tried the door-knob and found it still locked and with no signs of forced entry. "Should I go around back?" Thompson asked.

"I don't think that is necessary," Sean said as he put his gun away and withdrew a tool, with which he began to pick the lock on the door.

"Are you that sure he isn't here?"

"Yes," Sean answered as he opened the door. He put his tool away and then took out his weapon once again. He and Thompson entered quietly and began to look around and through every room. Thompson went up the stairs to the bedrooms while Sean checked the downstairs rooms and garage.

"Upstairs is clear. No sign anyone has been here," Thompson stated as he met Sean in the great room. Sean confirmed that his search had been uneventful as well. "I saw her briefcase in the foyer, just like she said," Thompson said as he went to retrieve it.

Sean walked over to the phone on Nicole's desk, which had an answering machine sitting beside it. There were six messages on the recorder. Sean found a piece of paper and a pen and pressed the button to listen to the messages. He took notes to give to Nicole when they returned. Thompson

*Blind Influence* | 151

walked in while Sean was listening to the messages. "She didn't tell you to listen to her private—" Sean cut him off by raising his hand. The first two messages were solicitations, but he wrote the names of the companies anyway. As the third message began, Sean began writing again.

"Nikki, this is Tony. I just heard about Carol. Honey, I'm so sorry. Call me when you get home, and I'll come by to visit. God, what a horrible way to die! Call me, Nikki—I'm worried about you." That call had been at one in the morning. The fourth message was another from Tony asking if she was all right and expressing again how worried he was about her. Tony went on to say that if he didn't hear from her shortly, he was going to talk with DC Police Chief Bailey to find out what was going on. The time on that call was five a.m.

"We'll need to call Bailey," Sean told Thompson quickly.

The next two calls were from people with names that Sean couldn't begin to spell properly. He tried his best to both understand the speakers and to spell their names. He figured that these must be the clients Nicole had talked about.

"Let's grab some of her clothes and get out of here," Sean said as he stuffed the paper into a pocket. As they were upstairs packing clothes into the suitcase they had found in the closet, the phone rang again.

"Should we answer it?" Thompson asked.

"I'm tempted," Sean answered, "but it is probably better if we didn't. This is good; let's go." They went back downstairs, and Sean paused in the foyer as he heard the answering machine connect. He walked over to the desk as the voice on the other end began to leave a message. "Nikki," the speaker said, sounding as if she were crying, "this is Ahnah. They killed one of our people. He confronted them after they put some pipes on his property. He just walked up to them and would not leave. They just killed him in cold blood … right there … in front of his children. Nikki, please call us. We need help!" The line went dead.

Sean walked back to the foyer, and both men left the condo, Thompson with the suitcase and Nicole's briefcase. Sean locked the door behind him. The two men moved quickly to the car to head back to Senator Jenkins's residence.

"What do you think that last call was about?" Thompson asked when they were safely away from Nicole's condo.

"I don't know, but there are two other messages that discussed happenings wherever these people are located. I would say Nicole doesn't lead a dull life," Sean remarked with a smile on his face.

"I don't know anything about her, really. Just her reputation when she worked for the DA's office." Thompson looked at Sean.

"What was her reputation?" Sean asked.

"She was one tough cookie, or so I'm told. She was a stickler for detail and a real headache to work with on a case. She had one of the best conviction rates in the office," Thompson answered. "Rumor has it that she quit the DA's to go to Rosen, Shafer, and Pruett because she and Tony Shafer were involved."

"That would explain the two calls from the guy named Tony," Sean stated.

"I'm not sure they're more than just friends," Thompson retorted. "She doesn't seem the type to go for a guy old enough to be her father."

Sean gave a little chuckle. "Based on what?"

"The way she looks at you," Thompson answered.

"I'm sorry. I don't think I heard what you said correctly." Sean was taken by surprise by his comment.

"Come on! You didn't notice how she was looking at you?"

"No. Kevin, I'm a little busy tracking an assassin right now. I don't need distractions," Sean answered somewhat annoyed but not exactly sure why.

"Well I'm not the only one who noticed. Jenkins did, too, and didn't much care for it. I think he has the hots for her."

"And I think you've been watching too many of your American soap operas. There is no love triangle here. If anything, since we are the only two in the world who can positively identify the Serpent, it creates a bond

*Blind Influence* | 153

or kinship of some type." Sean wanted to cringe at the words he was choosing. It seemed like he was trying to compensate or justify why there might possibly be a connection. Since Sarah's death, Sean had had little time for relationships. If it were a different time or place, he had to admit to himself that he would have been attracted to Nicole. For now, he found her fascinating.

"I think I'll skip that club if you don't mind," Thompson answered as they pulled up to Jenkins's condo.

"You aren't going to join Jenkins's investigation?" Sean asked.

"I didn't say that. I said that I don't want to know intimately what this guy looks like." Thompson opened the door to the car and got out. "The price is too high."

"That it is, Kevin." Sean grabbed the suitcase from the back seat of the car as Thompson reached for the briefcase. Locking the car door, they moved to the front door of Jenkins's condo.

As they entered the condo, they were met with the aromas of the breakfast that the senator was cooking. They put down the briefcase and suitcase in the great room. As they walked into the kitchen, Jenkins addressed Sean. "Charlie called. He wants you to check in with him. And we have problem."

"A problem?" Sean asked as he scanned the kitchen, looking for Nicole. "With Nicole?"

"No, she is upstairs. I assume she is sleeping. I wouldn't doubt it, actually," Jenkins answered as he continued to cook. "No, Jefferies issued a communique alerting the intelligence community that you are wanted for President Andrews's assassination."

"What?!" Sean and Thompson exclaimed at the same time.

Jenkins smiled. "I don't think you could have timed that more perfectly. I have been wrestling with my next step. I don't want everyone out there hunting you down, Sean, but at the same time, I'm not sure why Jefferies is hell-bent on nailing this assassination on you."

154 | *Linda Riesenberg Fisler*

"You mean besides the fact that it takes some pressure off the agency to capture someone quickly?" Thompson asked with a bit of sarcasm. "I'm sorry. I am just a tad bit jaded. I've seen the start of a number of cover-ups, most of which have blown up in the agency's face."

"This could play to our advantage," Sean answered. "But if the Serpent manages—or decides, rather—to leave before tying up the loose ends here, thinking that I'll be serving time for the president's murder, I won't be able to follow."

"And it puts Charlie in a very bad situation with your father and the Joint Intelligence Committee your father leads."

"Your father is Lord Peter Adkins?" Thompson asked, surprised. He hadn't put the connection together until this moment.

"Yes," Sean answered, "and Geoffrey Adkins is my older brother." Geoffrey had followed in the footsteps of his father, picking a life of politics to try to make a difference in their world. While Peter Adkins was in the House of Lords, Geoffrey had just been elected into the House of Commons.

"Wow! You're like royalty." Thompson was impressed. He knew of Peter Adkins only because of Peter being the chairman of the British Joint Intelligence Committee. Thompson was impressed with Peter Adkins. Sometime in the near future, he fully expected, Peter Adkins would be prime minister.

"No, we are not royalty, I assure you," Sean answered in a way that left Thompson wondering if he had insulted Sean. "They are more a pain in my ass than a help at times."

"I'm surprised they let you out of the country, much less track this assassin. I mean, if someone catches you, that is one heck of a bargaining chip," Thompson responded.

"Don't think that they haven't thought about that, Kevin," Jenkins answered. "Breakfast is about ready. Can someone wake Nicole?"

There was a bit of hesitation, before Sean spoke up. "I'll go." He turned and grabbed the two cases on his way to the stairs. As he reached the top of

*Blind Influence* | 155

the stairs, he heard a bloodcurdling scream from the bedroom where Nicole lay sleeping.

Sean threw the two cases aside and withdrew his gun from its holster. He barged through the door to find Nicole on the bed and sitting up. His entrance frightened her again, and she jumped and let out another scream.

A few seconds later, Thompson, with his gun drawn and with Jenkins a few steps behind him, rushed into the room. When Nicole realized it was Sean who had scared her the second time, she closed her eyes, looking up at the ceiling.

Sean put his gun in his holster and moved to Nicole's side. Thompson looked out the window, making sure all was secure before he reholstered his gun. Sean sat down next to Nicole. He didn't have to ask; he knew what had frightened her again. "The Serpent has a way of haunting you even when you sleep," he whispered. "I should know." She looked at him, unsure of his meaning. "You'll be fine," he responded rather flippantly, as if he were sure of everything.

"I'm sorry. I didn't mean to frighten all of you," Nicole said. "It was a bad dream that ended with those icy blue eyes staring at me."

"You're safe right now, Nikki," Jenkins answered. "Let's get some breakfast and decide what we need to do to keep you that way." He turned and headed back down the steps.

"Did you bring some clothes from my apartment?" Nicole asked, tugging at Jenkins's robe that she wore.

"Yes, sorry. I threw them aside when I heard you scream. I'll be right back." Sean returned with the cases and set them on the bed. He reached into his pocket and retrieved the paper with the messages written on them. "These messages were on your answering machine." He handed her the slip of paper. Nicole looked down at the messages. She looked up at Sean. "There was an additional one that came in when we were there," he told her. "It was from an Ahnah. She said that one of her people had been killed."

"May I call these people?"

"Not yet. Maybe you can before we leave," Sean answered as he turned to go downstairs.

"Leave?" Thompson asked. "Where are you going?"

"I don't know exactly yet, but she isn't safe in DC," Sean answered. Thompson looked at him, and Sean added, "Trust me, Kevin. I've been tracking this man for ten years. She isn't safe in DC, and we need to find a place that gives us an upper hand." He left the room, heading down to the dining room for breakfast.

"So, he will track me down." Nicole looked at Thompson when she made her statement.

"It sounds like it," Thompson answered as he motioned for her to leave the room.

"I'd like to change first. I'll be down in a few minutes. Don't wait for me," Nicole said as Thompson reached the door. "To start eating, I mean." Thompson smiled and gave a quick shake of the head. He closed the door behind him, and Nicole began to look through the suitcase for something to wear.

Thompson walked down to the dining room table and informed the two who were already sitting that Nicole would be joining them once she changed clothes. Reaching for his knife and fork, placing his napkin on his lap, he finished by telling them that she had said not to wait. The three followed Thompson's lead. "What's your plan, Sean?" Thompson asked as he reached for a biscuit. The senator had made a good old-fashioned country breakfast, including grits, biscuits, and gravy to go with the ham and eggs on each plate.

"We have to get her out of DC. I am just not sure where yet," Sean started. "Someone should try to warn this Sipes fellow and maybe even take him into custody if possible."

"Would it be possible to try and catch the Serpent over at Sipes's house?" Thompson asked.

"I originally thought so. We are running out of time to set a thorough trap. Would Sipes cooperate?" Sean asked.

*Blind Influence* | 157

"Norman Sipes is a bastard of a fellow to reason with. He won't go into custody unless you can prove he is guilty of something. He is an old warhorse. He'll think he can protect himself," Jenkins added to the conversation.

"Even if we warn him?" Sean asked.

"I'm afraid so," Jenkins answered. "And we simply don't have the evidence to arrest him. Shafer would be all over that, and he'd be released within an hour."

"Shafer?" Sean questioned.

"Tony Shafer, Nicole's boss, is his attorney," Jenkins stated. He laughed as he watched Sean trying to tie all of this together. "Rest assured, Sean, Nikki has no love for Norman Sipes, and while she works for Tony Shafer, she does not share his political views or desires."

"One can never be so sure," Sean answered. "I've just about seen it all when it comes to the Serpent and what people will do to save their lives."

# London, England

*C*harlie Dawson was on the phone when Kent barged into his office. Charlie looked up in midsentence to see Kent standing in front of him with a piece of paper in his hands. Charlie motioned for Kent to sit as he continued his conversation. "Our contact in the US has assured me that all is going well. I wanted to get you this information before you had the unfortunate experience of reading it in the intelligence briefings." Charlie paused as the person on the end of the line was talking. "I fully understand, Lord Adkins. If necessary, I can have our contact call you. Yes, I see." Charlie waited a few seconds. "Yes, of course, sir. Good-bye, sir." He turned his attention to Kent, who was now seated in front of him. "What brings you here, Kent?"

"I just read this. I wanted you and Sean to know that I can leave immediately to lend a hand," Kent responded, almost too rehearsed and too eager to get involved. This piqued Charlie's curiosity.

"What makes you think Sean needs assistance? After all, Kent, you know you cannot trust everything you read from the dispatches, at least not one hundred percent of the time."

"I got a call from a friend who works in the agency there. It sounds bad, Charlie, and from the accounts, it sounds like he has his hands full. He might welcome a little help from someone he trusted with his life at one time. There are times when I'd trust my own countryman over the Yanks."

Charlie smiled. Obviously, Kent had found out about the communique. "Are you sure, Kent? The United States has been our ally for a hundred years. We've shared intelligence, and while some of it wasn't worth the paper it was written on by either side at one time or another, I'd hardly say we couldn't trust them." Charlie studied Kent, who certainly seemed anxious to get involved with Sean's case. He watched as Kent, who wasn't the sharpest knife in the drawer, struggled to come up with another reason to leave for the United States. "Kent, I'll tell you what," Charlie finally said. "I'm to talk with Sean in a little bit. I'll tell him of your concern and ask if there is something you can do. In the meantime, I suggest you get back to your cases." Kent didn't move. "Kent, I am really busy. Do you mind?"

"Oh, yes, of course." Kent stood up and wadded up the paper in his hands. He tossed it into the trashcan by the door, then opened the door and left for his desk.

Charlie buzzed for his secretary. When she entered the room, he motioned for her to close the door, which she did. "I need all the files on Kent Chapman, all that you can find. And do it quietly and quickly."

"Yes, sir," she replied as she walked out of the office.

Charlie sat for a moment and wondered where Kent had come up with the highly classified communique. The communiques of that nature usually didn't go directly to the agents without a need to know. Kent was not in the need-to-know category. And just who was his contact in the United States who had called him? Maybe a quick call to his supervisor would shed some light on what Kent's assignments were.

Charlie dialed Kent's superior, an old friend. "Hello, Henry. Everything is fine. Actually, I'm calling about one of your men. Kent Chapman. Was wondering what he is working on, and if I need him, if he would be available?"

"I suppose if you needed the help, we could break him away. He is working on the Middle East. What are you thinking?" Henry asked his old friend.

"Oh, nothing specific really comes to mind. I am waiting to hear from Sean, and they had worked together some time ago."

"I see where you are going. Just give a call back if you need him. He's low enough on the totem pole that we really wouldn't miss him for a few weeks," Henry responded.

"That's all I need to know for now. Thank you, Henry." Charlie placed the receiver down on its cradle. He stood and walked over to the trashcan that contained the paper that Kent had discarded. There were only a handful of papers in the can, and Charlie wanted to look at each one of them. It was unusual not only that Kent had the dispatch but also that he had discarded the highly classified dispatch in such a manner. Charlie unfolded each paper, and his finding made him scratch his beard and think. Not one paper contained any information on Sean. He himself had discarded the other four papers. The fifth piece of paper was blank, leading Charlie to believe, as he had suspected, Kent had no information on Sean's situation from British intelligence. He sat back down and waited for Kent's files.

The secretary had returned with Kent's personnel files and performance reviews nearly five hours ago. Charlie had read through them three times in those five hours. There was nothing in them that would afford Charlie his suspicions of Kent's possible disloyalty to the Crown, but something still wasn't sitting right. The blank paper and his knowledge of Sean's situation were too much of a sign.

He was deep in thought when the phone rang. "Hello," Charlie said, still in deep thought.

"Hello, Charlie," Sean said. "We've got things pretty well figured out. I don't want to go into all the details, but I will say that Nicole Charbonneau is a wonderfully courageous woman. She has agreed to help us catch the Serpent. Since she can identify him, she, as well as I, will be acting as bait."

"Are you sure you want to bring someone else into your nightmare, Sean?"

"She is already in it, Charlie." Sean paused. "The Serpent will try to kill her. It is just a matter of being in the right place. A place where I can have the upper hand is of utmost importance. I want Kent Chapman to fly over to the States and lend a hand."

"Sean, I'm not sure that Kent is the right man," Charlie started. "I have some doubts about his loyalty."

Sean smiled as Charlie confirmed his suspicions. Sean's ten-year pursuit of the Serpent had begun on an assignment that had involved Kent. Although Kent may have saved his life when they had been a part of MI-5, Sean had always wondered if he had been meant not to do so, and Kent seemed to pop up at very interesting times in Sean's life, especially when he was getting too close to catching the Serpent. In conversations earlier in the week in Jenkins's home, he had begun to see a pattern that made him also suspect that Kent was working for the Serpent. "I do too, which makes him perfect for the job. Charlie, let it slip to Kent that Nicole can identify the Serpent and that I'm moving her to a safer location. Don't tell him where yet, just that I am and that I've requested his assistance, just like the old days. Have him fly into DC, and tell him that I'll be picking him up at the airport."

"Are you very sure about this, Sean?"

"Absolutely."

"Where will you be going?" Charlie asked.

"Charlie, for now, that remains a mystery to you. If you don't know, you can't let it slip." Sean waited. "Do you understand, Charlie?"

"Be careful, Sean. I'll get in touch with Kent now and get him to DC. I'll call you back with the details." Charlie hung up the phone and put Kent's files in his drawer. It was late, but he had Kent's home phone number. The sooner he got this started, the better. He dialed the number. Kent answered the phone on the second ring. "Kent, I just heard from Sean. As it turns out, he has requested your assistance in DC. I'm booking reservations for you, and I'll call Henry to square it with him. Can you be ready in a few hours? Sean will pick up at the DC airport when you arrive."

"Yes. That is not a problem at all. It will be good to work with Sean again," Kent responded. "I'll come by the office for the tickets and orders."

"Not necessary. Sean has full command of this. He'll fill you in when you get there. He told me to tell you that he is guarding someone who can identify the Serpent. Her name is Nicole Charbonneau." Charlie was interrupted.

"Wow! Sean has someone who can put the Serpent in DC at the time of the assassination and can identify the Serpent. What a break in his case!" Kent was almost too excited.

"Yes, well, part of your job will be to ensure her safety. Sean will fill you in when you get there," Charlie said. "I'm wishing you the best, Kent."

"Thank you, Charlie." Kent hung up the phone and smiled. He knew this was the information the Serpent wanted and he would be able to help the Serpent dispose of the two people who could positively identify him. He smiled, thinking his fortunes were finally turning around.

He reached into his pocket and pulled out a piece of paper that contained a phone number. He dialed it and waited for an answer. "Yes." This was the way he was greeted by the party on the other end of the line. The man never identified himself as the Serpent. Kent always assumed it was. "You'll be happy to hear this news," Kent started. "Nicole can identify you."

"And that would make me happy?" the heavily accented voice of the Serpent asked.

"Adkins has requested my assistance in securing her safety. I'm leaving shortly and will be working closely with him. You will be able to rid the world of the two people who can identify you. That should make you happy," Kent said. He wondered what this man looked like. He had never met him in person, and based on the line of deaths of those who could, he was in no hurry to find out. "When I know more, I will contact you."

"I have a few more loose ends to take care of here. You will be able to reach me at the original number I gave you. Is that clear?"

"Yes," Kent said as he heard the click that ended their conversation.

# Jenkins's Home

Sean stood up after he finished his call to Charlie. He walked into the kitchen. Nicole and Jenkins were seated at the kitchen table in deep discussion. Nicole's briefcase was open, and she had just taken out the photographs supplied to her by the Inuit clients. "I don't know if you recall, Bobby, the day we spoke briefly outside the Old Ebbitt Grill, that I was accompanied by three Inuit people?"

"No, I don't recall that," Bobby answered, acknowledging Sean, who joined them at the table.

"They delivered these photographs to me. Someone is drilling illegally in ANWR." She handed the photographs to Jenkins, who started to page through them. "Or more accurately, they are getting ready to drill there. The messages that Sean retrieved from my answering machine are from that client. It sounds like the situation there is escalating. I was wondering if it would be acceptable for me to call them and find out what exactly is happening. Sean told me that Ahnah called as he was leaving my condo and reported that they had shot one of their tribe. Obviously this is illegal activity."

Jenkins smiled. "You don't have to make your case to me, Nikki. Sean, this is your call."

"They are in Alaska?" Sean asked.

"Yes. I told them I could help them. Please let me talk with them."

"Go ahead, but don't mention anything about your situation," Sean answered.

"Nikki, would you mind making that call in my home office on speakerphone? I would like to listen to their story firsthand," Jenkins asked. "If someone is drilling there, I think that is something I'd be interested in knowing so that I can assist in shutting it down."

"Are you sure that is a stance you want to make, Senator?" Nicole asked. "It might hurt you in the future if you run for president."

"Nicole, for every oil company vote I lose, I would pick up a vote from a far more intelligent voter who knows that we need alternatives to oil and we need that research to start now."

Nicole smiled. "Then let's get this phone call placed." They left the kitchen for the senator's home office.

"Sean, you are welcome to join us. I sent Kevin over to Sipes's place to stake it out. Chris is typing up another subpoena. I've asked him to drop it off to Kevin to serve. I figure it would get Kevin inside the gate to maybe talk some sense into Sipes," Jenkins informed Sean as they entered the great room.

"I will need him in North Carolina on Monday or Tuesday at the latest," Sean replied. "I can head over if you think it would be helpful."

"That is up to you," Jenkins said as he started again for the office.

Sean followed them as he talked. "We'll stop to talk with Kevin on our way to the airport to pick up Kent. I'm sure Kevin will need some food and coffee by that time."

As they entered the office, Jenkins gestured for Nicole to sit at his desk and make the call. Nicole dialed the number, and then Jenkins depressed the speakerphone button. Sean sat in a chair across the desk from Nicole. The senator walked to the side of his desk and leaned against the bookcase. The phone rang several times until it was answered with a brisk hello from a female.

"Ahnah? This is Nicole Charbonneau. I'm sorry that I haven't been in touch."

"Nicole—we need help!" Ahnah cried into the phone. "I was just getting ready to send you more film. I've got about six rolls, including the cold-blooded murder of one of my cousins."

"Slow down, Ahnah. What is happening there? Start at the beginning and talk slowly."

Ahnah took a breath and began her story. "A few days ago, several of the company men began to set up the rig. They started to lay down pipe and

*Blind Influence* | 165

other equipment. I took photographs of that. My cousin, he saw that they were putting this equipment on his land, and he went down to tell them to remove it. They argued for less than a minute when one of the men pulled out a gun and shot him right in front of his family. Annakpok and Nagojut ran to the family's side to keep them from running to our cousin's body. We were frightened that they would shoot them too. We asked permission to remove his body, which they allowed us to do."

Nicole looked at Jenkins, who was intently staring at the phone, his arms crossed upon his chest. "We buried him today, and we have been trying to keep everyone away from the men building this rig. They march along the perimeter with shotguns and automatic rifles. They are constructing a chainlink fence around it. I suppose they think this will keep us out." Ahnah paused for a moment. "Am I on speakerphone?"

"Yes," Nicole answered. "I'm taking notes."

"Oh, I see. There still is no identification as to what company is drilling. A number of the people here have called the governor's office, but they are not talking and refuse to get involved. Whoever is doing this, they must have paid them off as well. Anyway, Nikki, I'm not sure how much longer we can keep everyone from going to war here. Our family and neighbors are stockpiling ammunition and food. Plans are being made, and it is going to get really bad quickly."

"Ahnah, are you going to send six rolls of film?"

"Yes."

"You still have them?" Nicole followed up.

"Yes."

Just as Nicole was going to tell Ahnah where to send them, Senator Jenkins moved forward, placing a hand on each side of his desk. He leaned in toward the desk to speak into the speakerphone. He interrupted Nicole before she could answer. "Ahnah, my name is Senator Robert Jenkins. I am very interested in what is going on there, and I am a good friend of Nikki's."

"I know who you are, Senator. Nikki, you know I don't like being lied to."

166 | *Linda Riesenberg Fisler*

"I'm sorry, Ahnah. There have been some unfortunate circumstances over here as well. You can trust Senator Jenkins," Nicole answered.

"Ahnah, Nikki will have to leave on other business, and she came to me with concerns that illegal drilling is occurring on your lands. I want to know who is doing that drilling. I need those six rolls of film as quickly as you can get them to me. I'll give you my mailing address in a second. I also will be sending up one of my aides to assess the situation."

"He better come with an armed guard, Senator," Ahnah stated flatly.

"I'm not sure I can provide that. I can assure you that he will have the ability to report directly to me. Are there any company signs on the equipment?" Jenkins asked.

"No."

"Have any of the men stated who they work for?" Jenkins was grasping at straws, but hopeful that something may have been overheard by someone in the town.

"No. They are very careful about that. They never leave the area right around the rig. They are never away from it. Everything is directly delivered to them at the site. We have asked over and over, but they just say it is none of our business and that we should contact Nikki's law firm."

Jenkins was taken by surprise and shot a look at Nicole. "Why would they contact your law firm?"

"I don't know. None of the partners know I'm in contact with Ahnah and her brothers. They came to the law firm demanding the drilling stop, and I intercepted them before any of the other lawyers could have them thrown out. I was taking on this case outside of the law firm until I could figure out what was happening."

"It's my case now," Jenkins answered. "Ahnah, do you have a pen and paper? I want to give you my phone numbers. We'll get to the bottom of this."

Nicole mouthed a thank-you to Senator Jenkins as she vacated his seat to let him take control of the phone call. The senator barked out his phone

*Blind Influence* | 167

numbers, along with other instructions. He ended the call with, "I'm going to call one of my aides, John Spencer. He will be on the first plane out of DC to Alaska. He will be calling you in a few minutes to get your information. Thank you, Ahnah."

"Thank you, Senator."

They ended the call, and Senator Jenkins picked up the phone to call John and dispatch him on his mission. When he had finished that call, he looked up at Nicole. "May I keep your information and those photographs?"

"Of course you can," Nicole answered. "Do you think you know who is behind this?"

"I have my suspicions, and I don't share those." Jenkins smiled.

Nicole looked over at Sean. "Can I call Tony and let him know I'm alright?"

"No," Sean answered without hesitation. "It will be better for all of us, and especially Tony, if he has not heard from you and doesn't know where you are."

"I'll get word to him that you are alright and that you decided to go on a vacation," Jenkins answered as Nicole looked his way.

"I'm sorry, Senator, but you can't do that," Sean protested. "Doing so could tip off the Serpent that there is a connection. It could present enough of a connection in the Serpent's mind that he may decide to question you on it, and we just can't take that chance for this to work the way I want it to work."

"Maybe I can send him a postcard," Nicole hopefully stated.

Sean chuckled. "I'm sure Tony will be a bit worried, but he'll survive."

The senator's phone rang, which he answered. "Hello?" It was Charlie Dawson asking for Sean.

"Hello, Charlie," Sean said. He listened intently. "No, we will be fine. I have backup here, and I know he will be of great service. We are headed to

North Carolina, and that's all I'm going to tell you. Good-bye, Charlie." Sean wrote Kent's flight numbers down and shoved the paper into his pocket. "We'll need to be leaving very soon. Kent's flight arrives in a couple hours."

# Sipes's Manor

Norman Sipes was sitting at his desk in his home office with a cup of coffee and the morning paper. Headlines screamed across the top of the paper, heralding the death at the upscale, exclusive nightclub. It seemed like a nightmare, but the paper confirmed that it had happened. The horrors of the night before flashed before his eyes: Carol's lifeless body falling to the dance floor. He recalled Nicole trying to get to her friend and the shots that seemed to be fired in every direction. He was actually amazed that there was only one person dead. He read the sketchy details in the paper, but there was nothing really there that shed any light on the incident.

David knocked on his office door and opened it. "I'm sorry to bother you, sir. There is a special agent at the gate with another subpoena and is insisting on giving it you to personally."

Sipes stood up and swore at his butler. "What the fuck is Jenkins up to now?"

"I have no idea, sir," David said, opening the door further for Sipes to walk through. "I tried—"

"Don't worry about it, David. The man is a jackass, and I'm sure he just wants to make sure I know I'm to be in front of his little puppet of a committee on Monday morning." Sipes continued to walk to the foyer and out the front door. He walked all the way to the gate, where Special Agent Kevin Thompson was standing.

"Sir, this isn't a good idea," Thompson said, looking around, wondering if the Serpent was waiting to take a shot at the retired general.

"Tell that to your boss, jackass," Sipes answered. "Now give me the damn subpoena and tell Jenkins I'll be there Monday morning with my counsel."

"This isn't for that committee. This is a different one. This is in reference to the investigation into the president's assassination," Thompson answered flatly.

Sipes stopped in his tracks. Thompson could tell that he was taken by surprise, and the guilt almost showed on his face. Sipes recovered quickly.

"Young man, I'm a retired three-star general. You can tell Senator Jenkins that this is quite an insult. I outranked that little pisser back then, and I had nothing to do with the assassination of my commander in chief."

"I'll tell him, sir. You still need to take this, and another agent, very familiar with the case, wanted me to pass along that your life is in danger. Would you like us to provide some protection for you?"

"I don't know what you all are smoking down there at the Capitol, but my life is not in danger, and I'm not involved in the assassination, so go fuck off."

"I will be right over there if you need anything or maybe want to tell me something," Thompson said.

"Suit yourself, buddy, but it is a waste of time," Sipes called to him as he turned to walk back to his home.

Thompson was still standing at the gate when he called to Sipes, "That's just what the other agent said." He returned to his car, got in, and watched Sipes quickly walk back to his mansion, slamming the door behind him.

Once inside, Sipes returned to his office. He sat down behind his desk as he started to read the subpoena. This indeed was a different subpoena. Sipes could feel his blood pressure rise and a sense of panic set into his chest. He got up and poured himself a whiskey. He had to think. What was he going to say? What would he have to tell his attorney? He returned to his desk and sat down. Trying to calm himself, he started to go down his very short list of options.

Meanwhile, Kevin Thompson sat outside in his car, keeping track of cars passing him on the street and a general eye on the manor. He found it odd that a van approached Sipes's residence and was admitted beyond the property gate. He took out his binoculars and watched as a man got out of the van and was greeted by the butler. After a brief discussion, the butler went back inside and the man started to wash and detail the general's car that was parked in front of the manor. Nothing seemed out of the ordinary, especially because the butler didn't show any signs of alarm. After a few hours, the man was done working on the car and left the premises. Thompson noted the license plate as the van pulled out and drove down the street.

*Blind Influence* | 171

Back inside the manor, in his office, Sipes was still beside himself. He had been making a list of possible escape plans. Everything he could think of was on that short list of options, including suicide. He felt trapped and ashamed, but if he was going to kill himself, he wanted to leave on his terms and he would not take full responsibility. He still felt what he had done was justified, and he wanted the world to know he had not acted alone. If he was going to take the fall for Andrews's assassination, he was going to take his partners in the crime with him. He locked his office door and then set up a video camera, running a microphone to the desk. He aimed the camera at the chair behind his desk. He turned it on and then walked to sit down behind his desk. He picked up the microphone and, looking directly into the camera, raised his whiskey-filled glass in a salute and said, "Tony, if you are viewing this, then I'm dead."

It was starting to get dark when a car pulled up alongside Thompson's car outside Sipes's manor. Sean and Nicole were in that car, and Nicole wound down the window when it stopped. "Hungry?" she asked as she handed Thompson a bag of fast food and a drink.

"Starving," Thompson answered, taking the food from her.

"Have you seen anything unusual or anyone unusual?" Sean asked.

"No. There really isn't anything going on. He came out, got the subpoena, and went back inside. There were some deliveries and he got his car washed, but other than that, nothing exciting." Thompson unwrapped one of the hamburgers in the bag. "He certainly looked guilty when I told him that this was for Jenkins's special investigation into the president's assassination."

Sean looked around the property. "It's not very secure," he said as he continued to look around.

"Do you have any idea how he might do it?" Thompson asked, taking a bite of the hamburger.

"The Serpent is resourceful. It could be something as simple as getting access to a roof and shooting him from long range, to a pipe bomb in his mailbox. The only thing I can be sure of is that he won't live," Sean answered. "In any case, we'll see you on Tuesday?"

172 | *Linda Riesenberg Fisler*

"Yes. I'll be there regardless of what happens or doesn't happen here. I'll probably fly into New Bern and drive down. I'll meet you at the Dockhouse Restaurant Tuesday evening around 6:30," Thompson said.

"See you then," Sean said. "Be safe."

"You do the same." Thompson returned to eating as Sean drove away. From time to time, he would get out his binoculars and scan the area as well as try to peer inside the manor. All was eerily quiet, and that gave Thompson the creeps.

Inside the manor, Sipes finished filming his video. He took the VHS tape out of the recorder and placed it on his desk. He took down all the video equipment and put it away. He walked behind his desk, sat back in his chair, and looked at the ceiling. In a way, he felt like a weight had been taken off his shoulders. After a few minutes, he opened the center drawer of his desk and removed a manila envelope. With a marker, he wrote, "For Tony Shafer's eyes only." He placed the tape inside the envelope and sealed it. He got up from the desk, walked to the door of his home office, and called for David.

"Yes, sir?" David asked as he walked into the office.

"David, if anything happens to me over the next couple days, if I die or am killed, I want you to take this envelope to Tony Shafer immediately. Do you understand?"

"Yes, sir, but I really wish you wouldn't talk that way. Nothing is going to happen to you," David answered, taking the envelope from him. "Is there anything else, sir?"

"I'm ready for dinner when you are. I'll eat in the dining room."

"Very well, sir. It will be ready in about five minutes." David retreated from the office and closed the door behind him. He tossed the envelope on the table in the foyer and shook his head. *The old coot is at it again*, he thought as he walked to the kitchen to finish up dinner.

Throughout the night, Thompson kept an eye out, but nothing really stood out to him as odd. He held vigil as he had been instructed even

*Blind Influence* | 173

though all involved thought it would be hopeless to try to prevent the inevitable. He played the radio from time to time to keep himself awake, and he occasionally got out to stretch his legs. He knew it was going to be a long night.

# Day Seven

# The Journey to a Safe Haven?

Sean and Nicole drove over to Dulles after leaving Thompson. The drive to the airport gave Sean time to give some final instructions to Nicole, cautioning her not to say too much to Kent, who was excellent at extracting information without someone being aware of it.

They picked up Kent at the curb in front of the baggage claim area. Sean, with help from Nicole, found their way to Interstate 95 heading south. After a short introduction, Nicole looked straight ahead. She really had no desire to learn more about Kent.

"Heading south? Where are we going?" Kent asked.

"We are going to North Carolina. A friend of Nicole's has a beach house there, and well, I figured that would be a safer place to keep her than in DC," Sean answered.

"I could go for a little vacation," Kent answered.

"This is no vacation, Kent. You know how the Serpent is. He'll find her, especially if he knows I'm with her."

Kent didn't answer, but he had to admit that Sean had done his homework. If the Serpent wanted Nicole dead, all he had to do was tell Kent to take care of it for him, but with Sean in the equation, the Serpent would be sure to show up. For some reason unknown to Kent, the Serpent couldn't resist the temptation to kill Sean with his own hands when the time was right.

Sean looked in the mirror to see if he could determine what Kent was thinking. Kent assuredly was thinking about how the events would play out. "Get some sleep, Kent. We have a long drive and, when we get there, some work to do," Sean instructed.

"You are quite a lady to let this guy use you as bait," Kent said to Nicole.

Nicole looked at Kent but did not say a word. The look was so stern that it caused Kent to think twice about trying to continue his conversation with her. He decided to sit back and close his eyes even though he had just slept on the flight over to DC.

176 | *Linda Riesenberg Fisler*

Sean had to admit Nicole's was the coldest stare he had ever seen. Nicole turned her head back to look out the front windshield. Out of the corner of his eye, Sean could see a little curl of a smile on her lips as she was certain Sean was looking.

The drive was uneventful and it was mid-afternoon on Sunday when they reached Emerald Isle. This particular barrier island of North Carolina ran east to west in direction and was situated across Bogue Sound from the city of Morehead. Its unusual position in the outer banks made it possible to watch the sun rise and set over water. The barrier island housed a number of quaint incorporated villages, and at one time in history, a large portion had been owned by the Roosevelt family. Emerald Isle was located on the southwestern tip of the island and was so named because of the emerald color of the ocean water. The beach was wide at low tide, and the surf was pounding. In the fall, the temperatures were warm, with the wind keeping it quite comfortable. The barrier island was dotted with a combination of beach houses, motels, and condominiums. There were a few restaurants on the island, and a grocery store located on the main island road close by Senator Jenkins's beach house.

Located right on the beach, nestled behind a sand dune, the Sand Castle was a majestic beach house. It stood proudly above the neighboring, older beach homes on either side. Constructed of cedar-stained wood, the Sand Castle had all the latest amenities.

Sean parked the car under the building. Exiting the car, they climbed the stairs up to the first level. He unlocked the door, opening it for Nicole to enter.

"Is anyone renting the other side?" Kent asked.

"No," Sean answered. "There is an adjoining door here, so we'll make a sweep and secure the outer doors. It should be fine. There are not a lot of renters this time of year."

"Your friend owns this? What do they do? This place isn't cheap," Kent remarked, looking around.

It was Senator Jenkins's respite, and he had offered it to Sean during their discussion about setting the trap. Nicole had never really thought of Senator Jenkins as a friend. "He's a CEO," she replied. She opened the drapes

*Blind Influence* | 177

that revealed sliding glass doors. Beyond was the sand dune that provided protection from the sea. "I suppose a walk on the beach is out of the question." Nicole looked at Sean.

"Not right this minute," Sean answered. "We need to get a list together for Kent to go shopping."

"Shopping? Let Nikki do it," Kent answered. "I'm not your patsy."

"You asked Charlie how you can help, Kent. I'm in the lead. If you don't like that, you can start walking to the airport," Sean answered. "We are going to need some food and other supplies." Sean walked over to a desk and removed some stationery that had been left for guests to use. "We'll take turns cooking." Sean didn't want the responsibility of cooking to be arbitrarily assigned to Nicole. He wasn't the best cook, but he could whip something together when he had to do so.

Nicole sat on the couch and flipped on the television. "Do either of you know how to cook?"

Both Sean and Kent looked at one another. "I wouldn't brag about my cooking abilities. It is edible sometimes." Sean answered looking at Kent, who just shrugged his shoulders.

"I didn't think so. How about grilling? There is a grill outside." Nicole asked.

"I may have done that once or twice," Sean answered.

"I order things grilled occasionally," Kent added.

"Hopeless," Nicole answered. "I'll do the cooking, thank you. You'll clean up after the meal." Sean had found a pen and started to write some items on the paper when Nicole started to add to it. "Bottled water, flashlights, batteries, canned goods, can opener, radio that runs on batteries—"

"What?" Sean said, turning to Nicole.

"Evidently, there is a hurricane brewing. Not a very big one, but there is one, and it seems to be headed this way."

"Oh, lovely!" Kent answered. "Didn't you check the weather before you created this plan?"

"It's a tropical storm. If it gets worse, we'll figure out a contingency. When are they projecting landfall?"

"Looks like either Tuesday or Wednesday."

"We'll keep an eye on it," Sean said as he turned his attention back to the list.

Indeed, there was a storm brewing in the waters of the Atlantic, and the weather forecasts were predicting no more than a category one. *In a strange way, that brewing hurricane with its churning water out at sea and preceding calm along the beach is much like what is occurring in my life right now*, Nicole thought. She turned her gaze out the sliding glass doors as she watched the sea oats sway gently in the breeze. She thought about Carol and how she was already missing her best friend. Her eyes filled with tears, and she swore that if she had the chance, she'd kill the Serpent herself. Visions of Carol danced in front of her, mimicking the sea oats. She could hear Carol's laugh and see her body swaying gracefully, embodying the very essence of her carefree spirit. She smiled at the image. Nicole was so deep in thought she didn't hear Sean and Kent disappear out the door to get their luggage. A few tears escaped Nicole's eyes as Carol's dancing image before her waned, and she was startled back into reality as Sean opened the front door. She quickly wiped the tears from her cheek, giving thanks for her long hair, which she hoped shielded her face.

"Nicole and I will take the two bedrooms upstairs. You can bunk in the one on this floor," Sean told Kent as he headed toward the stairs. Nicole stood up and started to walk to the stairs as well. Sean could see that she was upset. "Let's get unpacked, and Kent can head to the store. We'll go for that short walk on the beach," he added, looking at Nicole. He waited for her to go up the stairs first.

Kent looked at Sean. When Nicole was halfway up the stairs, he stated, "If I didn't know better, Sean, I'd say you're a bit smitten with Ms. Charbonneau." He winked at his former partner.

Sean looked at Kent. This was the second time now that someone had mentioned his having feelings for Nicole. "I have a job to do, Kent. So do you. Let's not get off track," Sean answered sounding a little annoyed.

"Relax. Sarah's been dead for ten years. It's about time you found someone else," Kent said flatly.

Sean wasn't sure if he was falling for Nicole, and he certainly didn't need to be distracted by the thought of possibly falling in love. His mission for the past ten years had been to capture or kill the man who had murdered the two most important people in his life. All he had felt for the past ten years was the hate that the Serpent had burned into his soul by torturing to death his wife and child. After that day, Sean had never been very sure he would ever be able to love again, but now, someone else was sharing his nightmare. Someone else could identify the Serpent and was living in the same hell he was living. Sean couldn't deny that Nicole was stunning and brave. He acknowledged to himself that he felt attracted to this lovely lady before him. He looked up to see that Nicole was almost at the top of the stairs. Could she be his savior? Could she reach into his soul and provide a way back to the living?

Sean swallowed back the thoughts and in a quiet, calm voice, answered Kent. "Sarah was the one, Kent. There will never be anyone else. And even if there was any chance of anyone else, this is not the time to muddy the waters with those thoughts. We have a job to do."

Kent smiled as he turned to pick up the grocery list and started for the door. "Whatever you say, old friend, but I don't believe it for a minute." Kent shut the door behind himself, satisfied he had planted the seed of doubt that could throw Sean off his game.

Nicole had stopped at the top of stairs when she'd heard Sean's answer. She was looking at Sean when he looked up at her. "He can be a real pain in the ass, you know that?" Nicole stated, skirting the whole issue of the attraction that she felt growing between them.

Sean laughed as he started up the stairs. "Much too well," he answered, still laughing. "Let's get these up in the room and go for that walk." Sean was relieved that Nicole was quite content to not address what they were feeling. There wasn't much daylight left, and a walk on the beach sounded nice to Sean as well.

# Washington, DC

*T*he Serpent had changed his identity. He was now a blonde, and the contact lenses changed his eye color to hazel. He was sorting through his passports to find the one that matched his new look. Finding what he was looking for, he replaced the other passports in a secret compartment of his suitcase. He walked over to the minibar, taking a small bottle of vodka and pouring its contents into a glass. His hand was slow to heal and still bothered him. He had stopped for an ACE bandage, which he had wrapped around his hand. He had been careful to keep it clean and wrapped. When asked by any nosy American, he would reply that he had slightly sprained it.

All he could do now was to wait for information. He always felt that waiting was his strength, but it seemed to be harder now. The assassination had happened days ago, and President Andrews had already been buried. The loose ends were still dangling out there in front of him, and he was growing restless, as he knew that the longer they were alive, the greater the chance of being caught. He took a drink of his vodka, cursing the loose ends that could place him here and could cause his identity to be known before he could leave the country. He knew Sean was here, and he knew the cat-and-mouse game was proceeding, but American law enforcement agencies may not want to sit idly by and let the game continue.

The phone rang and shattered the silence in the room. He walked over to the phone and picked it up. "Yes?" The Serpent listened intently to the voice on the other end. He took mental notes and then hung up the receiver when he had all he needed to know. His informant had performed admirably again. He gathered his things quickly, as he had a long drive ahead of him. Perhaps by midweek, he could return to his beloved France and enjoy the sanctity of his humble abode, admiring the view from his chateau in the Lot Valley. He paused as he thought of his peaceful refuge. *I'll be there soon enough*, he thought and forced himself to continue to pack. For now, he needed to secure a rental car and maps that could lead him to North Carolina.

*Blind Influence* | 181

# Alaska's North Slope

John Spencer, Senator Jenkins's aide who had been dispatched to Alaska, walked off the plane and was greeted by Ahnah. It was mid-afternoon, and John had traveled nonstop to Fairbanks, thanks to a favor owed to Senator Jenkins. John had managed to sleep a little on the plane until it had hit the turbulence that caused the motion sickness that he always dreaded. Ahnah drove them from Fairbanks to the North Slope, her people's homeland. Ahnah and her family welcomed the stranger into their home. There was nothing outlandish or ornate about this little home, but it was protection from the harsh climate. Although their home was isolated, it provided exactly what was needed. She showed John to his room. John almost felt embarrassed that he would have a bedroom all to himself. He told Ahnah that he would be quite comfortable on the couch, but she would not hear of it.

John unpacked and met them in the kitchen of the small home. He looked at Ahnah's mother and father, who were sitting at a small kitchen table. The years of hardship showed in their faces. Ahnah was young and shielded from the bitter weather and years of hard work. Working several jobs and saving every penny had allowed Ahnah's parents to send their children to college. Ahnah and her brothers had all returned to their homeland in hopes of making a difference. They hoped that the knowledge they had gained would help them preserve their land and way of life, shielding them from what was currently occurring in their backyard.

Upon entering the room he greeted Ahnah's parents. "Thank you for your kindness," he said as he bowed slightly. He was not real sure of protocol in this situation. The parents acknowledged John with slight head bows.

"I thought you might be hungry," Ahnah said as she presented him with a sandwich. "What can I get you to drink?"

"Yes. Thank you," John said, taking the plate from her. "Water will be fine." Ahnah fulfilled his request. John took a bite of the sandwich made of lunch meat, some kind of ham. He took a drink of water and then asked, "Tell me what you know about the people trying to drill on your land."

Ahnah sighed. "Not much. Did you see the photographs that we left with Nikki?"

182 | *Linda Riesenberg Fisler*

"Yes, the senator has those now," John said. "The equipment has no marking on it?"

"No, there are none. If we try to approach or talk to them, they threaten us with their weapons. Nikki told us not to engage them."

"But one of your people did?"

"Yes, my cousin did. They were laying this huge pipe on his land, and he wanted it removed. This wasn't far from his home, and it is clearly his land. He confronted them, and they shot him in front of his family."

"Where is his family now?" John asked.

"They are in their home. His wife will not leave. She has a rifle with her at all times, and if any of them even draws a gun on her children, she has made it known that she will kill them." Ahnah paused. "John, she will do it. She can do it from a far distance."

John smiled. "I have no doubt." He finished his sandwich and drink. He placed the dishes in the sink. "You have more photos of the progress."

"Yes." Ahnah walked past him and headed to the family room. She returned with a manila envelope that contained seven rolls of film. "I have seven rolls of film now. I had told Senator Jenkins we had six. We just finished shooting an additional roll earlier today."

"We need to get these sent back to Senator Jenkins. Do you have a box that I can use? I want to make sure they are protected."

"Yes. I have one in the other room." Ahnah said.

"I would like to pay the drill site a visit," John said.

"I'll drive you over to our campsite." Ahnah said.

"Thank you again for your hospitality," John said to Ahnah's parents.

"Thank us by getting them off our land," her father replied.

*Blind Influence* | 183

"That is what I am hoping to do." John turned to Ahnah. "Before we leave, I'd like to make arrangements to get the photos to the airport in Fairbanks. Is there someone you trust to run that errand for us?"

"Yes." Ahnah answered putting on her coat. John followed her lead.

John requested another of Ahnah's many cousins be dispatched to take the box of film to the airport in Fairbanks. Through a couple of phone calls, he arranged for the package to fly on the required flights and then for an aide to pick them up at National Airport in DC. From there, they would be developed and delivered to Senator Jenkins personally. Jenkins's aide Chris would be in the presence of the film from picking it up at National until it was in Jenkins's hands. Within twenty-four hours, those photographs, including those of the murder of Ahnah's cousin, would be in the hands of someone who could get to the bottom of this.

John and Ahnah left for the drill site. John instructed her to pull the car over a safe distance from the site. She took him to where Ahnah and her brothers were doing their observation of the drill site. As the car pulled up, her brothers, Annakpok and Nagojut, turned. They waved and walked back to meet the car. John got out of the car, taking notice of the campsite that the two men had assembled. Both of the brothers noticed his surveillance of their camp.

"I assure you, this is our land," Nagojut started, somewhat defensively.

John smiled. "That wasn't what I was thinking."

"What were you thinking?" Annakpok asked.

"How I would have liked to have had some of the luxuries you have here in Vietnam," John answered. He extended his hand. "I am John Spencer. I'm an aide to Senator Robert Jenkins. I served with him in Vietnam. He was my commander. We were both Navy Seals."

Both men shook his hand. Nagojut began, "I'm sorry for my defensiveness."

John held up his hand. "No apology needed. I would feel the same if I were in your position." They walked to where they could observe the drill site.

John was shocked to see that the platform was almost complete. "They aren't wasting any time, are they?"

"It is almost as if they were told to speed things up," Annakpok started. "They have been working through the night for the past couple of days."

"Well, I think it is about time for me to say hello." John retreated a bit from their vantage point. He opened his coat and suit jacket to reveal a .357 Magnum in his shoulder holster. He removed the gun and put it in the pocket of his coat. He grabbed his congressional credentials out of his breast pocket and placed them in the other hand. At this point, Nagojut and Annakpok retrieved their rifles, meeting back up with John as he started for the drill site. "Whoa! Where do you think you are going?"

"We are going with you," Nagojut stated flatly.

"No," John said. The brothers started to protest. "They won't shoot me here. Not when I tell them that I have been sent by Senator Jenkins and he knows I'm here. They won't cooperate, either, but they will get word back to their bosses that they have been found out. That will buy us some time. If they do shoot me and kill me"—he turned to Ahnah and gave her a card from his pocket—"call Senator Jenkins directly and tell him what happened. If that does occur, all hell will break loose on Capitol Hill, believe me."

Ahnah took the card. "You are that sure of yourself?"

John looked at Ahnah. "I know the senator very well. He only sends me on missions like this because we both know there is a risk of being killed. It is what I do for him. If I die here, I know it won't be in vain." John started to walk toward the drill site. He stopped and turned. "Of course, if you have a clear shot at the bastard who shoots me, take it." He gave a smile and started walking again.

Nagojut and Annakpok took their positions to provide cover for John, and they did so in clear sight of the men at the drill site. Ahnah stood above them, the wind blowing her long black hair. She stood above her brothers in clear sight, almost a dare for the men to shoot her. Just as confident as John, she knew they would not shoot her—not because she was a woman, but because their rifles could not reach her. Their armaments were limited in distance, and she and her brothers were at a safe distance.

*Blind Influence* | 185

John walked down to the drill site, which caught the attention of some of the men. "We have a visitor!" one of the men yelled down to the foreman. The foreman turned and looked in the direction in which the man pointed. He grabbed his rifle and started out to meet John. He knew by looking at the man that this was not one of the Inuit that he had been dealing with over the past few weeks.

When John saw the man starting to approach with a rifle, he raised his hands. Ahnah swung her satchel around and removed her camera. She began taking pictures. In one of John's hands were his credentials. Nothing was in his other hand. "I'm showing you my congressional credentials." John yelled loud enough so even the men on the drilling platform could hear him. "I've been sent here by Senator Robert Jenkins."

"His jurisdiction isn't recognized here," the foreman called back and then spit some of his chewing tobacco on the ground in defiance.

"Well, we'll let Congress decided that," John said as he kept walking. He and the foreman met halfway, and the foreman looked over the credentials. John was close to the platform and about ten yards from the ring of trucks. He was five yards from the chainlink fence that completely circled the drilling site.

"You know, I wouldn't know a fake congressional credential from a real one." The foreman spat again, squinting while he looked John over.

"It's real. I'm John Spencer. I'm an aide to Senator Jenkins, who has been informed that you are about to drill on land that doesn't belong to you."

"No one owns this land. It's an easement," the foreman shot back.

"Oh, I see. So you work for the State of Alaska?" John asked. The foreman spit his tobacco dangerously close to John's shoe. John smirked at the man's attempt to scare him. "You want go there?" John retorted. "I don't think so."

"We don't work for the State of Alaska."

"Who do you work for?" John asked. "Just so you know, this is an official congressional inquiry. As we speak, Senator Jenkins is creating a formal investigation." John felt that providing the information might open the door of communication a slight bit. He quickly found out he was wrong.

"That's none of your fucking business," the foreman answered. "And unless you have some kind of subpoena, I don't have to answer your questions."

"That is true, I don't have a subpoena, and I don't have any kind of an order to make you stop yet. I thought maybe you'd tell me who you are working for and we could work this from Washington between the big guys."

"I'm not answering your questions, and until my bosses tell me to stop, I'm not stopping. Even an order from Congress won't stop that."

"Well then, you'll need to tell me what company you are with so that I can send them the order."

"That isn't going to fucking happen," the foreman said as he shifted his weight.

As the conversation between the foreman and John continued, a man from the platform walked down to one of the trucks that circled around the drill site. This particular truck seemed to be a storage truck and was in John's sight. As the man opened the back door of the truck, John moved his hand to the pocket of his coat, grasping his gun, unsure of the man's actions. The man slid open the tractor trailer's door and then jumped up into the trailer. John realized that in his peripheral vision was the answer he wanted. There in plain sight was the logo for an oil company. The man who had opened the trailer's door turned, looking right at John, as if he wanted John to see which company was responsible.

John looked in the opposite direction as he started to frame his next statement. He wanted to make sure that he didn't draw any attention to the man's clearly rebellious act. "So, I suppose we are going to stand here all day. You're telling me"—John heard another truck door opening in the opposite direction and acted like he was trying to see what was in it, purposely drawing attention from the first man's effort—"it's none of my business."

The foreman shifted his position, looking in the direction that John was now looking. "I'm not standing here all day, and neither are you." The foreman cocked the rifle and pointed it at him. With the attention off of

*Blind Influence* | 187

him, the man who had provided the help climbed down from the truck, closed the truck door quietly, and returned to the drill platform with the needed tool. "I think it is time for you to go." The foreman moved the rifle, indicating the direction that John should take his leave.

"Yeah, I guess it is." John started taking steps backward from the foreman. "But one thing is for sure."

"What's that, jackass?" the foreman asked.

"I'll be back," John said as he smiled at the foreman.

"Now that wouldn't be too smart, and you look like a really smart man."

"I'll be back, and you'll be packing up then," John said as he continued to walk backward, still facing the foreman.

The foreman grew tired of watching John back away from him, so he turned his back to John and returned to his work. He disappeared inside one of the trailers that had been set up for the men to live in.

When John reached Ahnah and her brothers, he was smiling. "I need to call the senator as quickly as I can." He noticed that Ahnah had been taking photographs. "You didn't happen to get a shot of the guy in the truck, did you?"

"What guy in the truck?" she asked sincerely.

"Damn," John answered. "Well, doesn't matter. We got 'em!" The three looked at John like he was out of his mind.

"He told you who they are working for?" Annakpok asked.

"No. I have something even better. When I was talking to the foreman, a guy opened a truck there on the southern side. It had the logo of the company on the inside. He meant for me to see it." John headed back to the car. "Let's go, I need to call Bobby."


It was late Sunday night, and Senator Jenkins was seated at his desk, working on the questions he wanted to ask Norman Sipes. Sipes was scheduled

188 | *Linda Riesenberg Fisler*

to appear before his committee on Monday morning around ten o'clock. Jenkins had a number of reports laid across his desk, and he reached over to pick up one of the financial reports. It was late, and he rubbed his eyes. His phone rang, and he looked up at his clock. He wondered who could be calling him at eleven o'clock at night. He reached for the phone and answered it. It was his friend and aide John Spencer.

"Yes, John. Good to hear from you," Jenkins said. "Yes, Chris said that you had called and he will be meeting the plane in the morning." Jenkins listened intently. "Are you sure?" Jenkins sat forward in his chair as he listened to John's findings. "Well, this is most interesting. Is there any way to get a photo of that logo?" Jenkins listened to John's answer, which basically was that if there was a will, there was a way. "John, I don't want you putting yourself in harm's way. Well, do what you can, but don't take any risk that puts your life in danger. After all, I have Norman Sipes in front of my committee tomorrow. If I play my cards correctly, those photos should be available for me to use in the afternoon session. It makes perfect sense. His finances are in shambles, and drilling in the ANWR with the only access to that oil would put him in a better position financially. It is absolutely mind-boggling that he actually thought he could get away with drilling illegally." Jenkins listened to John's comment. "Well, that is true that he has no business sense and feels entitled. Well, see what you can do, and be very careful. I have no doubt they have shoot-to-kill orders. Thank you, John. Good night."

The senator sat back and pondered the information he had just been given. This information changed how he wanted the proceedings to go in the morning. He looked up at the clock and decided it was time to go to bed. He was very anxious for morning to come, and he wanted to get some rest.

# Day Eight

# Sipes's Manor

Kevin Thompson was extremely happy to see the first rays of sunlight. It had been a real hardship trying to stay awake through the night, and he was happy to get the little bit of relief that came from Chris, Senator Jenkins's aide, in the wee hours of the morning. He drove around the property, walked around the outside of Sipes's property, looking for any signs of mischief. There were none. He looked at his watch and figured that in a few minutes, Norman Sipes would be on his way to either his lawyer's office or to the congressional hearing he had been subpoenaed to appear in front of. He was actually looking forward to this part of his duties ending and to be on his way to join back up with Sean and Nicole.

After fifteen minutes had passed, Sipes exited his home and walked to the Lincoln Town Car that had been parked in the same spot since Thompson had arrived. Sipes turned to say something to his butler and then walked around to the driver's side of the car. He opened the passenger-side door to the backseat and threw his briefcase onto the backseat. He opened the driver's side door and maneuvered his big body behind the steering wheel. He reached out and closed the car door. Then it happened. With the turn of the key to start the car, the car bomb exploded. The very loud explosion rocked the windows of Sipes's house and Thompson's car. A plume of black smoke and orange flames reached as high as the roof of Sipes's manor.

House alarms, set off by the shockwave, began to screech all around Thompson, who was just now uncovering his head, which he had shielded out of reaction more than necessity. There was no escape for Norman Sipes. Thompson watched the flames and knew that nothing would be left that would point anyone in the direction of the Serpent. Through the flames he could see someone peering through the door and figured it had to be Sipes's butler. Thompson started his car, leaving the scene to inform Jenkins of the incident.

David rushed to the door after regaining his footing in the hallway of the mansion. He broke the door off the last hinge to see the town car engulfed in flames. He quickly retreated inside to call for emergency help. As he headed back to the front door, he saw the envelope that Sipes had given him two nights before. He picked it up and placed it with some personal possessions in his room. He would do as Sipes had requested. He would deliver the package to Tony Shafer as soon as he could get away.

David stood watching the car burn, and when he heard the sirens of the fire engine approaching, he pushed the button that would open the front gate. It was like a dream. Everything was moving in slow motion. One of the firemen moved him out of the manor's doorway to the back of one of the ambulances. He had not even been aware that he had injured his hand removing the door from the hinge.

While David was sitting on the bumper of the ambulance, a police officer approached him. David tried his best to answer the questions being asked. He was visibly shaken, and as the reality that his employer had just been murdered began to sink in, he could feel his fears begin to grow. He wanted to flee. He hadn't done anything wrong, but he also didn't want to think that he could be next. The police officer said his name a number of times to get his attention again. No, he didn't know of anyone who wanted his employer dead. No, there had been nothing out of the ordinary over night or the day before. He provided the police with the names of those who had visited over the past week. Although David was not intentionally trying to omit anything except the manila envelope, he did forget to mention the car detailer who had insisted that Sipes had made an appointment with him and had just forgotten to tell David. The man had come during the time when Sipes had given David strict orders not to be disturbed, so he had let the gentleman in to wash and buff the car. He paid the man very little attention, and the man had been gone within two hours. The old coot was strange that way; he often forgot appointments. David truly gave it no thought.

The forensic unit arrived. The gory, meticulous search for clues and evidence would begin shortly. The police conducted a few searches around the premises to secure them, placing the yellow crime scene tape in plain view. Neighbors were gathering, and the press began to circle and report from the scene. The firefighters had extinguished the flames, but the remains were too hot for anyone to touch as yet. A smoldering blue wispy mist eerily circled the embers of the car. David wondered if that was the soul of Sipes hanging around in confusion about what just occurred.

A police officer informed David that the property was being considered a crime scene and that he could no longer stay at the mansion. David asked if he was allowed to return to his room to pack a bag and gather some personal items. He was granted that opportunity, and he walked, still in shock, to his room. Into the suitcase went some clothes and the mysterious manila envelope.

The police escorted him to a squad car, which drove him to a nearby hotel. He of course was told that he shouldn't plan on going anywhere, as the police were sure to have additional questions as the investigation proceeded. He was free to come and go, but not allowed to leave the DC area.

David checked in to the hotel. He unpacked his bag and decided to shower. He thought the shower would help clear his head. He knew he needed to get that envelope to Tony Shafer, but it could wait until after he showered.

# Capitol Hill

$\mathcal{T}$hompson arrived at Senator Jenkins's office and walked in to see Chris on the phone. He hung up the phone in a few minutes, finishing the conversation with an aide in another Senator's office. "Is Senator Jenkins in his office?" Thompson asked when Chris hung up the phone.

"No, he's in the committee room, waiting for Sipes to arrive," Chris answered.

"Sipes won't be appearing before the committee. He's dead," Thompson said. "Where can I find the senator?"

"You'll need clearance, but I can make those arrangements." Chris gave him directions to the committee hearing room. He then picked up the phone and made a call. Thompson waited until Chris nodded his head to acknowledge that his clearance was granted.

Thompson walked into the committee room and directly to Senator Jenkins, who saw him enter and excused himself from the conversation he was having with two other senators. "Senator Jenkins, might I have a word in private?" Thompson asked as he met Jenkins in the center of the committee room. The senator took him by the arm and motioned to an area where they could have a quiet conversation.

"I assume since you are here and Sipes is not that our friend was successful in his mission?" Jenkins asked in whisper.

"If you mean that Sipes is dead, then you are correct," Thompson answered bluntly.

"How?"

"It was a car bomb. I'm sorry I missed this. There was a visit from a car detailer, but I didn't put two and two together," Thompson answered.

"It seems the Serpent is very resourceful. Sean was certain Sipes wouldn't be alive for very long, so I don't think it is a reflection on you." Jenkins thought for a moment. "In any case, you need to get down to North Carolina, as Sean requested."

*Blind Influence* | 195

"Yes, I do," Thompson agreed. "The DC police are securing the scene, and if you need anything, call Chief Bailey and tell him I sent you."

"Thank you. Will you give a message to Nicole? Tell her that we have some interesting evidence coming in from her friends in Alaska. We need to obtain a few more photos, but we are pretty sure we know who is drilling there. Also tell her we are actively working the case."

"You know she is going to ask who you suspect is doing the drilling."

"Yes, but until I see it with my own two eyes, I won't say who it is." Jenkins smiled. "I just want to reassure her that we are actively working the case. Safe travels, and you have my sincerest wishes that I see the three of you again." He extended his hand, and Thompson accepted it.

"Me too. Keep sharp," Thompson answered as he left the committee room.

Jenkins headed to the front of the room where the senators and congressmen were standing, discussing various legislation. Jenkins took his spot behind the chairman's desk and gaveled the room to order. Everyone moved to their seats, and a silence fell over the room. Jenkins sat for a second, letting the weight of the silence linger. "My fellow senators, congressmen, and congresswomen ... " He paused, looking at the members of the committee. "It is with sincere regret that I have to inform this committee that Norman Sipes was killed this morning." Gasps filled the committee room, with exclamations of disbelief. "There is an investigation occurring as I am addressing you, by the DC police. At this time, I am adjourning this hearing for today. Thank you for your time and understanding"

Jenkins gaveled the committee hearing to a close and rushed out of the room, not stopping to talk to anyone. He quickly walked back to his office, where he met Chris, who was just leaving the office. "I'm on my way to National, sir. Do you need anything?"

"I just need that important cargo as quickly as you can, Chris. I am asking you to be very careful. There is a lot here that just isn't adding up," Jenkins said as he headed into his office. After he walked into his inner office, he picked up the phone and began dialing.

---

196 | *Linda Riesenberg Fisler*

When the line was picked up, he said, "Hello, this is Senator Jenkins. Is John available?" He waited for the answer on the other end. "Yes, could you get word to him that I need to talk with him as quickly as he can call me back? Perfect! Thank you, Ahnah. I appreciate all you are doing to help us. Yes, well, we really need to shut this down. Thank you. Good-bye." He hung up the phone and pulled out a folder from his desk drawer. He opened another drawer and retrieved a legal pad of paper. He began to write down some names, starting with President Andrews.

# Washington, DC

*D*avid arrived at the offices of Rosen, Shafer, and Pruett, paying the taxi before heading inside the building with what he could only surmise to be Sipes's last will or maybe some last-minute changes to his will. It was all too surreal for David. He just wanted to deliver this envelope and get back to his hotel room. He wanted this all to end. He rode the elevator up to the fifteenth floor, where the doors opened to the reception area of the law offices.

Tony was at the reception desk, and he wasn't happy. "Jean, I don't care who you have to call. Call Chief Bailey or that ex of hers, the Secret Service agent. Hell, I don't give a fuck if you call Senator Jenkins. Someone has got to know where she is!" He paused when he saw David. "David, what are you doing here?"

"You haven't heard, then?" David asked.

"Heard what?"

"The general's dead. It was a car bomb."

Jean gasped, and a desperate "Oh no!" escaped her lips.

"What?" Tony exclaimed in disbelief. His world was falling apart. First, the president's assassination, then Carol Gartner's murder, Nicole's disappearance, and now his friend Norman Sipes murdered by a car bomb. He wondered who would be next. "Just what the hell is going on here?" He yelled, his trademark composure still eluding him.

"I have no idea," David answered. "I was instructed on Saturday by the general to deliver this envelope to you if anything should happen to him. I have no idea what it is, and frankly, I want to keep it that way." He extended his hand that held the envelope toward Tony. "So here it is. This is my last official duty for General Sipes."

Tony accepted the envelope and watched David turn to the elevator and wait for the doors to open. When the doors finally opened, David entered and depressed the button to the ground floor and what he now considered his freedom from all that had happened.

198 | *Linda Riesenberg Fisler*

Tony stood looking at the envelope, then at the elevator doors. "Amazing," he uttered. "The elevator never gets there that quickly when I need it!" He looked at Jean, who was giving a little smirk behind the hand over her mouth. Tony shook his head and headed back to his office. As he opened the door to the aisle that led to his office, he turned to Jean and demanded. "Get me Senator Jenkins on the phone now! I'll be damned if he gets away with this."

Tony reached his office and grabbed his remote. He turned on his television to a local news station. There was the live report outside of Sipes's manor. He could barely see the burned-out shell of Sipes's town car through all the commotion, police, and forensic vehicles. The reporter was giving sketchy details, but it was true. Norman Sipes was dead, murdered by what appeared to be a car bomb.

Tony walked to the bar and poured himself a whiskey. He opened the mysterious envelope delivered by David. He shook the contents onto his desk. It was a VHS tape. On the label was Tony's name, followed by a phrase that Sipes like to use far too often in their conversations. They were four little words that drove Tony crazy: "For your eyes only," Tony read them out loud. "Even from the grave, you still manage to drive me crazy." He took a drink of his whiskey. "All right, you old coot, let's see what this is about."

Tony walked over to his VHS recorder, turned it on, and inserted the tape. There was Sipes's desk in his study. Sipes appeared as he walked to his desk and sat down. He lifted his drink and said. "Tony, if you are viewing this, then I'm dead." Sipes saluted him with the glass in his hand and then took a drink. Tony sat down in disbelief. "If you are not sitting down, my friend, I suggest you do so," the recording of Sipes said. "I have a lot to tell you. You may need some paper, so I'll wait until you get your typical yellow legal pad. I always wonder if you were just doodling on that paper." Sipes laughed. "Go ahead. I'll wait." Tony did as Sipes instructed and returned to his chair. "Hold on, my friend! What I'm about to tell you is going to really rock that Puritan world of yours."

*Blind Influence* | 199

# Capitol Hill

*T*he phone rang in Senator Jenkins's office. Jenkins answered it, knowing his aides were dispensed elsewhere. "Senator Jenkins's office."

"Bobby? It's John."

"John, thanks for getting back to me so quickly. I just wanted to tell you of a development here and caution you. Norman Sipes is dead. A car bomb went off this morning in his driveway. He was on his way to my hearing, but obviously, he never made it off his property."

"Are you shitting me?" John answered in disbelief.

"No, unfortunately. I need to ask this. Do you think that any of the—"

"No. No way. These folks up here aren't like that, Bobby. They have been very helpful and from everything I can tell are adhering more to our laws than the fucking oil company is," John answered before Jenkins could finish his question.

"OK. John, get what we discussed, and then get the hell out of there. Don't take any unnecessary chances," Jenkins warned. "I don't like how this is going down, and I honestly don't think I can influence any of it."

"I'll do that," John confirmed. "Has Chris received the package yet?"

"He is retrieving it now," Jenkins answered.

"Good! I expect that I'll be back within twenty-four hours. Good-bye, Senator." John didn't wait for Jenkins's good-bye. The line went dead before Jenkins could utter another word.

As soon as Jenkins hung up the phone, it rang again. "Senator Jenkins's office." He got a strange kick out of answering his phone that way. There was always a pause on the other end as the caller recognized his southern accent.

"We need to get you more help," came the response from the other end of the call. It was Senator Barker. "It's almost lunchtime. What do you say we get a bite to eat and discuss next steps?"

"I think that would be a very good idea. I'm expecting my aide back shortly. Give me about thirty minutes. I suppose I don't have to emphasize that it be a private location."

"Those are my thoughts too. Meet me in the rotunda in thirty, then." Barker hung up.

*It seems no one has the time to say good-bye anymore,* Jenkins thought. He returned the phone to its cradle. The list of names that he had been scribbling while talking to John and then Senator Barker included all who had been killed since President Andrews. These names were on the left side of the paper. There were lines leading over to a column of names on the right of people whom Jenkins had had contact with over the same period. He then started listing names in the center. First was Senator Barker, who mentored Jenkins. He was very well respected on Capitol Hill and beyond. Under Barker's name he wrote one more—one he had hesitated to put on the list from the beginning. He wrote *Nicole* just as the phone rang once more. "Senator Jenkins's office."

Jean sounded every bit as shy as she was in person. "I have Mr. Tony Shafer for Senator Jenkins," she said. She had been trying to reach the senator for more than thirty minutes, always receiving a busy signal. She hadn't been expecting what she heard next.

"This is Senator Jenkins. Can I help you?"

"Oh, Senator. I'm sorry. I wasn't expecting you to answer your own phone." This made the senator smile. "Can I ask you to hold one moment for Mr. Shafer? I'm sorry for the inconvenience."

"The inconvenience of talking with Mr. Shafer or being put on hold?"

He could almost hear the laughter in Jean's voice when she answered. "I was referring to the inconvenience of making you wait while I put you on hold, sir."

"I'll wait. Thank you," Jenkins answered with a smile on his face.

Jean buzzed Tony's office. Tony turned the television off. He had been sitting in shock, watching the snow that had been dancing on the television screen since the tape from Sipes had stopped playing. The phone ringing had broken his shock at what he just viewed, bringing him back to the present. He walked to his desk and depressed the speaker button. "Yes?" he asked, somewhat perplexed.

"Mr. Shafer, I have Senator Jenkins for you."

"What? Oh, yes. Jenkins," Tony reminded himself. "Thanks, Jean." The phone signaled that Jenkins was on the line with a short beep. "Senator Jenkins. Thank you for taking my call."

"It is my pleasure, Mr. Shafer. What can I do for you?" Jenkins answered, detecting that there was something different in Tony's voice. "Allow me first to offer my condolences on Norman Sipes's death."

"Yes, thank you. I was about to … " Tony wasn't thinking clearly. "I'm sorry, Senator. Would it be possible to schedule some time with you later today or even tomorrow?"

"My aide isn't in the office right now. Can I have him call you back to arrange a time?"

"Yes, of course," Tony answered, trying to regain his composure.

"May I inquire as to the topic of our discussion?" Jenkins asked, curious about the confused state in which Tony seemed to be.

"I think I am now in possession of some information that you will be interested in reviewing." Tony shook his head. He really wasn't thinking clearly. "And secondly, have you heard from Nicole? I haven't seen or heard from her since her friend's murder, and quite frankly, I'm a bit concerned about her safety."

"No, I have not heard from Nicole. While that is concerning, my office isn't in the habit of running down missing persons," Jenkins answered rather sarcastically and coldly.

The senator's tone seemed to jerk Tony back to reality. "I wasn't asking you to look for her, and I didn't say she was missing. I just said that I have not seen or heard from her. I was just curious if maybe you had tried to contact her or if she had contacted you over the last few days," Tony snapped back.

"As I said, I have not. I've been a bit busy between the president's assassination and now Sipes's murder. You do remember he was to appear before my committee," Jenkins reminded him as a way to get the conversation away from Nicole's whereabouts. "I'll have Chris call you to set up a time. Thank you, Mr. Shafer." Jenkins hung up the phone and added another name to his list. Underneath *Nicole*, he added *Tony Shafer* and drew a line to Norman Sipes.

Chris entered the outer office, and Jenkins placed the pad of paper in the folder, securing it in the drawer of his desk. He stood up and grabbed his coat, meeting Chris in the outer office. "Chris, can you call Tony Shafer's office back and arrange a time for me to meet with him here in my office? Either later today or tomorrow will be good. I'm heading out to eat lunch with Senator Barker."

"What would you like me to do with these?" Chris showed him a thick manila envelope, which contained the photographs sent by John from Alaska.

"I'll take them with me. Thank you, Chris. This is a job well done," Jenkins said as he exited the door. He was already a few minutes late meeting Senator Barker.

Jenkins waved to Senator Barker as he entered the rotunda, and then the two disappeared from Capitol Hill. Barker had called his wife to arrange for the two of them to have a late lunch in the privacy of Barker's study. Barker's limo met them just outside and whisked them away to the senator's home in Georgetown.

Upon their arrival, Mrs. Barker greeted them at the door, and they exchanged pleasantries. Then Mrs. Barker said she would have their lunch brought in to them. The two gentlemen walked to the study, and Senator Barker closed the door behind him.

"So, Bobby, I've been curious about that manila envelope you have there in your hands," Barker started as he sat down in one of the two chairs opposite each other at the table where they would be having their lunch.

"As well as I am, Senator," Jenkins answered as he sat down. There was a knock on the door. The butler opened it. The staff brought in two plates of food, which they placed in front of the senators along with their drinks.

*Blind Influence* | 203

"Well, this looks very nice. Thank you," Jenkins said to the staff. The staff retreated without a word, shutting the door behind them. "Senator—"

"Please, call me Larry." While Barker was a senior senator and Jenkins's mentor, he appreciated Jenkins's show of respect by addressing him formally. Barker felt it was time for Jenkins to start considering him a friend as well.

"Larry, you certainly remember Nicole Charbonneau."

"Yes, Tony Shafer's associate, and I believe that you have an interest in her," Barker remarked as he began to eat.

Jenkins could almost feel his cheeks blush, but he cleared his throat and focused his thoughts. "I will grant you that she is a very attractive woman, but I assure you, there is nothing between us. She came to me the other day with a bit of an issue. It seems that one of her clients claim that an oil company is drilling on her clients' land illegally."

"Is her client from Texas?"

"No, Senator. Her clients are the Inuit tribe living on the North Slope." Jenkins waited as that information registered with Barker, who stopped eating and looked at Jenkins. Assured that he had the senator's full attention, Jenkins continued. "An oil company is drilling or preparing to drill in ANWR. In this little envelope are photographs of the construction of that illegal rig. They were taken by her clients, and my aide is in Alaska, conducting a more thorough investigation."

There was a knock on the door, and Mrs. Barker poked her head around. "I'm sorry to bother you, dear, but Senator Jenkins's aide is on the line. He said it is very important—so important, he told me that the senator wouldn't mind the interruption."

Jenkins stood up as Senator Barker directed him to take the call over at his desk. Jenkins walked to the desk and answered the phone. "Hello. Yes. You did! It was! Fabulous! I will dispatch a plane for you right away. No ... no. This evidence is far too precious to risk that. I'm calling Jefferies, and we'll get you back with FBI protection. That's right. Great! Thank you!"

---

204  |  *Linda Riesenberg Fisler*

Jenkins looked at Barker, who gave him an inaudible OK to make the call. "Jefferies, this is Senator Jenkins. I need you to dispatch a plane to Fairbanks, Alaska, to pick up my aide. He has some very important information. It has to do with illegal oil drilling in the ANWR, and I need this back quickly. Yes, that will be fine. Thank you."

"I take it that was good news," Barker said as he continued to eat.

"Yes," Jenkins answered as he sat back down. He opened the envelope and started looking at the pictures. "Larry, we have everything we need to nail Sipes and his colleagues. And if we play our cards correctly, the country may be so infuriated that it may be a long time before we see another Republican president any time soon." Jenkins smiled as he handed some of the photographs over to Senator Barker.

# Emerald Isle, NC

*N*icole and Sean had just returned from a walk on the beach. Kent greeted them on the boardwalk, asking for help with the groceries he had been dispensed to acquire. They all grabbed what they could and head up the stairs of the Sand Castle and into the kitchen, setting the bags on the counter. Nicole began to put the perishable items in the refrigerator, while Sean and Kent returned to the car to retrieve the bottled water as well as a few six-packs of beer.

"I hope you picked up a bottle or two of wine. Nicole doesn't strike me as the type who drinks beer," Sean remarked as he picked up the two six-packs.

"There's a bottle or two in the bags somewhere," Kent answered as he closed the trunk on the car and picked up the bottled water he had placed on the ground. They headed up to the kitchen where Nicole was putting things away.

Almost on cue, she looked at the additional items and sighed, "Guess this means I won't be eating out any time soon."

"If you play your cards right, I might be able to arrange something," Sean chimed in with a wink of his eye. "Kent will be able to keep the place secured."

"I can't come along?"

Sean gave him a look as if to reinforce the comments about Nicole's interest in him. "I think I'd rather like to be alone with Nicole," he answered.

Nicole moved over to the family room, touching Sean's arm as she passed, and turned on the television. She flipped on the news as it was getting close to six o'clock. The lead story caught her attention, and she called out. "Sean, look! That's Norman Sipes's home."

Sean and Kent moved toward the television as Nicole turned up the volume. "Norman Sipes, CEO of Sipes Oil Company, was the victim of a car bombing just outside his front door. The police are still investigating, and according to the DC police chief, there are many leads that they are investigating at this time. Moving on to our next big story, we bring in meteorologist Sonny Walters to tell us about the tropical storm that is forming off the coast. Sonny?"

The scene moved to a young blonde-haired man who was ready to talk about the storm brewing. "Thanks, Connie. There is a tropical disturbance south of us and still pretty far out to sea. I don't see this growing to a hurricane. It still is a little bit too early to tell, but there are a couple factors that will, I believe, hinder that development into a hurricane. But that doesn't mean we won't feel any effects from it. We are going have four to five inches of rain, sustained winds possibly as high as forty-five miles per hour, lightning, and some spin-up tornadoes may be possible. I don't expect any mandatory evacuations from the beaches, but you may want to make sure you have plenty of bottled water, flashlights, and batteries. I believe that Hatteras will see the worst of this, but there is a slight chance that its path could vary, with the barrier islands a little further south getting hit a bit more. Either way, Hatteras will take the brunt of the storm as it moves up the coast. We'll have more in about fifteen minutes, including the conditions over the next couple of days."

Nicole turned the sound down. "Well, that was just full of good news."

"Nothing we didn't expect regarding Sipes," Sean said. "I'm more concerned about that storm."

"It's just a little wind and rain," Nicole joked. "Is anybody hungry?"

*Blind Influence* | 207

*Day Nine*

# Jenkins's Home

Tuesday morning arrived with the rain hitting the window of his bedroom. Jenkins didn't seem to mind the rain. He lay in bed for a few more minutes after shutting off his alarm. He had a very busy day scheduled. It started with meeting John and the evidence he had been waiting for at Andrews Air Force Base in the early morning. When he had last spoken to John, John had been about to board the jet that had been sent to retrieve him. Jenkins had scheduled a special meeting to present the evidence for ten o'clock this morning. It was now seven o'clock, and he needed to shower, eat breakfast, and head to the Air Force base. His meeting with Tony Shafer was immediately following the committee meeting.

Jenkins swung his legs around and sat up on the edge of his bed. He secured his prosthetic leg and walked to the master bath to begin getting ready. He thought about Tony Shafer and how Tony's world must have been shaken by losing three people within days of each other. Jenkins wasn't sure what he was going to tell Shafer. He decided he would think about that when the time came. Right now, he needed a shower and he needed to feel the water refreshing his body.

After a long time in the shower, he dressed and ate breakfast. During this time, he received a call from Chris, who informed him that the plane was going to be late and that Chris would meet the plane and escort John to the committee meeting.

Jenkins headed to Capitol Hill, deciding to arrive just before the committee meeting. He walked into the conference and greeted everyone on his way to his appointed committee chair. Each member expressed surprise that they were meeting again so quickly, given the death of Norman Sipes. The camera crews were all in their place, and the news reporters were milling around looking for their assigned seats as Jenkins reached his chair. He gaveled the room to order.

"Good morning. Thank you for clearing your schedules for this special meeting of the Finance Subcommittee." Jenkins was surprised to see Chris frantically entering the room and briskly walking up to him. Chris paused at the table where those being questioned typically sat. He waited for the senator to direct him further. "Chris? You have something for me?" Chris shook his head. "Excuse me, gentlemen and gentle ladies." Jenkins waved for Chris to approach him.

When Chris arrived by the senator's chair, the senator pushed his chair back. Chris bent down to whisper into Jenkins's ear. Jenkins was visibly shaken. They talked a few minutes longer. Chris stepped back as Jenkins rolled himself in his chair back to the microphone. He gathered his courage and cleared his throat. "Excuse me." He tried to clear his throat again. "My aide has just informed me that the witness that I had hoped to question has died in an airplane crash earlier this morning."

All the members of the subcommittee were in disbelief, and there was almost one cohesive gasp. Jenkins continued. "I had hoped to provide you with evidence of an illegal operation occurring in Alaska. My aide John Spencer had been in Alaska the last few days gathering evidence. I have just been informed that it was his plane that went down this morning. One pilot is in critical condition, and all the others onboard were killed." The senator's voice cracked as he mentioned John. "At this point, I have nothing more to add but will keep you informed as I find out more. I apologize for all the work you did to reschedule for this meeting. I apologize for the inconvenience."

"Senator," one Republican senator called out, "may I address the chair?"

"Of course," Jenkins answered.

"I don't mean to sound harsh, but why is it that all your witnesses seem to be dying? Is there something that is being covered up?"

This particular senator always seemed to be drumming up drama, but this time, it almost seemed to be a valid question. "At this point, I don't have enough information to confirm or deny any kind of cover-up," Jenkins replied. "However, my aide was traveling on a plane dispatched by the FBI. I suppose we all can and will draw our own conclusions."

The committee broke out in loud disapproving remarks and mayhem. Jenkins gaveled, trying to restore order. "At this juncture, I gavel this subcommittee to dismiss." His gavel struck twice, and he quickly left the chamber, not stopping to talk to anyone. Chris led the way through the senators trying to address Jenkins.

*Blind Influence* | 211

Chris walked with Senator Jenkins all the way back to his office, running interference so Jenkins did not have to talk with anyone. As Jenkins entered his inner office, his sanctuary, Chris closed the door to allow him time to gather his thoughts and regain control over the emotions that he knew the senator had been fighting ever since he had learned of John's death.

Jenkins sat down at his desk, gasping for breath, his heart pounding. He broke out in a cold sweat, and he reached up to loosen his tie. He unbuttoned his jacket, still trying to catch his breath. He was losing his battle to control his demon, his nightmare. It was rearing its ugly head again, and Jenkins knew he was going to relive the night that had cost him his lower right leg. The pain in his leg was pulsing with each rapid heartbeat. The bittersweet metallic taste in his mouth suddenly appeared, and Jenkins reached for a glass of water, but his hands were shaking too much for him to grasp a glass. He sat back in his chair, knowing there was nothing he could do to stop the adrenaline. It always started that same way. He sat back, just trying to breath.

Jenkins closed his eyes, telling himself it would be over soon. In the darkness of his mind's eye, there was a flash of lightning. There he stood with his men on the narrow strip of beach, so narrow that the water was lapping at their feet. Directly in front of them was the 400-foot cliff they had to scale to carry out their top-secret mission. Another flash of lightning, and Jenkins was at the top of the cliff. He began to walk through the dense jungle. His team moved swiftly and quietly through the night. He winced at the rain hitting his face and the cuts to his hands from the jungle leaves. Jenkins looked to his left and saw John, his second on this mission, shadowing his movements. Another flash of light, but this time it was not lightning. Someone had been alerted to their presence, and at that moment a decision had to be made. Jenkins and his men struck quickly, killing the enemy. The now dead men were manning one of the many sentry posts.

Jenkins and his men continued to move toward the village. Suddenly, in front of Jenkins, appeared a young man—a boy, really. He stood up with a semiautomatic rifle in his hands. The boy pointed the gun at Jenkins, who froze. The boy looked scared; the hesitation cost Jenkins. He was conflicted about shooting a boy. The boy, however, had no such conflict. The small, seemingly innocent, boy pulled the trigger but was unable to control the gun's kick. The sound of the rifle scared the boy more than standing in front of Jenkins had. He dropped the gun and ran for the village, but not before damage had been done.

212 | *Linda Riesenberg Fisler*

Jenkins felt the sting of multiple bullets entering his lower right leg. He tried to avoid being hit with more bullets in those few seconds and ended up on the ground. He called out to John via his radio, telling John that he had been hit and to continue, as the boy would be alerting the village. John did charge ahead as he and the remaining men quickened their pace. The boy never made it to the village; he crossed the path of one of Jenkins's men, who shot him without any hesitation.

He heard his men calling back on the radio that the boy was dead. Another flash of lightning allowed Jenkins to see his lower right leg, bleeding profusely, the pain almost unbearable. He ripped some material from his sleeve to make a tourniquet. He tied the material just below the knee to try to slow the bleeding while he continued to command his men. He saw the blood, and his leg throbbed. He became lightheaded from the blood loss, but he continued to command his men. Jenkins could feel himself losing consciousness as he heard explosions and gunfire coming from the village. He remembered John finding him and lifting him into a fireman's carry as they headed back to the cliffs.

That was where his demon left him. Jenkins remembered waking from the surgery that had taken his lower right leg. Surrounded in white and feeling the softness of the pillow that his head was resting on as well as the clean white sheets that encapsulated his body, he opened his eyes. He remembered waking to John's face and to John telling him that the raid had been a success. In fact, it had been very successful. The village had been the nerve center of the Viet Cong, and their capture of enemy combatants as well as the destruction of equipment would wreak havoc for the enemy for many months. Both men received medals for their brave service and sacrifice. John was the one who had informed him of his missing lower leg, and John was the one who had pushed him during his rehab.

Jenkins owed John his life, and now John was dead.

Jenkins removed his handkerchief to wipe away the cold sweat from his face. His breathing was slowing, as well as his heart rate. The episode was over, and Jenkins was slowly gathering his courage. Reliving that hellish raid had ended, and now he had a couple of tasks ahead of him. One was to help John's family with the funeral, and the other was to determine just what had happened to that jet. He needed more information. He buzzed Chris in the outer office. Chris answered promptly, and Jenkins could hear the chaos emanating from his outer office. "What in the hell is going on out there, Chris?"

*Blind Influence* | 213

Chris cleared his throat and in a loud voice announced, "Nothing I can't handle, sir." He motioned for Jenkins's third aide to start dismissing the press and senators out of the office. "How can I help you, sir?" When Jenkins asked him to join him in his inner office, Chris said, "I'm on my way, sir." He rose and entered the sanctuary, closing the door quickly behind him. He waited to be addressed by the senator.

"What the hell was that about?" Jenkins asked, exasperated.

Chris ignored the direct question and started the conversation with the details of what had transpired to date. "Jefferies called about ten minutes to ten and said that the plane had gone down over Minnesota. He wasn't informed until he arrived at his office this morning. He said that the pilot is in critical condition and that all else were dead upon arrival at the hospital. The plane caught fire on impact. The pilot in critical condition isn't expected to make it. He somehow crawled out of the cockpit and has sustained third-degree burns over ninety percent of his body. He is on life support but is not conscious. Jefferies said he is sending some agents up to gather information and if the pilot gains consciousness, to question him. He wanted me to tell you that it is an active investigation."

Jenkins bit his tongue. He did not want to lash out at Chris, the messenger. He drew in a deep breath and exhaled. "Get me Ahnah on the phone. Is there any media coverage on the crash?"

"There was no national media at the crash site. I'm not sure what the press in the subcommittee room will be reporting or if they have already reported it."

Jenkins acknowledged the answer. "Is Jefferies sending a detachment to tell John's family?"

"He didn't say. Would you like me to ask Jefferies?"

"Yes, please. And if he hasn't, I'll go," Jenkins answered. "Actually, call Jefferies and tell him I'm heading over to John's home to talk to his family."

"I'll do that right now." Chris left the inner office and dialed Jefferies the minute he got to the desk. "Director, this is Chris in Senator Jenkins's office. The senator asked me to tell you he was on the way to the Spencer home to talk to his family." Chris listened for a second, and then he hung up the phone. He looked at the other aide. "What a slimy little bastard!" He turned and knocked on the senator's door, then entered. "Senator, I talked with Jefferies. He has not sent anyone to talk to John's family. I don't think he had any intention of sending anyone."

"Get me a car. I need to get over there," Jenkins barked.

"I'll drive you, sir," Chris said.

"No, you need to stay here and hold down the office. Have Andy drive me." Andy, short for Andrea, was the other aide in Jenkins's office.

"Yes, sir. I'll have her meet you outside the rotunda in five minutes. Would you like me to reschedule your meeting with Tony Shafer at two?"

"No, I need to see him, especially in light of all that is going on."

Chris left the senator's inner office to carry out his orders. A half hour later, Senator Jenkins found himself walking up the front walk to his best friend's home to inform John's wife of her husband's death. He was not looking forward to this conversation. He had requested that Andy join him during this meeting. As they arrived on the porch, Andy depressed the doorbell.

An attractive woman in her mid-thirties, her blonde hair pulled back from her face in a ponytail, answered the door. She didn't look first but was looking over her shoulder at the toddler in the other room. Her head swung around as she finished her last instruction to the toddler. "Yes?"

"Karen, I need to talk with you," Jenkins said.

Karen focused on the senator now. "Bobby—oh my God … no!" Karen started to walk away from the opened door. Jenkins and Andy entered the house. The senator motioned to the room with the toddler. Andy quickly directed the child back to the television, asking him what he was watching.

"Nooooo!" came an anguished cry from Karen as she felt John's presence leave her. Jenkins gathered her up in his arms and shut the door behind him with his good foot. Karen felt the emptiness, a feeling she had hoped to never feel in their relatively young lives. John was no longer among them, and she continued to scream, "No!" through the heartbreaking sobs that seemed to jolt her entire body.

*Blind Influence* | 215

Jenkins held her tightly and blinked back more tears. She continued to sob, her body finally becoming limp, and Jenkins directed her toward the couch, still holding her in his arms. He managed to get her to the couch before she totally collapsed in uncontrollable tears. Jenkins sat down on the floor next to the couch, taking her hand in his as she sobbed with every part of her body and soul.

"I'm so sorry, Karen," Jenkins said in a whisper. "I'm so very sorry."

Karen continued to sob for a few minutes more, as if to get it all out of her. She knew that she had to be strong for the rest of her life, and especially for her family. She started to quiet her crying and realized that Jenkins was sitting on the floor next to the couch. She wiped her eyes with a free hand, and without lifting her head, she looked at Jenkins out of the corners of her now bloodshot eyes. She whispered, "How?"

"He was in a plane crash," Jenkins answered.

"I haven't heard anything about a plane crash."

"It was a private charter. I sent an FBI plane to retrieve him," Jenkins answered quietly. "I promise you, Karen, I will get to the bottom of this."

Karen lifted her head. "You think there is foul play?"

"Yes," Jenkins answered, feeling a small amount of anger beginning to kindle inside of him. "And I swear I will make them pay."

Karen sat back, putting her head down on the back of the couch. "That won't bring John back to me." A tear rolled down her face. "Damn it, Bobby! We made it through Vietnam, and I thought that was it. I thought that we'd grow old together." There was a long pause. "I don't care what you do to them, Bobby, but just make sure his death was not in vain. He loved you like the brother he never had."

A tear formed in Jenkins's eyes. "I loved him, too. You all are the family that I never had." Jenkins waited a few moments before he continued. "I'd like to have him buried in Arlington, Karen, unless you have another preference."

Karen looked at Jenkins. "He always said he wanted to be next to his parents back in North Carolina. Does that have to be decided right now? I have family that I have to talk to, and the kids." She sat up. "I don't know how I'm going to get through this."

Jenkins smiled. "It starts by putting one foot in front of the other."

Karen looked at him, and they both gave a little chuckle. That was the comment that John had kept saying to Jenkins when he had been learning to overcome the loss of his leg and learning to walk with his prosthesis. Karen's smile grew a bit larger. She gave Jenkins the answer that he had given to John. "Fuck you."

Jenkins smiled a bit bigger as they fell together in a hug. "I'll be here if you need anything."

Karen answered, "You have an inquiry to run and a country that needs you, but call me to check on me when you can." She stood up and walked to the room where her toddler was being entertained by Andy. Jenkins was only a few steps behind her. "Thank you," she said to Andy as she picked up the three-year-old.

"Would you like Andy to stay and help you?" Jenkins asked.

"I'd be honored to help," Andy added.

"That would be great," Karen answered. "Now go find out who killed my husband."

With that, Jenkins took the keys from Andy and was out the door to the car and back on his way to his office.

# Emerald Isle, NC

*N*icole woke up mid-morning to a quiet beach house. She determined that Kent and Sean were still sleeping. She got up, dressed, walked down the stairs to the kitchen where she made coffee. She began to gather and cook breakfast. The aroma woke the rest of those still sleeping. She heard Kent moving around in his bedroom a good ten minutes before joining her in the kitchen to pour a mug of coffee. Nicole was cooking scrambled eggs and bacon. "Morning," he mumbled as the eye-opening liquid filled his mug.

"Morning, Kent. Breakfast will be ready shortly." Nicole turned her head to look up the stairs as she heard Sean's footsteps. "Good morning, Sean," she called.

"Good morning." Sean walked to the sliding glass doors that led to the boardwalk and beach. He looked up at the skies, noting the broken clouds. "Is there any news on that tropical storm?"

"I haven't had the TV on since last night," Nicole answered as she started to plate up some of the bacon and scrambled eggs.

"That smells wonderful," Sean said, now behind her, looking over her shoulder at the food. "Thank you." He grabbed a cup and poured himself some coffee. Nicole handed him his plate of food. He took it and moved to the table to eat. Nicole followed him around the counter with two plates. She set one plate in front of Kent.

Kent looked at the plate of food in front of him. He looked at Sean, then back at the food. "I don't think I've ever ate this good when bunking with you in the old days," he commented. "I think I'm going to like this."

Nicole and Sean laughed. Sean looked at Nicole. "With that storm moving in, maybe you and I better go grab that promised dinner out. We might be stuck inside after this."

"That would be nice," Nicole answered, but she wasn't going to let the comment about the men's past go. "Just how did you two meet?"

Kent looked at Sean while he answered. "We were a team way back when. Our first assignment was to penetrate the IRA."

218 | *Linda Riesenberg Fisler*

Sean thought that Kent was being very free with his information.

"I saved his life like every other week, if I remember correctly," Kent finished.

"You don't," Sean responded as he placed a fork full of food into his mouth.

"Oh, is that right? Well, let's see. What about the time when we were to set up that bomb in—"

"Kent," Sean interrupted, "first of all, I don't think Nicole needs to hear about MI-5 business, and secondly, you didn't save my life in that situation. I saved yours."

"How do figure that?"

"You originally had the bomb wired incorrectly," Sean answered flatly. "That was something that our partners would have noticed right off as they examined your so-called handiwork. So I rewired it for their inspection. Had you made that final connection the way that you wanted to, we both would not be sitting here today."

"OK, I'll give you that one. But there were plenty of other times."

Sean gave Kent a look that stopped him. It was clear that Sean didn't want it discussed. "Well," Kent started, changing the subject as he shoved the rest of his breakfast in his mouth, "if you two are going to skip out at dinner, would you mind if I get in a run on the beach?"

"No, go whenever you want. Just let me know when you will be leaving," Sean answered.

Kent stood to leave the room, turning to Nicole before exiting to his bedroom. "That was a great breakfast, Nikki. Thank you!" He was out of the room before Nicole asked her next question.

Nicole wasn't about to let it go. "Seriously, how many times did he save your life?"

"Drop it, Nicole. I really don't want to talk about it," Sean said, finishing up his breakfast. He stood up and gathered up Kent's plate to take to the

*Blind Influence* | 219

kitchen. He noticed Nicole's stare. "We are probably about even. It's just that the night that he should have killed me, he didn't," Sean answered as he turned to the kitchen.

"Whoa! Wait a minute. Run that past me again."

In the kitchen and starting to clean up, Sean was trying to squelch the flow of adrenaline that always surfaced when the thoughts of his wife's and daughter's deaths entered his mind. He tried to stop the vision of how he had found them from entering his consciousness. He was leaning hard on his hands on the kitchen counter; his body was tense. He had his back to Nicole, but she could see that something was wrong, and she moved to his side. He didn't notice that Nicole was beside him as he tried to stop the visions. He shook his head as if that would clear it. He was coaxed back to the present moment by Nicole's calm voice calling his name. "Sean. Sean, what's happening? What's wrong?"

He turned his head to look at her. "It's nothing. I'm fine."

"No, you are not fine. What was that?" Nicole looked at him with much concern.

"It's nothing you need to know." Sean started working on cleaning up.

"I beg to differ. My life is in your hands, and if this happens in the wrong moment, I'm dead. As much as I don't have a lot to live for right now, I'm entirely sure being dead is not the right answer." She watched Sean as he turned to the sink to wash off the dishes, ignoring her comments. She reached across angrily and shut off the water. "Damn it, Sean! Talk to me! Did you hear me? My fucking life is in your hands, and you just blacked out for over two minutes! Talk to me, or I'm out of here!"

Sean set the dishes down in the sink. He turned to look at her. "Senator Jenkins didn't tell you?"

"Tell me what?"

"How we met? The circumstances surrounding how we got to know each other so well?" Sean asked, looking directly into Nicole's eyes.

220 | *Linda Riesenberg Fisler*

"No," Nicole answered in a low voice, now suspecting that she did not want to know.

Sean turned his whole body to face her, resting his hip against the counter. "The Serpent murdered and mutilated my wife and kid," Sean said quickly with a forced distance in his whispering voice. Nicole was shocked and started to back away from him. "That night, Kent was supposed to kill me as well, but for some sick reason, he didn't. I had always thought of us, Kent and I, as close, maybe like brothers. At first, I didn't think Kent was involved in the plot, but over the years, I've come to find little facts that point to his involvement."

Nicole was still backing away from Sean when he reached out and took her arm gently, pulling her toward him again. He continued to talk in a low voice. "I never said anything to Charlie until now because I used Kent, much the same way that the Serpent uses him. I got messages to the Serpent through Kent, and no doubt, this afternoon, Kent will be hightailing it down the beach to a phone, where he will be telling the Serpent where we are and other details like the layout of this beach house."

Nicole looked at Sean. "When you disappear with that look on your face ... like you had in Jenkins's condo and just a few minutes ago ... "

"I relive the discovery of what that cold-hearted bastard did to my wife and child," Sean answered.

"Why?" Nicole shook her head, trying to clear it. "How?" She put her hand up to prevent Sean from answering. "The relationship between you and Senator Jenkins, why would you think he would tell me this, and how does he know about it?"

"I was recovering from the murders at Director Kensington's vacation house. Jenkins flew in for some summit or meeting, and Kensington asked me if it would be a problem if Jenkins stayed there as well. It was a big vacation house, so I said it wouldn't be an issue. Jenkins has his demons, too. We spent a lot of time talking and became good friends, but we've kept that very quiet. We trust each other immensely and with our lives."

"You were cleared to go back to work, right?"

Sean smiled. "Yes. Nicole, it won't happen when the times comes. Trust me."

"I don't have a choice, do I?" Nicole turned to go to her room, but before heading up the stairs, she turned to address Sean. "You know, it would have been nice to have known about this before I signed up for this little charade." With that, she ran up the steps and slammed the door. She sought the sanctuary of a shower, hoping the water would cleanse her mind. Maybe she wished it would change this whole situation, just wash it way. All along, she knew that this nightmare was not going to end. Not right now, anyway.

Sean finished cleaning the kitchen. He wondered what Nicole's state of mind actually was and wondered if, with all that had happened, she had reached her breaking point. As the hours ticked by, the showdown between the Serpent and Sean was getting closer. Sean played out in his head the many scenarios for how it was going to go down. What did he need to do to turn the odds in his favor?

He went outside and looked at the balconies on the backside of the building. He climbed up on top of the railing of the first balcony and practiced clamoring up to the second balcony. If he needed to, he now knew he could get up to the second floor. He climbed back down and reentered the beach house. He continued on to the unoccupied side. He walked up the steps and to the second floor bedroom balconies. He examined the sliding glass doors, making note of the locking mechanisms and glass. He walked out to the balcony closest to Nicole's room—an easy jump, if need be, to access her room. It was almost too easy for the Serpent to get into the beach house. Sean retreated back down the stairs and into their side of the house, locking the unoccupied side's adjoining door behind him.

Nicole was coming down the steps, fresh from her shower. She saw Sean coming over from the unoccupied side and asked, "Everything all right?"

"Yes," Sean answered. "How are you?"

"I'm all right. Any more surprises that you want to get off your chest?"

"I didn't want to tell you," Sean reminded her. He walked around the corner just as Kent was exiting his bedroom. "Are you going for that run now?"

"I thought I might," Kent said as he walked to the kitchen for a glass of water. He eyed Nicole, who was dressed very sharply. He began to wonder just how the Serpent was going to kill her. "You look very nice," he said in a voice that almost made Nicole shiver.

"Thanks," she answered as she walked to the couch and sat down.

"Do you think we have enough bottled water?" Kent asked as he grabbed a bottle and headed to the sliding glass doors.

"We can stop and get some more if you think we need more," Sean said.

"That might be a good idea," Kent answered. "I'll be back in a little while."

"Enjoy your run," Sean answered. He looked at the clock, realizing it was the middle of the afternoon. "I've made reservations at 6:30."

Kent acknowledged Sean's comment as he closed the door behind him.

Sean walked over to join Nicole on the couch. He asked Nicole in a low voice, "Are we okay?"

"In what way are you referring?" Nicole asked, confused.

Sean wasn't sure how to answer that. He had felt close to Nicole, but that seemed to have disappeared after she had learned about his past. "Do you still trust me?" This was the best question that Sean could ask as he struggled to understand his feelings.

"I would say that is a stretch, but I don't have much choice. I certainly trust you more than I do Kent," she answered. "Sean, I don't want to die, so if you think you can't do this, get me out of here at dinner and don't look back."

"I can do this. I won't let him kill you," Sean answered. "I mean that."

"That's all anybody could ask, I suppose." Nicole shook her head. "One day, I'm going to look at this and laugh, right? I mean, how the hell did I get here? One minute I'm talking to clients about nailing an oil company to the wall for drilling in the ANWR, and the next, I'm the bait for some international assassin who just happened to kill my best friend. If that isn't fucking crazy, I don't know what is!"

Nicole stood up and retreated up the stairs to her bedroom. Lying on the bed, she cursed herself for doing something she despised in others. She was feeling sorry for herself and allowing that to dictate her feelings. She promised herself that was the last of that attitude.

She stood up and opened the sliding glass doors that led to her balcony. She returned to the bed, lying down and listening to the sound of the surf. After a few minutes, she was asleep.

# *Capitol Hill*

*J*enkins returned to his Senate office about thirty minutes before his scheduled meeting with Tony Shafer. As he entered the outer office, he greeted Chris, who followed him into his office. Chris closed the door to the outer office. "How is Karen? Is there anything I can do?" he asked.

Jenkins smiled. "She's a fighter. She's doing as well as can be expected. Andy is staying there to help. Do I have any messages?"

"A number of the senators, who were not at the hearing, have determined that John was killed in the plane crash. The national news agencies are beginning to cover it."

"You might want to ask the DC police chief to get some police officers over to Karen's house to keep them a distance away from her and her children." Jenkins paused and smiled. "But on the other hand, I pity the reporter who asks her the wrong question." Chris joined the Senator in the smile. "Am I to guess that certain senators are demanding answers?"

"There have been a lot of deaths since the president's," Chris confirmed. "Senator Barker would like you to call him as soon as you are free. He said it was a follow-up to your lunch meeting." Chris placed all the messages and notes on the senator's desk before him.

"Thank you. Get me Jefferies on the phone," Jenkins demanded. He wasn't sure how he was going to handle this or what exactly he was going to say, but he was becoming very certain that there was indeed a cover-up. He didn't have the puzzle pieces quite yet, but he felt that putting a little pressure on Jefferies just might be the proper thing to do at this moment. Chris was out of the office and placing the call before Jenkins had his coat hung up. His phone rang when Chris had Jefferies on the line.

"Jefferies, what the hell is going on?" Jenkins asked.

Jefferies' annoying little voice stuttered when he attempted to answer the senator. "I ... we ... are still investigating the crash." That was all he could muster.

Jenkins wondered how this shell of a man had ever passed his confirmation. "That's not good enough. You knew that Spencer had information I

*Blind Influence* | 225

needed. You and I were the only ones that knew what he was carrying. I suggest you find out what happened to that plane before I decide what happened to that plane. Do you understand me?" Jenkins made it clear that he knew something was amiss. "I will have your job for this, Director." With the final threat, Jenkins slammed the phone down. Now it was time to wait and see who called him back.

Jenkins sat down in his office chair and started to look through the messages Chris had left for him. He sorted the piles into three: the ones he would respond to, those from the media, and those he had no intention of returning. When he was done, he shredded the last pile and placed the other two piles to the side of his desk.

He took out a pad of paper and started to write down all that was in his head, just to clear it. He had done this often, as it served as a way to let his mind release the thoughts. He wrote feverishly, his emotions pouring out of him, captured on the coldness of a yellow legal pad. There was a buzz on the phone. He finished the final few words before he answered it. "Yes, Chris?"

"Mr. Shafer is here to see you, sir."

"Yes, of course. Give me a minute to straighten up my desk, and show him in. Thank you." Jenkins opened his briefcase and placed in it the yellow legal pad that contained his raw emotions and thoughts. He snapped the briefcase shut and placed it on the floor next to his desk. He tidied up a few things on his desk and straightened his tie and clothing.

There was a knock on the door, and it opened, with Chris showing Tony Shafer into the inner office. Jenkins stood as Tony entered. "Mr. Shafer." He extended his hand, and he noticed the manila envelope that Tony shifted to his other hand to shake the senator's hand. "Please sit down."

"Thank you." Tony sat down and then quickly shifted his position. "Senator, I don't know what to do or where to turn." He shifted again. He was clearly uncomfortable. Jenkins had never seen Shafer behave this way before.

"Come now, Mr. Shafer. It can't be that bad."

"Well, I think I need to disagree with you." Tony placed the envelope on Jenkins's desk. "That may change even *your* mind." It was then that Jenkins noticed that all the color was drained from Tony Shafer's usually suntanned, weathered face. It was as if he had aged twenty years since the last time Jenkins had seen him at the state dinner the night before the president's assassination. The man sitting in front of Senator Jenkins had lost his swagger and his confidence. Just what was in that manila envelope?

Jenkins did not make a move to the envelope. Instead, he quietly studied Shafer. Jenkins looked again at the envelope and then finally spoke. "Mr. Shafer, obviously, the envelope's content has shaken you to the core. Would you like to tell me what is in it?"

"No," Shafer said flatly. "But I do want you to know that I had nothing to do with it and I knew nothing about it until that tape appeared in my office yesterday." Shafer stood up. "Senator, I know Nicole really liked you and felt that you were an upstanding politician. Personally, I'm beginning not to trust the lot of you." He walked to the office door and then turned for one final word. "I'm only going to add that I have a copy of what is in the envelope, in the event that I need it to clear my name. I leave what you do with that information after you have reviewed it up to you. I can only hope that you act responsibly. Good day, Senator."

Jenkins watched Shafer leave his office. He looked back at the envelope, wondering just what bombshell Tony had just delivered to him. He continued to look at the envelope as a smile crept across his lips. He smiled because he knew that whatever was on that tape, he was now in control of. Seeing how Tony was handling his newly acquired knowledge gave Jenkins an indication that it was something powerful. Having that power made him smile.

# Emerald Isle, NC

Kent had returned from his two-hour run and showered before Sean and Nicole left on what Kent teasingly called a dinner date. Kent made these suggestions as part of a mind game. Sean knew that, but there was a part of him that really didn't like it. Sean didn't like that he felt a need to dismiss the notion every time Kent mentioned a possible romance between him and Nicole. He actually wanted Kent or the Serpent to think there was some kind of bonding between the two of them. Sean knew the Serpent couldn't resist killing another woman Sean cared for, and that was part of the plan to ensure that the Serpent would show. To make sure that Kent would continue to think he was falling in love with Nicole, Sean decided to play along with Kent's assertions. As he was leaving and with Nicole already out the door, Sean turned to Kent just before exiting, winked, and said, "Don't wait up." He then closed the door behind him and walked down the stairs to the car.

Sean and Nicole arrived at the restaurant just before the appointed time for meeting Kevin Thompson. Thompson was already waiting, seated at a table and enjoying a cold beer. Sean and Nicole were escorted to the table, where they joined him.

"Good to see you two," Thompson said as they sat down.

"Good to see you," Sean answered. "We saw what happened to Sipes."

"I should have seen that coming. Only vehicle in and out was the personal car detailer. I gave Bailey all the information. I'm sure it will lead to a dead end, though."

"It will," Sean confirmed.

"How are things going at the beach house?" Thompson asked, looking at Nicole with a smile.

"It's just peachy," Nicole answered sarcastically.

Thompson laughed. "What happened to all that enthusiasm?"

"I was never enthusiastic about this," Nicole reminded him.

"It's going fine. It is going according to plan, actually," Sean answered quickly as the waitress arrived.

"Can I get you anything to drink?" the waitress asked.

"I'll have a gin and tonic, please," Nicole answered.

Sean smiled. If anyone deserved to have a drink, it was Nicole. "Make that two," he added. The waitress went to retrieve their drinks after informing them of the menu specials. After the waitress returned with their drinks, she took their food orders.

Knowing that it would be a little bit of time before she returned with their food, Sean took the opportunity to talk about the plan. He slid an envelope over to Thompson that contained a key to the unoccupied side of the beach house. "We've been keeping the unoccupied side locked," Sean said. "I have been checking that side a couple times a day. Kent hasn't shown any interest in it, so this could go down one of two ways."

"You think Kent will have the Serpent enter through my side?" Thompson asked. "Now wouldn't that be cozy, both of us hiding on the unoccupied side of the beach house?"

"That would be the best scenario, but I'm not sure that will be the way. It is something for you to consider, though. Do you have everything you need?"

"Yes. I went shopping at one of the Army surplus shops down here. Night-vision glasses and scope were just a couple things I picked up," Thompson answered.

"Good," Sean answered. "No matter which side he enters, I am expecting it to be from the beach side. There is less chance of being seen. I'm sure Kent has told him which room is Nicole's. His goal will be to make sure none of us walks out of there alive."

"Including Kent?" Nicole asked.

The waitress arrived with their food, and Sean waited until she was gone before answering. "Yes, including Kent. If I'm dead, he doesn't need Kent any longer." Sean looked at Thompson. "Your job, Kevin, is to make sure that Kent doesn't make it upstairs."

*Blind Influence* | 229

"I've got it," Thompson answered as he ate.

"When do you expect this to go down?" Nicole asked.

"Anytime in the next twenty-four to forty-eight hours. It will be at night, in the cover of darkness," Sean answered as he began to eat.

"I'll enter the unoccupied side this evening," Thompson stated.

"Good. I'm sure Kent will know that I'll make another walk-through tonight before we go to bed," Sean answered. "I suppose you heard about the tropical storm?"

"Yeah, I did. Just looks like high surf and big thunderstorms for this area," Thompson answered. "You don't think that will change his plans about a beach entry?"

"No. If it were a full-fledged hurricane, it might. He's been in worse situations," Sean answered, thinking back to all the dangerous situations he had been in while chasing the Serpent in the past. A tropical storm was nothing in comparison to a few of those situations.

"We said we would pick up some extra water," Nicole reminded Sean.

"Yes. Do you have any other questions?" Sean looked at Thompson.

"No. If I have a shot, I'm going to take it. You know that, right?" Thompson was looking at Nicole, even though the question was to Sean.

"I would expect no less," Nicole answered. She continued to eat her dinner as did Sean and Thompson. Thompson passed on Senator Jenkins's information about the oil rig in Alaska. Nicole was intrigued by the little tidbit of information that Thompson provided. She was disappointed that it was just a tidbit and nothing more. As they began to finish up their meal, Sean went over the plan once more. Thompson smiled as he listened and confirmed that he understood what he was to do.

Sean put some money on the table as Nicole took her last drink of the gin and tonic she had ordered. "It's good to know you have our backs, Kevin."

230 | *Linda Riesenberg Fisler*

Sean extended his hand, which Thompson shook. "You won't have a shot at the Serpent. Just focus on Kent and keep him downstairs."

"Stay safe," Thompson replied.

Sean and Nicole left for the beach house, stopping to get the water as they had promised. While in the store, Nicole spotted the board game Monopoly and suggested it might be a fun way to pass time in the evening and during the day if the electricity went out. The store had also put out camping-type lanterns, and Sean decided it would be good to have them on hand as well. Assured that they had proper supplies, they paid for the items and returned to their car.

Upon their return to the beach house, the first thunderstorms from the outer bands of the tropical storm were visible offshore. Lightning bolts danced among the ominous clouds and the wind began to blow in stiff bursts that subsided into a gentle but constant breeze. They hurried into the beach house, placing their items on the kitchen counter after they entered.

"Looks like the wind gusts are going to be a bit higher than originally thought," Kent said. He spotted the lanterns in Sean's hand. "Good, those lanterns should help. Voluntary evacuation for our area has been issued. Cape Hatteras has a mandatory evacuation."

"Is the Cape still going to receive the worst of it?" Nicole asked.

"Yes, it appears that way," Kent answered. "Where do you want those?" He pointed to the lanterns.

"Right here for now. There is one for each of us," Sean answered. "Since we'll all be down here for a while, I think keeping them here will be good. Just take one with you when you go upstairs," Sean said to Nicole, who nodded an acknowledgment.

"How was dinner?" Kent asked.

"Enlightening," Nicole answered.

"Really? How is that?" Kent asked, intrigued.

*Blind Influence* | 231

"I had the pleasure to learn all about you, Kent," Nicole said, deciding to play with Kent a bit. "I was treated to the story of how you and Sean met and how you saved his life. Yes, it was quite interesting."

"He admitted to you that I saved his life, did he?" Kent was genuinely surprised.

"Yes, he did." Nicole looked at Sean, who was rather uneasy about Nicole's declarations. "But he also added that there was a time when he saved yours, maybe a few times. He was rather bashful about his actions, though. I'm not sure I got the whole story."

Kent looked at Nicole and smiled. "No doubt he told you about the time that an IRA member shot me because he found out I was with MI-5."

Nicole looked coy. "Was this before or after you saved his life?"

"It was before," Sean answered quickly.

Nicole looked surprised. She played it very well. "You mean there are multiple times he has saved your life, Kent?"

Kent looked at Nicole suspiciously. "Yes, there have been many times. I guess that is why I think of him as my brother."

"Yes. I'm sure you are close. In your line of work, it is always good to know that there is someone you can depend on," Nicole said as she started to slip something out of the brown bag. She could feel the tension in the room that her line of questioning brought. She suddenly pulled the Monopoly game from the bag. "But in Monopoly, no one has your back."

Kent seemed to exhaust a short breath and gave a chuckle. Sean held his reaction inside, choosing only to shake his head at Nicole when Kent wasn't looking. "Monopoly? I have never heard of it," Kent said, taking the game from Nicole to look at. "Oh, this won't do. It involves buying properties and acquiring money. Two things MI-6 agents never get a chance to do."

They all laughed.

"It is a fun little game of chance. Something you agents deal with every day, right?" Nicole pressed. "I think you both deal every day in the world of chance. Of course, there are times when you are in control of someone's fate, but that isn't the kind of chance you deal in daily—or at least I hope you don't." Neither Sean nor Kent knew what Nicole was trying to say. "Well, I guess since you are both guarding me, I do hope that you have all the experience in the world at keeping me protected."

"Of course we do," Sean answered. "Isn't that correct, Kent? That's what we signed on to do."

"Yes, of course," Kent answered, not able to look either in the eye. That was all the proof Nicole needed to know that Kent would indeed betray his friend and her in the coming days.

Kent put the game down on the counter. There was an awkward tension in the air. He hoped that he was the only one who felt it.

"Good," Nicole said as she seductively walked toward Kent, brushing him as she passed. She whispered, just loud enough for Sean to hear, "You don't know how having you here makes me feel." She lingered just long enough, close to Kent's body, to imprint her perfume on his conscious, long enough to draw Kent into believing she might be attracted to him. Then she gave a cooing, coy laugh as she reached around him to grab a lantern. "Is it getting warmer? The humidity must be on the rise," she said as she headed to the stairs, giving a quick wink at Sean. She gave a breathy sigh and said as she started up the stairs, "I do believe I need a cold shower."

Sean swallowed and closed his eyes to keep from laughing as he now knew what she was up to with her advances toward Kent. He opened his eyes as quickly as he had closed them to see Kent's reaction. He could see that Nicole had Kent wondering about her: What it would be like to be with her, inside her? Kent was always quick to jump in bed with any skirt that gave him any provocation.

*Good job, Nicole!* Sean thought. He walked to the sink to retrieve a glass of water. "She has a way of getting to you, doesn't she?" he asked between sips of water.

"She's hot, all right," Kent admitted. "How do you keep your mind on the job?"

*Blind Influence* | 233

"I do so by telling myself that I want to keep her alive. It wouldn't be much fun if she doesn't live through this, now would it?" Sean asked as he filled another glass of cold water and placed it on the counter in front of Kent. He slapped Kent's back as he almost ran up the stairs, giving the impression that he was hot after Nicole.

# Jenkins's Office

Jenkins turned off the VCR and television. He was stunned at what he had just witnessed. Sitting back in his chair, he contemplated his next move. The tape from Tony had not been what he had anticipated at all. He finally had his answers, and he cursed when he realized that the call to Jefferies had possibly been premature. All the pieces were fitting together now, and he didn't like to whom it was pointing. He stood up and ejected the tape from the VCR. He placed it back in the manila envelope and then walked to his safe. He dialed the combination, opened the safe, and placed the videotape inside. This was definitely something he didn't want falling into the wrong hands. He knew now he had to proceed with caution.

There was a knock on his office door that jolted him back to reality. He walked back to his desk before answering. "Yes?" he said as casually as his could. Chris opened the door and walked into the office.

"I thought you might be interested in this, Senator." Chris picked up the remote.

"Here," Jenkins said as he took the remote. "I had an old tape on, doing some research," he said as he flipped the remote to work with the television. He flipped on the television and handed the remote back to Chris. Chris changed the channel to the weather.

"There is a tropical storm that is projected to hit Cape Hatteras. Tropical storm warnings are out for the area where your beach house is, sir."

"Is there?" Jenkins answered, surprised, and now worried about Sean and Nicole. "That snuck up on the coast pretty quickly. Any evacuations ordered?"

"There are for Ocracoke, Cape Hatteras, and up to Kill Devil Hills," Chris answered.

"Issue a statement from the office encouraging my constituents in the area to heed any warnings or evacuations. The statement should include how we will work with FEMA and the Red Cross to get them aid as quickly as possible. Thank you, Chris."

*Blind Influence* | 235

Chris acknowledged the senator's instructions, quickly leaving Jenkins alone in his office. Jenkins sat down at his desk and called his beach house directly.

## Emerald Isle, NC

When the phone rang at the beach house, Sean was on his way back down the stairs with Nicole behind him. They had had a good laugh at Kent's expense, and Sean had to admit to himself that he had felt a pang of jealousy when Nicole had made her advances to Kent. She admitted to Sean that she intended to keep Kent off balance as much as she could. She honestly didn't think it would be so difficult to do. She admitted to herself that she could channel Carol for a little help. After all, she had seen all of Carol's moves in the past.

Kent reached the phone first and picked it up. "Hello? Yes, he is here, just a second." Kent stretched out the receiver to Sean, who started walking toward it. "It's for you."

"Thank you. Hello? Oh yes, hello, Bobby," Sean said, looking at Nicole. "Yes, we did see that. The last I saw, gusts up to forty-five or fifty, I think. It didn't seem to be all that bad. It is raining now, and the storms are gathering a bit in strength. I agree. Thank you." Sean hung up the phone. "That was Bobby. He owns the beach house. He wanted to make sure were prepared."

"Is he a friend of yours?" Kent asked Sean.

"He is a friend of mine," Nicole answered. She wanted to make sure the secret friendship between Jenkins and Sean remained that way. She also recalled the discussion when they had first arrived when Sean had indicated that the house belonged to her friend.

"How does Sean know him?" Kent asked.

"He found me at his house, and I said I needed to get away from DC. You see, my best friend was killed in an unfortunate accident … " Nicole let her voice trail off, knowing that Kent knew the circumstances leading to how she could identify the Serpent. She ended her sentence with a rather upbeat, "and that's how we all got here. Who wants something to drink?"

"I'm fine," Sean answered. Nicole moved to the kitchen and looked out the window. She saw a man walking on the street. It was dark, and a burst of lightning lit up the outside. The man's build looked familiar, and she knew instantly it was Kevin Thompson.

"You know, I feel like dancing. Turn on some music or something, will you, Sean?"

Nicole grabbed a glass to pour herself some wine as Sean did what she asked. "Oh, dear Lord, *not* country!" she said as she finished pouring the glass of wine. She walked past Kent, who was watching her, wondering what had gotten into her. She walked over to the radio and started searching for a rock station. She turned the volume up as she searched for some rock music. She wanted to make sure that any noise Thompson was going to make while getting into the other side of the beach house would not be heard. She searched the radio band until she heard a song from the Allman Brothers Band, "Jessica," playing. She set her glass down. She turned the volume up even louder and shouted, "Air guitar jam! C'mon, Sean. Show us your best air guitar!" She started pretending to play the guitar, and Sean began to play along. "Kent! Don't be left out!" she called to him. Kent thought that Sean looked pretty ridiculous, but he didn't want to be left out.

Nicole started to move toward him, and before Kent knew it, she was leaning on his back, moving up and down as she played her air guitar. Kent joined in, and the three of them jammed to the song. It was followed by another Allman Brothers Band song, and they continued their jam session, although Kent had had enough. He watched Sean and Nicole carry on throughout that song until Nicole ended up in the chair, exhausted from the dance.

"Can I turn this down now?" Kent asked, somewhat annoyed.

Nicole figured that Thompson was in by that time and nodded. "Sorry. I just had to get that out of me," she said as she stood up to retrieve her wine. "Carol always said I was only good for a song or two. I think she was right."

"Should we start that board game?" Kent asked.

"Not yet," Sean answered. "Maybe in a little bit. I want to have another look around."

"It's pouring rain outside." Kent stated. "And I hesitate to mention some pretty terrifying lightning." Sean could tell that the thought of Sean doing a sweep set off an internal alarm with Kent. Was the Serpent going to make his move this evening instead of tomorrow evening?

"You're afraid of lightning, Kent?" Nicole chided.

"Yes, indeed," Kent answered.

"I find that fascinating. You are not afraid of bullets, terrorists, or assassins, but you are afraid of lightning," Nicole stated. "Why is that?"

"I can usually control when and where I get shot at, but I can't control when lightning will hit me," Kent refuted.

"Do you know the odds of lightning hitting you?" Nicole prodded.

"Yes, I know."

"I would think that a bullet hitting you, given the situations you are in, has a far better chance of happening," Nicole continued. She looked at Sean, who shook his head at her as he put on a raincoat and headed out the sliding glass door. "I mean, think of it."

"I'd rather not," Kent answered.

Nicole smiled. "Oh, sorry, you probably think it is bad luck to talk about it."

Kent walked over to where she was sitting and joined her on the couch. "Yes, just a little. It is kind of silly, isn't it? I mean, they are just words." With Sean outside, he wanted to confirm Nicole's interest in him.

"I don't think it is the words that bother people like you. It is the intention behind the words," Nicole answered. "It is funny how sometimes the most innocent thing can be mistaken for something awful. The intention and the way that it is said is all that it takes, you know what I mean?"

"Yes," Kent said. "Like earlier today. I could have sworn that you had a thing for Sean, but yet there you were, obviously flirting with me right in front of him."

Nicole smiled. "Yeah, well, I've learned a lot about Sean in the last few days." Nicole leaned in to Kent. "You know, he is just fucked up. All that

*Blind Influence* | 239

shit with his wife and kid. I'm not into saving someone from themselves." Nicole's comments hit Kent harder than she expected. "I mean, he is a nice guy and all, but I pity the woman that gets involved with him." She looked at Kent and knew that her words were causing a conflict in him. "Seriously, the woman that gets involved with him better be really strong to pull him out of his pain. I guess a person doesn't get over this kind of shit. Do you regret any of the decisions you made when it came to killing someone?"

Kent's head was spinning. A confluence of emotions was running through him. "What?" he asked, trying to clear his head.

"I said, do you regret any of the decisions you made when it came to killing someone?" Nicole asked again, looking directly into his eyes.

"Yes. I mean no. They were our enemies," Kent answered, still a bit taken aback.

"All of them? You never made a mistake and killed someone completely innocent, like my friend Carol was? You know, she had no idea what she walked into, and the next minute, she was dead. You wouldn't have regrets if you had done something like that?"

"Why does it matter to you how I feel?" Kent started to get defensive. He wasn't sure why. He just knew that Nicole didn't seem to be the woman he had thought she was. Maybe the damsel in distress that Sean had painted her as wasn't true.

"Well, I'm kind of attracted to you, and I'm just trying to get to know you better. I could never be interested in anyone who couldn't feel some kind of remorse for the innocent bystander that gets caught up in the fight. I mean, isn't that the difference between the bad guy and the good guy?" Nicole smiled as she repositioned herself on the couch, brushing her breasts "accidentally" against Kent's arm as they talked.

"God, Nicole! You are so blind! In our line of work, there is no good or bad guy if you use your definition. Remorse will eat you alive in this game."

Sean entered the room from the outside at Kent's last words. He looked at Nicole, how close she was to Kent. He wasn't sure if he was maybe interrupting something. "You can't have feelings," Kent stated.

---

240  |  *Linda Riesenberg Fisler*

"So you couldn't have any type of compassion or love for anyone?" Nicole asked, running her fingers through her long cinnamon hair. Sean paused to hear Kent's answer, wondering how this conversation had come up.

"I didn't say that. I said that I can't look back on who I have shot with any kind of regret or remorse." He looked at Sean.

"I'm going to have a look on the other side," Sean said. "It is really raining out there now. I'm going to secure the other side once more, double-check that everything is locked up in the event we lose electricity," he said, wanting very much to stay out of the conversation between Nicole and Kent, and yet very thankful for Nicole keeping Kent off balance a little. And yet again there was a pang of jealousy that he was trying very hard to ignore.

"Thanks, Sean," Nicole said. Her tone gave the impression that Sean was intruding on her private conversation with Kent. "I always find this so interesting. Have you ever shot someone that you later found out was not the bad guy? I mean, I know killing someone who was that bad guy can be justified. How can you justify shooting someone who wasn't bad?"

Kent looked at Nicole. "Nicole, we usually are only after the bad guy."

"Usually?" Nicole asked playfully.

"We have evidence that points to their being on the wrong side," Kent said.

"So you have shot and killed people?" Nicole felt like she had Kent on the stand in a courtroom, and he kept playing into the confusion. She felt his bicep, running it seductively down to the crux of his arm.

Kent looked down at Nicole's hand. "Yes, in the line of duty," Kent answered, placing his other hand over Nicole's.

"And all of them, up to this point, have been bad guys?" she questioned softly, leaning into him as she spoke.

Kent wasn't sure where she was going with this. Who would have thought that she was the kind of woman who got turned on by this type of discussion "Yes, of course, they have all been bad guys," Kent whispered, inhaling the scent of her perfume.

*Blind Influence* | 241

"You never accidently hit a bystander?" Nicole recoiled slowly, as a tease.

"I did once," Kent said. "And yes, I felt bad, but I couldn't dwell on it. They happened to cross into the line of fire. It was split seconds. It happened so fast." Kent suddenly felt like he had to defend his decision all over again.

"Oh, I'm sure it was," Nicole placated him, squeezing his arm with her hand. "I just hope you use better judgment when push comes to shove here." She stood up in a way that provided Kent with a quick view down her shirt. She brushed her legs against his as she passed between him and the coffee table. Then she walked to the kitchen, exaggerating her hip swing ever so slightly, knowing that he was watching her.

The storm was getting worse, and Nicole knew, somehow; she could feel that tonight was going to be the night the Serpent was going to attack. She glanced out the window in the kitchen a couple of times but saw nothing but an empty street. She didn't realize that Kent had gotten up and moved into the kitchen, essentially cornering her against the cupboards.

Kent decided it was time to give a little back. "You know, Nicole," he whispered in her ear, "I'm only here to protect you." He kissed her neck, putting a hand on her shoulder. "When this is over, I would look forward to disappearing with you for a few days."

Nicole closed her eyes as Kent kissed her neck again. She tried with all her courage not to tense up her body. She wondered how much longer Sean was going to be. Kent caressed her arm, moving his hand down to her hip.

Sean opened the door from the other side just as Kent was about to wrap his arm around Nicole. At the sound of the opening door, Kent moved away from Nicole to the other side of the kitchen. He wasn't fast enough for Sean not to catch what was happening. Sean's small pang of jealousy grew almost into a flame. He decided not to give in to it. He needed to stay sharp, and these feelings needed to be ignored. He had to ignore what he had seen. He had to stop questioning what Nicole had said to bring on such a situation. He closed the door behind him. "Everything looks good over there," he said as he looked at Kent.

"Good. I think I'm going to take another shower before the hot water is all gone." Kent started for his bedroom. He had to walk past Sean.

242 | *Linda Riesenberg Fisler*

"I don't think you need a hot shower," Sean shot back just loud enough to be heard by Nicole as Kent passed him. Kent paused slightly but continued on, closing the door to his bedroom.

"Sean, I'm sorry," Nicole whispered as she walked toward him. She oddly could see that she somehow had wounded Sean. The tone in his voice wasn't an act. She hadn't expected Kent to react the way he had. She clearly hadn't anticipated Kent's action.

"What happened?" Sean asked, meeting her halfway. He was not sure why he had gotten her apology.

"I'm not sure what happened, really. I guess that was pay back for the shit I'm doing to him." Nicole whispered as Sean met her in the kitchen.

"Well, maybe it is best to let it be," Sean answered. "He has been deceiving people a lot longer than you have."

"Is everything in place?" Nicole asked, ignoring his last comment.

"Yes. Kevin says hello," he whispered before moving to the fridge to retrieve a beer. A lightning strike hit close to their location. "Wow! That was close!"

Without a second passing, Kent's bedroom door flew open and he ran from the bedroom zipping up the pants he had not had the chance to remove yet. He had yet to get in the shower. The sight made Nicole and Sean laugh. "You better wait a little bit before you take that shower," Sean said through a few chuckles.

"The storm has made it so dark out," Nicole observed, looking out the back glass doors from her vantage point in the kitchen. It was quiet, and the three of them listened to the wind howling through the streets and down the beach.

"I think you are right about waiting a while on that shower," Kent said, breaking the silence. The lights began to flicker. They went out but flickered back on within a few seconds. "We better check the last of the weather reports before we lose power." Kent moved to the television and turned it on.

Nicole moved to the wine she had opened and put the cork into the neck of the bottle. She moved the bottle to the other side of the countertop. She

*Blind Influence* | 243

could tell by Sean's actions that the trap was set and now it was just a matter of time. She wondered what Thompson was doing and if he was ready for what might take place.

As Kent listened to the reports of the winds picking up and the track of the storm, Sean removed the gun from his holster and checked the bullets.

"It sounds like the worst of the storm is still a bit away," Kent announced as he turned the television off. He looked out the sliding glass door. It was pitch black. He could barely make out the whitecaps on the ocean farther out at sea. Like Sean, he knew the Serpent would be striking tonight. He wondered if the plan was still the same or if the Serpent would approach a different way. He just knew that the darkness was in the Serpent's favor. "How about we get that game going?" Kent asked nervously.

"What's the matter, Kent?" Sean asked. He thought back to a time in Ireland when a rather bad storm had been pounding around them as they had waited in a flat for instructions from the home office. "I had forgotten how much you dislike storms. Are you alright?"

"Yes, I suppose so," Kent answered. "I just figure having something to do would take my mind off it."

"We can play if you want," Nicole answered. "I'll get it set up." She grabbed the box and moved to the table, ripping off the cellophane cover and placing it in the trash. She then opened the box and began setting up the board. She looked for the game pieces as the two men moved to the table.

Sean stood by the chair he was going to sit in, selecting the one that provided a view of the sliding glass door. He was still convinced that the Serpent was going to approach from the beach. This seat also provided Sean with a view of the front door via the reflection in the dark glass doors.

Kent sat on the end of the table, his back to the stairs and the door that joined the two sides of the beach house. He felt this position would give him the ability to look at the glass doors and the front door.

Nicole, content with not knowing what was going on, sat with her back to the sliding glass doors. "Let's see," she said as she started looking at the game pieces, "I think Sean should be the car. Kent, you get the hat."

244 | *Linda Riesenberg Fisler*

"I'm afraid to even ask the reasoning behind those choices," Kent said, accepting his fate.

Nicole smiled. "I'll be the battleship."

"Are you sure?" Sean asked. "I thought maybe the iron or thimble would be—"

Nicole looked at Sean, interrupting him. "You really want to go there?"

"I wouldn't if I were you, my friend," Kent advised. Sean just smiled and sat down. Nicole distributed the starting funds. The rules were discussed, and the game began.

The storm outside continued to strengthen, adding to the tension growing with each roll of the dice. At first Nicole wasn't sure if the tension was because of the intensity the three of them had to win at all costs or because of the uncertainty of not knowing when or if the Serpent was going to strike. The storm's sustained winds were growing, and the howling that was produced as it funneled through the tightly nestled beach houses reminded Nicole of a lone wolf howling on a cold night. The shrillness raised the hair on the back of her neck, and even though the winds were warm and humid, she felt the coldness of all that was happening around her.

The lights flickered at times but remained on, even with the increasing sustained winds. The gusts were over tropical storm force now and materializing more frequently, which ratcheted up the tension in the room. It was getting late, and yet there was no sign of the Serpent. As the storm's eye grew closer to Hatteras, the ocean churned with bubbling waves. They pounded the beach, stretching foamy fingers to the sand dune that protected the building behind it. With each wave, little by little, the safety that the dune provided was etched away. With each wave and gust of wind, the sand was fated to the whims of each element. Hopelessly, the defense of both the sand dune and the inhabitants of the beach house beyond it were at the storm's mercy.

It was around midnight when the lights flickered out for a few seconds again before coming back on. "I forgot that my lantern is in my room. I better go get it," Nicole said as she stood up.

"I'll get it," Kent volunteered. He was up and out of his seat before Sean could stop him.

*Blind Influence* | 245

Sean looked at Nicole, who was sitting down now. "Here we go. Are you ready?"

"Would it matter if I said no?" Nicole asked. "You better light one of those lanterns in case the lights go out."

"Good idea," Sean said as he got up to do just that.

In the meantime, Kent was retrieving the lantern from Nicole's room. Before leaving the room, he unlocked the sliding glass door, flipped the light a couple of times, and headed downstairs. He had no idea if the Serpent was out there. He had been relieved when Nicole had mentioned the lantern because he had made arrangements with the Serpent to do just what he had done. The Serpent had assured Kent he would be approaching the beach house from the ocean side and needed to know in which room his victim would be residing. Like Sean, Kent had tested out the climb from below using the railed balconies to reach the second floor. Kent had informed the Serpent that it could be done and had given him a short list of equipment that would make it even easier, considering that the storm would be in full swing.

Kent was about to head downstairs when he, at the last second, decided to unlock the sliding glass door in Sean's room as well. Mission accomplished, Kent headed down the stairs. "Here you go." He set the lantern down on the countertop. "Nice rooms up there."

"This whole beach house is really nice," Nicole said. "OK, Kent, it's your turn."

Kent sat back down and rolled the dice. Play resumed as if nothing had happened. In fact, Nicole was beginning to think that she was wrong about the Serpent coming this evening. The tension in the room seemed to be easing.

It was getting very late, close to two in the morning, when Nicole announced that she was going to go to bed. She had been yawning for an hour and was battling to keep her eyes open. "Really, I'm exhausted," she said, standing up.

"So, that's it. The game is over?" Kent asked.

"No. We can just leave it and resume play tomorrow," Nicole answered. "This game could take days." She laughed. "Now I remember why this game never held my attention for very long."

"You aren't happy because you can't sue someone," Sean joked.

Nicole looked at Sean, taking in what he had just said. "You know, I think you are correct, Sean! I'm going to have to figure out how to incorporate that aspect into the game." She smiled as she turned to the stairs. "Good night, all."

"I'll be up in a minute," Sean called after her as she started for the stairs.

After Kent bid good night to Nicole, she left the room. Flipping the light on to her bedroom, she entered it. She stretched as she walked to the bathroom and prepared for what she hoped was a good night's sleep. Maybe Sean was wrong. Maybe it wasn't going to happen tonight. In any case, she was tired and wanted to get to bed. She walked over to the chest of drawers and retrieved her nightgown. She walked over to a desk, which had a large mirror hanging above it. She picked up her brush as she sat down, and she began to brush her hair. Lightning struck very close, with a deafening boom that immediately followed. Startled, Nicole jumped. She tried to calm herself and somewhat succeeded in doing so as she tried to slow her fast-beating heart. With that lightning strike, little did she know that the dreaded and anticipated event was just about to begin.

A few seconds later, the lights didn't flicker; they just went out. She sat in the dark, holding her brush. Her heart had barely slowed from the lightning strike and now it started racing again. She clutched the hairbrush to her chest. She cursed as she remembered that her lantern was downstairs. It was very dark, and her eyes had not adjusted yet. Her heart started to pound even harder—so hard, she thought it was going to burst through her chest. She was motionless from the fear she felt in each and every inch of her body. She noticed that she was in a cold sweat. She needed to gather her courage.

As her eyes began to focus in the dark, she could see a light from the lantern that was reflecting up the staircase. It was dim but would be enough to guide her downstairs to retrieve her lantern. As she started to stand up, another flash of lightning struck. She jumped again at its unpredicted flash

*Blind Influence* | 247

and accompanying thunder. She cursed at herself for letting the storm and darkness affect her so badly.

Suddenly, the shrill howling of the wind became overbearing, and she felt the gust of wind and rain assault her back. She slowly turned to face the storm, and another bolt of lightning flashed, exposing the man with the icy blue eyes who had haunted her dreams of late, for only a second. Turning away from him, Nicole let out a bloodcurdling scream as the Serpent reached for her in the darkness. The lantern down the stairs had been extinguished. With one hand, she tried to grab the desk where she had been sitting. She could feel the man securing his hold around her thighs as he tried to pull her through the open sliding glass door. The Serpent removed her feet from the floor, desperately trying to grab her thighs. Still holding her hairbrush in her right hand and almost parallel to the floor, she hit the man in the head with as much force as she could. She continued to fight him and started to kick wildly. The desk she was desperately grasping started to move and wedged itself between the wall and bed.

The Serpent cursed at the pain Nicole had inflicted with the brush, taking one of his hands from her thigh to rid her of the brush. She screamed another blood-curdling scream. "Sean!" she yelled as she secured her grip to the desk with her other hand. She continued to kick the Serpent.

Then, something unimaginable happened—something she hadn't counted on or even thought about. How could she have been so stupid! She heard gunshots echoing up the stairs. She thought that Kent had managed to kill Sean. "Oh my God! Sean!" Nicole screamed. "Sean!" She continued to fight the Serpent, kicking and grabbing at the desk. She could feel her fingernails trying to etch themselves into the desk. "Sean!" she screamed again as another couple of shots went off downstairs. "Sean! Help me!" she screamed.

"He's dead, you dumb bitch!" the Serpent screamed at her as she hit him with a can of hairspray. He was, in a way, amazed at her strength, and her resistance heightened his desire for her.

Nicole continued to grab for items. *Think, or you are going to be dead!* she thought. She knew she had to get out of his grip, but how? As the Serpent grabbed one of her arms, she grabbed, at the last possible second, her perfume bottle. Just as the Serpent gained the upper hand, he flipped her around so they were face to face. He wanted to steal a kiss. Nicole found herself paralyzed by the icy blue eyes staring into hers. The Serpent started to pull her closer to him. His desire for this captured beauty was raging. He continued to pull her to him, repositioning his arms around her and at the same time roughly caressing her.

Nicole had not given up as he thought she had, however. Instead, she brought up her hand that held the perfume. She held his gaze. She smiled to keep his interest and for a slight moment felt the Serpent soften his grip. Although this only took a couple seconds, it felt like an eternity. Before the Serpent could react, Nicole started to spray the perfume directly into his piercing blue eyes. She continued to spray his eyes until she heard him scream from the pain the perfume inflicted.

He loosened his grip, and Nicole started to wiggle free. As she moved her left hand down the Serpent's arm, she felt the bandage on his hand and remembered that Sean had shot him there. She buried her fingernails deep into the wound. Blood started to flow from his hand, and the pain was intense, causing the Serpent to release her as he fell to his knees. He screamed from the pain she was inflicting.

With the perfume still in her hand, Nicole sprayed it in his mouth just for good measure. She was free from his grip, and she needed to get away from him. He coughed from the foul substance a few times. He alternated between coughs and screams of pain, wiping his eyes with his uninjured hand. As Nicole fled, he wildly grabbed in the darkness, knowing he had let his prey escape. He was amazed at the pain that the substance was causing in his eyes. From his mouth came a litany of curse words as his anger erupted.

Nicole started down the steps, but more gunfire broke out, keeping her from heading down to the first floor. She could think only about hiding. She ran into Sean's room. She could hear the Serpent struggling to his feet. She didn't have many options, and time was running out. She thought about going outside on the balcony but dismissed it. The bathroom was the only other option. She closed the door of Sean's bedroom behind her and opened the sliding glass door, hoping it might buy her some more time, and then headed for Sean's bathroom. She closed the bathroom door, hearing another scream of agony escape from the Serpent. She locked the bathroom door and climbed into the tub. She didn't know what else to do, and she knew she wasn't thinking very clearly. There really wasn't anywhere to hide that didn't present a trap for the Serpent to grab her and kill her. She

*Blind Influence* | 249

was frightened, and her heart was pounding. Her adrenaline had helped her escape, but now she needed to calm down and think. She had never felt this scared before in her whole life. She had to slow her breathing. She had to think about what else she could do. "Damn it, Sean! Where are you?" she said quietly to herself.

In the first few seconds of darkness, Sean had managed to douse the light of the lantern. He cursed that he had been distracted, forgetting to tell Nicole to take the lit lantern with her. That thought didn't last long, as he knew he had to gain the upper hand in this gunfight with Kent. He drew another round of gunfire from Kent even though Kent could not see him as he unlocked the adjoining door.

Thompson heard the door unlock, and he opened it slowly to provide Sean some cover fire. He heard Nicole scream Sean's name.

Sean crawled toward the door and hoped that Thompson could see him. When Sean was within reach of Thompson, he felt Thompson's hand on his back, letting him know he was safe.

"You OK? Are you shot?" Thompson asked.

"No, I don't think so," Sean answered. His adrenaline was flowing, and if he was shot, he wasn't feeling it. All he could hear was Nicole's screams for him and the raucous noise her struggle was causing. "I got to get up there." Sean looked at Thompson and smiled when he saw that Thompson had night-vision goggles on.

"You can't go up the stairs over there," Thompson answered, referring to the stairs where Kent had a perfect shot at Sean. "I got this asshole. Go get her." Thompson grabbed Sean's arm as Sean started for the stairs on the adjoining side of the beach house. Thompson reached behind him and said, "You'll need these." He handed Sean a pair of night-vison googles.

"Thank you. How did—" Sean started to ask.

"Who do you think turned out the lights?" Thompson whispered. "Now get out of here."

Sean could have given Thompson a hug, grateful to know that his ally was in control of the lighting and that it wasn't the Serpent's doing, but he settled for

250 | *Linda Riesenberg Fisler*

a pat on the back instead. He put the goggles on and headed up the stairs to rescue Nicole. He took the steps two at a time and was at the top of the stairs and out on the balcony in a matter of seconds. Sean could hear the Serpent's screams, and he wondered what Nicole had managed to do to him. He stood for a second on the balcony, trying to determine where the Serpent was. The rain was heavy, and he needed to get inside before a lightning strike blinded him. He removed the glasses as he prepared to jump from his balcony to Nicole's. As Sean landed on Nicole's balcony, he heard another round of gunfire from downstairs. The sheer curtains were blowing in the wind. Sean put his night-vision googles on again. He scanned the room for the Serpent but could not see him. He removed his gun from its holster as he peered into the room. He looked around and found nothing. He looked into the hall and saw a tall figure in the dark. He knew that man's build anywhere.

The Serpent had been looking out of the sliding glass door in Sean's bedroom but saw no indication that Nicole had gone that way. He was now moving to the closed bathroom door, smiling that Nicole had made it so easy for him to kill her by trapping herself in the bathroom.

Sean moved quickly and quietly into Nicole's bedroom and took aim at the Serpent. He could feel the adrenaline rushing through his veins, but this time, instead of the images of his wife and daughter appearing, his head was clear and his hand was steady. Sean had a clear shot of the Serpent. Just as he was getting ready to shoot, he heard Kent yell in pain as another round of gunfire started. "Sean, how could you?" Kent yelled. Sean now knew that Kent still thought Sean was downstairs firing, as Sean hoped Kent would believe.

Sean moved into the hallway between the two bedrooms to get a better shot at the Serpent. The Serpent was about to move around the bed toward the bathroom door. Sean took aim again and slowly pulled the trigger. The gun went off, and the Serpent fell to the ground as the bullet struck his head. Sean quickly moved to his bedroom, his gun trained on the Serpent. He shot the assassin again and again, feeling the emotion of losing his wife and child drain with each pull of the trigger. He was stoic as he pulled the trigger each time, hearing the gun discharge a bullet. With each bullet that landed in the body of the Serpent, he felt the anger leave him. He finally had his vengeance. His shots were fatal, and the Serpent's blood began to flow out of the bullet wounds.

*Blind Influence* | 251

Thompson counted the shots and knew that Sean was exacting his anger on the Serpent. The gunshots were all from the same gun. Thompson knew the Serpent was dead. He decided it was time to surprise Kent. "So, asshole, did you figure out that I'm not Sean yet?"

Thompson's voice yelling at Kent brought Sean back to the present. Sean almost smiled at Thompson's comment.

"Who are you?" Kent yelled into the darkness.

"Eyes off!" Thompson yelled. Sean removed his goggles just as Thompson threw the switch he had rigged earlier in the evening. The flickering lights had not been because of the storm. Thompson had rigged the electricity so he had control. "Kevin Thompson, special investigation for a certain US senator," Thompson said as he entered the other side of the beach house with his gun trained on Kent.

"Nicole?" Sean called. "Nicole, where are you?"

"Sean?" Nicole questioned from the bathtub. With each gunshot, she had sunk farther down in the tub, covering her ears and head. Washing over her now was a feeling of shock as the adrenaline started to reside.

"Yes. He's dead, Nicole," Sean answered as he moved around the dead body of the assassin and toward the bathroom door.

Nicole unlocked the door and swung it open, running into Sean's outstretched arms. "Thank you," she whispered. She held Sean tightly as she let the news of the Serpent's death sink into her confused brain. Her head was buried in Sean's shoulder. Her brain was not going to allow her to process the information without seeing it with her own eyes, however. She slowly lifted her head to look over Sean's shoulder at the lifeless body bleeding onto the beige carpet beneath it. He was dead. It was true. The nightmare was over. "Thank you," she repeated as she buried her head again in Sean's shoulder.

Sean continued to hold Nicole, shifting her so he could see the Serpent's body. He had taken the Serpent's gun as he had called for Nicole, and he had felt the Serpent's neck for a pulse. The man was dead. He still could not believe that his nemesis was dead. Like the storm outside, Sean's emotions were swirling. He felt the release, as if his wife and daughter had left him. His ten-year pursuit had just ended, and he felt as if the spirits of his family were resting easy now. He had avenged their deaths, and the realization of that goal had not hit him yet. He smiled when he heard Nicole's whispered thank-you. He had succeeded in preventing the death of someone he cared for, even thought they had just met. Should he even dare to think that he was falling for the cinnamon haired beauty? His mind raced as he tried to determine just what he was feeling. There were so many emotions. He was lightheaded from it all. His thoughts were darting about in his brain. The fact that it was over was beginning to sink into his consciousness.

"Are you two all right up there?" Thompson yelled up from the first floor. In the distance, sirens from the local police department were barely audible. He knew he had to get Sean out of the beach house.

"Yes," Sean answered. He continued to hold Nicole. He moved so he could look Nicole in the eyes. "Thank you. You were so brave," he whispered to her. He felt something that she was holding in her right hand. He gently released her so he could see what it was. He saw the perfume bottle she was still grasping.

Nicole looked at Sean and saw that he was looking at the perfume bottle with confusion. "I don't suppose you've ever accidentally sprayed perfume in your eyes, have you?" Nicole asked. Sean shook his head. "It burns like hell and makes the eyes water profusely. I don't recommend it."

Sean smiled at Nicole and then tenderly kissed her forehead. He brought his hand up and caressed her cheek allowing himself to run his fingers through her hair. It was a tender moment that he didn't want to end.

Thompson had secured Kent with his handcuffs. He knew Kent wasn't going to go anywhere. The one shot he had landed on Kent had probably shattered the man's kneecap. Kent had lost a lot of blood, as well. Thompson had performed a little triage on the wound before he quickly headed up the stairs. "Sean," he started as he rounded the corner to see Sean kissing Nicole's forehead. "You need to get out of here," he said.

He could tell his words weren't registering. "Get the hell out of here!" he yelled. "You don't have clearance to be here. The little memo from Jefferies … " he reminded Sean.

Sean acknowledged Thompson's comments. "He's right. I have to go." Sean said to Nicole. "Go with Kevin." He walked her past the Serpent's body to deliver her to Thompson. He stopped by the open door to the balcony.

Nicole knew that he was not going to leave by the front door. She watched as he started out the door leading to the balcony. "Sean!" she exclaimed. Sean stopped, looking over to her when she called him. "Will I ever see you again?" she asked as Thompson put an arm around her.

Sean wasn't sure, but he thought he could see a tear welling up in her eye. He smiled as he answered. "Let's hope so. And let's hope it is under much more pleasant circumstances." He watched as Nicole nodded her head in acknowledgment. A faint smile came across her lips as she watched him disappear.

"Let's get downstairs. While I wounded Kent pretty well and have him cuffed, I don't want him escaping," Thompson said, knowing full well that Kent wasn't going anywhere. The sirens were getting closer.

The storm seemed to be subsiding and appeared to be nothing more than rain and some gusty winds now. Thompson escorted Nicole downstairs to where Kent was wincing from pain. He was sitting on a chair at the table where they had been playing Monopoly earlier. Thompson had cuffed one of Kent's arms to the table.

Nicole didn't say a word to Kent as she walked past him to look out the door to the beach beyond the sand dune. She was straining to see Sean, but it was too dark. She felt as if a very important part of her was now lost.

"Nikki, it would be better if you wouldn't do that," Thompson said.

"Let her look, jackass," Kent chimed in. "I'm going to tell the authorities he was here, anyway."

Thompson smiled. "I'm sure they will believe an MI-6 agent who was working for the Serpent over a special agent working for a federal investigation. Your days are numbered."

Nicole had moved away from the glass doors as Thompson requested and sat down on the couch just as the sirens reached their highest pitch before

254 | *Linda Riesenberg Fisler*

they were shut off. Red lights were flashing through the windows as police-men surrounded the building. Nicole shot a nervous look at Thompson. He winked at her and walked to the door.

Thompson opened the door just as a policeman with his gun drawn reached it. Thompson had his badge in his hand and held it up for the offi-cer to see. "Special Agent Kevin Thompson. I am working on a special investigation for Senator Robert Jenkins," he told the officer. "You can stand down." He stepped aside to let the officer pass.

"What went on here tonight?" the officer asked.

"We apprehended those responsible for the assassination of President Andrews," Thompson answered. "You'll find the dead assassin upstairs in the bedroom on the left. This is his accomplice, Kent Chapman, former MI-6, but we'll keep that to ourselves. We don't want to embarrass our partners across the pond, now do we? Oh, and he'll need some attention to the gunshot wound there." Thompson pointed to Kent's knee.

The officer got on the radio and told his men it was all clear. One by one, they filed into the beach house to get out of the storm.

Thompson phoned the senator from the beach house to give him the news. He asked the senator to call Charlie Dawson and also the local police to keep the red tape at a minimum. Senator Jenkins was relieved to hear that Nicole was alive and that the only casualty was the assassin. He informed Kevin Thompson he would make the necessary phone calls and asked him to fly back to Washington as soon as he could. There was still a need for his services in the investigation.

With the first rays of light, all that was left of the storm was clouds reflect-ing an array of yellows and pinks, a beautiful offering of peace from Mother Nature after a turbulent night. The police were finishing up their work, vacating the beach house in a slow parade back to their police cars.

Thompson was the last to leave, with Nicole by his side. He secured the building and walked to the remaining police car. They were driven up to New Bern, where they caught a flight back to Washington, DC, later that afternoon.

*Blind Influence* | 255

Nicole was very quiet on the flight back. The adrenaline had stopped pulsing through her veins, and she was beginning to realize how tired she really was. It was just a little hop to Charlotte and didn't provide an opportunity for her to sleep; however, the flight into DC provided an opportunity for a two-hour nap. For the first time since Carol's murder, Nicole fell into a deep sleep, knowing those frigid blue eyes would never haunt her again.

*Seven Weeks Later*

# Jenkins's Home

"**H**appy New Year, dear," Jenkins said as he put his arms around Nicole, who was looking out the window. "It has been quite a year, hasn't it?"

Nicole thought to herself that she spent a lot of time looking out windows lately. She knew she was hopeful that she would see Sean. She didn't know why exactly, except that they had formed a bond that would always be there. He had protected her, and in that act, he had saved himself. Conversely, she also wondered if the dangerous life of a secret agent was attracting her. She thought that she would never be attracted to that kind of life, seeing firsthand the damage it wreaked on innocent people. She was, after all, one of those victims. All of these factors were a part of why she hoped so desperately that she would see Sean again. She smiled and responded, "Happy New Year. Yes, it was a pretty wild ride these past couple months."

"Do you feel like going out? We can stay in if you prefer. I'm rather indifferent about the whole thing," Jenkins stated. Nicole turned around in his arms.

"I know you'll hate me for this. Have you heard anything from Sean or Charlie?" Nicole asked.

Jenkins released Nicole and stepped away from her. He was annoyed that she had asked him again. "Nikki, I assure you, when I hear something from either of them, I will tell you. Sean is probably off someplace getting his head on straight. He'll turn up someday." To Jenkins, it seemed like she asked every day. "I'm beginning to think I should be a bit jealous. Do you love Sean?"

Nicole smiled. "I don't really know him, Bobby. He saved my life, and I do care for him. It doesn't seem unrealistic that I would have concern for him, does it?"

"No. But it seems like you ask me at least once a day." Nicole gave him a look that told him that he had hit a nerve, and he said, "Nikki, Sean has a lot of things to work out mentally. He's held this hatred for the Serpent for over ten years. Take it from someone who had to work to control his demons." Jenkins caressed the top of his right leg. "It takes a while to grab hold of life again. You can't help him with that. Trust me."

258 | *Linda Riesenberg Fisler*

"I know you're right," Nicole responded. "Can you understand, though, that he helped me and I want to help him?"

"Yes. But you can't," Jenkins reiterated.

Nicole smiled. "I don't know who is more stubborn, you or me."

Jenkins laughed. "I think it is a stalemate."

"Part of me just wanted everything wrapped up by year's end," Nicole said as Jenkins's phone began to ring. "The investigation, the drilling, and then I thought that I'd be able to start new on January first. It is frustrating that things are just so slow."

"Welcome to Washington politics," Jenkins said as he walked to the table next to his favorite chair to answer the phone. "Happy New Year!" he exclaimed as he answered it.

"Yes, indeed it is, Senator! Happy New Year!" Ahnah answered cheerfully.

Jenkins was not quite sure who it was on the other end of the line. "Ahnah?" he asked. Nicole walked toward him at the sound of her client's name.

"Yes!" came the confirmation.

"Ahnah, let me put you on speaker. Nikki is here with me." Jenkins depressed the button and put the receiver down. "Why is it indeed a happy new year?"

"Hello, Nikki! We are celebrating here," Ahnah started.

"Hello, Ahnah," Nicole answered. "What is going on there?"

"The men on the rig, they left today. They said they had not been paid in weeks, their supplies stopped coming, and they just started walking off. As a matter of fact, they were asking us if we could give them a ride to Fairbanks! Isn't that wonderful news?" Ahnah was elated.

"That is wonderful news, Ahnah! I don't think I have ever heard you this happy!" Nicole said with a smile on her face.

*Blind Influence* | 259

"Senator, I have another question. They left the equipment behind. Is that our equipment now?" Ahnah asked.

Jenkins looked at Nicole with a confused look. "I think that is a question for your counsel to answer."

"Why do you want to know, Ahnah?" Nicole asked, fearing the answer she might hear.

"It's perfectly good drilling equipment," Ahnah said.

"Ahnah, technically, the company men abandoned it when they walked off. It is on your land, so by default, it would become part of your people's assets. However, if you are thinking of drilling for oil on that land, you can't do that," Nicole answered.

"Nikki, that oil would benefit us," Ahnah started.

"Ahnah," Jenkins interrupted, "you understand that federal law trumps your own laws. Right now, it is illegal to drill for oil in ANWR," Jenkins reminded her.

"But you could help us with that," Ahnah stated flatly.

"Why would I change my position on this legislation? Ahnah, if it wasn't in the best interest of your tribe to drill on the land when your tribe was not doing the drilling, it is still in the best interest not to drill for oil by anyone, for all the reasons that have been stated regarding the ecological impacts and diversity of the land. I will not be changing my position just because someone deserted an illegal drilling rig in your backyard." Jenkins was firm in his judgment.

"Also understand that if you drill for oil, you are setting a precedent that basically says that anyone can drill there. Before you could blink your eye, every oil company around the world would have you in court, petitioning for rights to drill there as well. You could very well lose your land," Nicole added.

"I have a geology degree. Couldn't we be the ones that are providing the research that is needed?" Ahnah asked.

260 | *Linda Riesenberg Fisler*

Jenkins did not like where this was going. "Ahnah, you don't understand who you are dealing with in this matter. Yes, I suppose we could write something up granting you a research permit. I'd have to do some research on that, but again, that is changing my position, and I still feel that no drilling is best. Even a research grant is a slippery slope. Every oil company will have a reason to question your work and request that their own team conduct their own findings. The strongest voices against drilling there were the voices of your people. If we lose that, we have lost this fight. We just don't know the ecological impacts of drilling there."

"We love our land, Senator. We would do nothing to harm our land," Ahnah started. "We would be more responsible than those who do not live off the land."

"Accidents happen. You are not exempted from that, Ahnah. There would be accidents and spills. Drilling for oil, whether a major oil company or the Inuit people conducting the drilling, will affect your lands. The accident factor increases exponentially without experience," Nicole said, a bit surprised at this request as well as disappointed. "Am I to believe that the protest all along has been that you are in favor of drilling as long as it is you that is doing the drilling?"

"No, but think about the money it will generate for our people," Ahnah argued.

"It would generate money for your people regardless of who is doing the drilling," Jenkins chimed in. "I believe Nikki is correct in saying that the equipment is yours because it was abandoned; however, it is still illegal and will continue to be until that law is changed. I beg of you to not let money and greed steer your people away from your connection to your land. We need to think of other ways to help your people. Drilling for oil is not the answer for many reasons. It was wrong when you didn't have the equipment, and it is still the wrong decision now that the equipment is there. The temptation is great, but don't let it mislead you. In fact, drilling equipment isn't cheap. Your tribe could benefit from the sale of the equipment."

"That might not be a good idea," Nicole added. "We don't know which company was drilling, and they could file an injunction. If you were to sell it, I would have to look into how long you would need to wait before selling it legally."

Ahnah seemed a bit disappointed. "I guess it comes down to whether that law is passed, Senator. If it does change, then we will be starting an oil company and drilling for oil here."

"I hear your disappointment, Ahnah," Jenkins said, confirming her feelings. "I can't leave this conversation without expressing my disappointment in your people. I would like to believe that your connection to the land was so strong that you would not even think of this option."

"Well, it is not all our people. My brothers and I were discussing it. We have not said anything to anyone because we wanted to check with you first."

"Then I will restate my position again. I am not for drilling of any kind in the ANWR. That will not be changing," Jenkins answered.

Ahnah knew when she was defeated. "So we just have to look at this ugly thing?"

Both Nicole and Jenkins laughed. Jenkins then said, "I might be able to persuade a company to come up and take it down. I would suggest, though, that you have Nikki check on when and if you could sell the equipment. You might also find other uses for some of the equipment. Now that they are gone, have a walk around and see what could benefit you. Give Nikki a call after you create a list of everything and what you want to sell."

Nicole was surprised that Jenkins seemed so sure of himself that the company would not want their equipment back. Puzzled, she told Ahnah, "Call me on Wednesday."

"I'll do that. It really is good news, though, that the fight is over," Ahnah said, cheering herself back up.

"It is excellent news!" Nicole confirmed. "Let's keep it that way."

"Have a happy New Year. Thank you for all your help." Ahnah hung up the phone before they could wish it back to her.

Nicole looked at Jenkins. "You are awfully sure of yourself. How do you know that the oil company isn't going to want that equipment back?"

"Did I sound sure of myself?" Jenkins said, realizing he had almost committed an error. Nicole affirmed her assertion with a nod of her head. Jenkins gave a sigh. "I really can't tell you. It's part of the investigation."

"Bobby, that investigation has been going on now for a month. Surely you have all the information you need to indict someone. You have got to know how all the pieces fit together, and if it was an oil company behind all of this, then nail their asses to the wall and let's get on with it."

"If it were only that simple," Jenkins murmured to himself.

"What? I didn't hear you."

"I said it is a rather complicated web, Nikki. There are a few more witnesses to call. There is no reason to rush to judgment. The assassin has been killed. The intelligence community is learning something new on the Serpent's network thanks to Kent's shall we say willingness to talk." Jenkins took Nicole in his arms. "There is no reason to rush this through committee. After all, it took the Warren Commission a year to issue its finding. I want to be as thorough as needed."

Nicole put her arms around Jenkins. They kissed. Then she said, "Yes, but look at all the conspiracy theories that commission spurred."

"That is my point exactly. We owe it to ourselves to ensure that we benefit from the investigation." Jenkins kissed her again.

For a few brief minutes, Nicole wasn't sure if Jenkins was speaking about the American people or just the two of them. *Only time will tell*, she thought as she kissed him.

For now, Nicole was safe and she wasn't thinking about conspiracies. She was thinking of her happiness and how life could be blindly influenced by the people around her: people she thought she knew, people who knew her, and people she didn't know at all. She at times wondered if there were something she could have done differently that would have shielded her from this ordeal. At those times, she heard Sean's voice in her head, saying, *That warning meant nothing. You could have not said a word about those Secret Service men to Bobby. As long as you went to the nightclub this evening, you would still be right here.* Over the last few weeks, she had begun to accept that she would not and could not have done anything differently. She had been fated to live the experience she had lived and to discern the lesson that she had been meant to learn. She hoped that she was a bit wiser and a little less blind to the influences around her. She couldn't help but wonder if a healthy dose of suspicion was a good thing, although she reminded herself of Henry David Thoreau's quote: "We are always paid for our suspicion by finding what we suspect." Her senses were heightened now, and that would never change. She could only discern by using the knowledge she had in front of her at the time. It was all anyone could do.

Jenkins's mind was racing as he remembered the confession given on the tape that he had concealed in his safe in his condo. He certainly didn't want to rush his decision and knew that the only other person who held the secret had no desire to entangle himself in politics. In fact, Tony Shafer had retired from the firm and now spent most of his days sailing on his yacht.

There were many options on the table for Jenkins now that he possessed the tape. He smiled as his kiss with Nicole ended, but he wasn't smiling at Nicole and the pleasure that she had given him.

Instead, Jenkins was recalling a quote that he had recently read in a book by Hunter S. Thompson: "In a closed society where everybody's guilty, the only crime is getting caught. In a world of thieves, the only final sin is stupidity." Sipes had certainly been stupid and out of his league. Jenkins knew he lived within a society where, to some degree, guilt was easily assigned at the whim of the media or of his colleagues, unfortunately. Knowledge was power, and he was holding a lot of power via the tape confession. He just needed time to figure out how it could best be used. There was no room for stupidity among the thieves he worked with on a daily basis.

Still, he knew that he was walking on a thin ice. He was truly falling in love with Nicole, and if he didn't live up to her expectations, her naïve expectations, he would lose the only person he truly cared about in his life of power, greed, and alliances. He desperately needed someone he could trust unconditionally in his life, and he was falling madly in love with Nicole. He wasn't sure he could handle her walking away from him. He had fallen for her the first night they had met at the White House dinner. He hoped that through their relationship and with time, her naivety would wane and she would become his ally as he worked for the greater good. The greater good came with negotiations. He could only hope that she would in time love him as much as he loved her.

And they say love is blind.

Thank you for joining Nicole on her journey of personal discovery. I hope that you have enjoyed meeting Nicole, Sean and Bobby as well as the rest of the cast of characters. This little tale started many, many years ago and it has been a joy to finally get it into my readers' hands!

If you loved the book and have a minute to spare, **I would really appreciate a short review.** Your help in spreading the word about this novel is gratefully received and appreciated.

**What's next?** I am currently writing the sequel to *Blind Influence*. I can let the secret out now that you have finished this book. The title of the second book is *Love Is Blind*. So many questions left to be answered, aren't there? Will Bobby Jenkins do the right thing when it comes to the evidence he has hidden in his safe? Will Nicole find out about Bobby's secret? Will she see Sean again and when she does how will she feel about him? Where is Sean and how does he feel about Nicole? And these are just a few of the questions we are left with at the end of this book!

To make sure you are notified of future releases in the *Blind Series,* sign up for my free newsletter at http://www.lindafisler.com/blind-series/sign-up-for-my-newsletter/.

I would like to invite you to stay in touch as I write the sequel and other books (did I mention the fantasy series I'm working on? Oh dear, well-quickly it is called *Tales of Reginnis.*) Please do stay in touch! I can be found on

## Facebook (https://www.facebook.com/lindafisler)

## Twitter (@lfisler)

email: lfisler@lindafisler.com
Thank you with all my heart for reading ***Blind Influence***!
Respectfully yours,
—Linda Riesenberg Fisler

CPSIA information can be obtained at www.ICGtesting.com
Printed in the USA
BVOW05s0146240315

392980BV00001B/1/P